PRODIGAL LOVER

Margo Gregg

A KISMET ™ Romance

 METEOR PUBLISHING CORPORATION

Bensalem, Pennsylvania

To Brett and my darling Bryan

MARGO GREGG

From closet scribbler to published writer has been a lifetime dream for Margo Gregg. Along the way, she has enjoyed a career in medical transcription, both teaching and writing. She paints in her spare time and is an accomplished amateur landscape designer. Gregg was born in Ohio, but now lives in San Diego, California, taking inspiration from a romantic setting and a growing family.

ONE

The letter was lying beside her plate when she came down to breakfast.

Some things never change—death, taxes, and the tyranny of the morning mail, Keely reflected with a resigned twist of her lips. She sat down and picked up her napkin, the signal to the hovering housekeeper that the mail would wait again until after breakfast—a delay that never failed to infuriate the insubordinate Lida Maguire.

Long before Keely came to Easton Manor, her publishing magnate father-in-law began the ritual, using the same antique silver letter opener that now lay beside Keely's plate; and after Alfred Easton's death, his widow Helen assumed not only the reins of power in the family business, but all the traditional routines. And when Helen Easton suffered a debilitating stroke last year, thrusting upon a reluctant Keely the responsibility for the family fortune, Mrs. Maguire appointed herself guardian of the flame.

Coolly ignoring the mail, Keely addressed the chauffeur standing by unobtrusively for his orders. "Sikes, please close the draperies as soon as the table is cleared; I think we're in for a heat wave. Then you may bring the Bentley around."

"Very good, ma'am."

"And you must meet Mr. Preston at the airport at ten.

7

Mrs. Maguire, he'll be dining here tonight, so we'll have dessert after all. A fresh fruit compote will do—anything but strawberries, you keep forgetting I'm allergic to them. And serve our coffee upstairs."

"Yes, ma'am. When you're finished with the mail," the housekeeper said pointedly, "I'll be serving your breakfast."

"You may serve breakfast now," Keely responded firmly, knowing she had hit another sore spot by inviting Vern for dinner tonight. Mrs. Maguire thought that Keely's seeing another man while living in her deceased husband's house was nothing short of scandalous.

For Keely, the struggle for power ended at the bottom line—insulating Helen from any stress that could trigger another, possibly fatal, stroke. So in order to avoid head-on confrontation with a domestic who, by virtue of her forty years with the Eastons, considered herself a member of the family, she had learned to assert her authority in more subtle ways.

This morning, for instance, the mail would languish while Keely breakfasted in solitary bliss, with a smile of appreciation for the golden June melon served on emerald-hued plate enamel. While she loitered over a second cup of coffee, she would run through her appointment book before issuing household instructions for the day. Nothing would escape her eye, the smallest blue haze on mirrored surfaces, a hint of dust on oiled walnut, a fragment of frond from a ruffled fern. There would be no quarter given and none would be asked. Such matters Mrs. Maguire understood and expected from the chatelaine of Easton Manor, and had Keely not taken these household duties seriously during Helen Easton's illness, the housekeeper would have held her in open contempt.

As it was, the truce was a tenuous one; Mrs. Maguire would always believe that young Bryan Easton would be alive today, and sitting in his rightful place at the head of the table, if he had not married the little golddigger from the wrong side of the tracks eight years ago. Though her manner remained tolerably correct (for that was tradition, too), Keely was well aware of the housekeeper's resentment and disapproval.

The ringing telephone was a welcome reprieve. Keely now hurried through the mail, anxious to finish and to quit the mansion for the friendlier haven of her offices in Manhattan. Quickly the stack of envelopes was sorted into piles: household, stray office mail, junk, Helen and Keely's personal mail.

It was then she noticed the letter. It was marked personal, but what caught her eye most was not the Mexican stamp, which was of the utilitarian metered-mail variety, but the return address itself. It said: "Amnesty International."

She knew instantly.

TWO

Fingers trembling, Keely slit open the envelope and extracted a crisply folded sheet of paper. The letterhead bore the logo and address: "Amnesty International–London–New York–Mexico City." She skimmed the contents quickly.

"During the course of routine investigations of human rights violations in countries all over the world, we have obtained important information concerning Bryan T. Easton . . ."

"It's Mr. Preston, ma'am."

"What?" Keely blinked, dazed at the interruption. "Oh. The phone . . . of course. Yes. Tell him . . . later . . . I'm afraid I've . . . forgotten something upstairs . . . excuse me. Excuse me!" Keely rose, clattering the dishes in her haste, aware of nothing in her confusion and panic, driven by the pounding of her heart up to the privacy of her suite.

With the door shut tight behind her, she removed the letter from her pocket with shaking hands, tearing the envelope in her haste. It continued:

"Since this is a matter to be discussed in person, a suite has been reserved for you at the Hotel Internacionale in Mexico City for June 12. Please telephone our office if this date is not convenient."

It was signed, Ricardo G. Castillo, Associate Director,

10

Central American Affairs, Amnesty International—Mexico City.

Keely sank down on the bed, her composure shattered in a thousand directions, her mind a kaleidoscopic whirl of thoughts and memories, past and present.

Bryan Easton died seven years ago in May; alone, violently, scattered to the four winds in the wreckage of a helicopter over an implacable jungle in Nicaragua. There was no funeral because there was no body; a brief memorial service was arranged by his heartbroken, newly widowed mother in this very house in Westerby, New York. In her grief over losing her own husband and then her son just months apart, Helen reached out to her estranged daughter-in-law, and eventually Keely came to live in the mansion to try to fill the void in both their lives.

Of course, because of her precarious state of health after carotid surgery and a postoperative stroke last month, Helen could not be told that her son's body had finally been found. Dr. Houten was adamant about keeping her calm. Keely would have to fly to Mexico City alone to make arrangements to ship the body back. She wished Vern could go with her, but he was too much in the public eye and busy with his campaign for the Senate.

A tap on the door startled her out of her frantic reverie. "I don't want to be disturbed," she called out. Then, "What is it?"

"It's Mr. Preston again, ma'am," came the housekeeper's muffled voice. "I tried to tell him—"

Keely ripped open the door. "Never mind, I'll talk to him after all. Will you transfer the call to my private line?"

"Yes, ma'am."

Vern's deep voice was a godsend. "Darling, what the hell is going on up there this morning? Since when does that dragon Maguire woman decide whether I will or won't speak to you? I keep telling you to get rid of her—"

"Vern!" she interrupted impatiently. "They've found Bryan's body."

He was shocked into silence. Then he asked, "Who did?"

"Amnesty International. I just got the letter. They want me to fly to Mexico City to discuss arrangements. I've got to go right away, today—"

"Damn. I called to tell you I'm stuck here in Washington until Friday. Why don't you wait a few days so I can go with you?"

"I'm too upset to wait. By Friday I'd be a basket case. Besides, I don't want the newspapers to get wind of this, or we'll have a three-ring circus on our hands again, and that could kill Helen. And if you go with me, they'll think we're eloping to Mexico or some such nonsense—"

"Nonsense?" Wounded, he pounced on the word. "Keely, don't tell me that this development means you're backing out of your promise to marry me after the election—"

"Vern, please! How can you press me about marriage when I've just received this shattering news about Bryan?" Her voice began to tremble, but Vern could be like a bulldog at times and he did not intend to give in on this sore point.

"Keely, you've done your penance, and so have I—seven goddamned years of it. Bryan was declared legally dead last May. How much more time do you need to get him out of your system? Until you're all shriveled up like an old prune?" His voice had risen until it was almost a shout.

She stood hugging the phone receiver listening to his diatribe, struggling with long pent-up emotions and self-righteous anger at his insensitivity.

"I could understand it if you still loved him, but you say you don't," he ranted bitterly. "If that's true, then why am I so far down on your list of priorities—after Bryan's memory, after the company, after your mother-in-law? I'm beginning to realize all I am to you is a suitable, non-threatening escort for your public functions."

"Is that what you think?"

"What else can I think? You won't come out and endorse me for the Senate because of ethics. You won't marry me and formalize our relationship because of Helen's objections. What the hell do you even want me for, Keely?"

"I'm just asking for a little more time, Vern—"

"More time! In seven years, even Jacob got Rachel. If someone had told me I'd wait this long for a woman, I'd have said they were crazy. But I love you, dammit."

Keely's own temper was beginning to rise. "If you loved me, you'd understand my position . . ."

"And what about my position, Keely? I can't put my life on hold indefinitely waiting for you to make up your mind. If you'd given me just one ounce of the passion and energy you've expended on a dead man, I'd have been satisfied."

Her temper snapped. "Tell me again, Vern. Tell me I'm a maneater, devouring your pride and self-respect and making a laughingstock out of you. I have an idea. Why don't you just take what's left of your career and your precious manhood and say goodbye?"

"Keely—"

She severed the connection.

THREE

Keely emerged from the terminal into the warm afternoon of a smoggy Mexico City summer. Her taxi idled in smelly fumes through the snarl of traffic leaving the busy international airport. There was no air conditioning and the windows were down; she was sickened by the reek of diesel, carbon monoxide, and stale tobacco, but she leaned back, trying to relax. Any attempt to watch the traffic, or her own progress through it, left her nauseated in her present state of nervous exhaustion.

The hot afternoon sun slanted lancelike over the familiar city skyline, now growing closer. Despite her mental preoccupation, she reflected that every time she saw Mexico City its disordered sprawl seemed greater than it had before. And yet, in spite of the grime and smog, there was an indefinable ambiance about it that welcomed the traveler like an old, comfortable *zapato*.

It seemed hours before they arrived at the hotel. The doorman, his uniform complete with gold braid and visored cap, bounded over to open the cab door. The young mustachioed driver unloaded the luggage and was rewarded with a flash of long, slender legs as Keely stepped out of the cab to the pavement. A uniformed porter ran out of the hotel and seized her bags.

From under the hotel canopy, Keely got a glimpse into the opulence of a richly furnished lobby as she entered the enormous marble vestibule, her swinging stride projecting more energy and sense of purpose than she felt. The guests standing around the curved, burled walnut reception desk melted aside, not knowing who she was, but knowing she was somebody, sliding discreet looks at the sleek black hair, Saint Laurent cream shantung suit and emerald silk blouse, and the matched and monogrammed Vuitton luggage. When she gave her name, the clerk immediately handed her a cable, which she tucked into her purse for private reading. Soon, an entourage of porter and concierge escorted her by elevator to her suite on the third floor.

The room was not lavish, but was tastefully decorated. A spectacular arrangement of pink-dotted imperial lillies graced a carved escritoire—from Vern, she discovered from the card. When she was alone at last she tore open the telegram and read the message:

"FORGIVE A FOOL IN LOVE. VERN."

Suddenly, she of the cool dry eyes, who thought she had forgotten how, threw herself across the bed and wept.

Restlessness woke her the next morning just after daybreak. After a fruitless attempt to go back to sleep, Keely rose, wrapped herself in a white satin peignoir and pulled the draperies open, hoping for reassurance in a spectacular sunrise. But the horizon was obscured in mist, and lying over the city was a dirty scum of smog which would soon sting and bite the eyes. It looked as if it had not rained in weeks. Impatiently, she closed the drapes.

She wrote a note to Vern, reread it, wadded it up, and threw it in the wastebasket. Cooped up with her thoughts, she felt jittery and distracted. It was too early to call Amnesty International. She decided to dress and go downstairs to the hotel restaurant rather than eat breakfast in her room alone with her memories.

While waiting for the captain to seat her, she surveyed the well-appointed dining room. The Hotel Internacionale was frequently her own choice for its convenience and fine reputation in cuisine, as well as accommodations. Most of the business people she knew also liked this "central watering hole" where Americans were understood and welcomed, yet not treated like tourists.

"I am sorry for the inconvenience, senora, we seem to have no suitable table—" The captain looked around, wondering if he should rout out a less important person in favor of this unescorted but important *americana*.

Before she could reply, a man rose from a table nearby. "Pardon," he said politely to her in English. "You are most welcome to share my table. I am almost finished with my meal."

Keely looked around to see a tall, slim Mexican gentleman in his late thirties, with a grave, handsome face. His expressive black eyes observed Keely with quiet courtesy.

"You're very kind," she accepted, but kept her manner reserved.

The relieved captain beamed and escorted her to the table, seated her, and signaled for a waiter.

Her benefactor was having his coffee after completing breakfast. He waited until she gave her order for coffee and *bunuelo* to the waiter, then asked politely, "Is this your first visit to Mexico City?" He added quickly, "Forgive me. I do not mean to infer that conversation is my price for sharing the table."

Keely smiled then, appreciating his sensitivity. "Not at all. I've visited Mexico City many times on business. I'm returning to New York tomorrow."

He hesitated, his somber dark eyes questioning. "I do not mean to pry, but you are Keely Easton, are you not?"

Keely looked up at him, at first startled to be recognized in a foreign country, then upset that she could have been taken in by his courtly manners when he was obviously a reporter who had gotten wind of the story of the decade. But before she could respond, he touched his napkin to his lips and extracted a business card from his inside jacket pocket. "Allow me to introduce myself." He laid the card on the table so she would not have to touch his fingers. She read: Ricardo G. Castillo, Associate Director, Amnesty International, London–Mexico City.

Relieved, Keely managed to recover her aplomb and held out her hand. "Mr. Castillo. Yes, I'm Keely Easton."

His eyes flickered over her in an objective, assessing way. "I am surprised that I recognized you; your photograph certainly does not do you justice."

She arched winged eyebrows. "Photograph?"

Once more his hand went into his inside pocket, this time bringing out an envelope containing a studio photograph. He laid it down on the table in front of her. Immediately recognizing a wedding picture of herself and Bryan, Keely felt an ice-cold finger of apprehension down her back. The photograph was old—yellowed and dogeared, cracked and peeling. The couple, like strangers to her now, stood under a trellis of plastic flowers, smiling for the camera. She did not have to touch the photograph or turn it over to know that embossed on the back was the wedding date and the name of the cheap little chapel in Atlantic City where she and Bryan eloped in defiance of his father's wishes all those years ago.

"May I ask how you got this?" Her voice was deceptively calm. Inside she felt as if she were speaking through a long wind tunnel.

Castillo leaned forward and spoke in a low tone. "Perhaps a public restaurant is not the best place for our discussion, and you have not finished your breakfast."

"I don't care, I couldn't eat a thing now."

"Then—shall we adjourn to my office, Mrs. Easton?"

He made a move to rise, but she stopped him with a hand on his sleeve. "Please. I've been in suspense ever since I got your letter, and I've come thousands of miles prepared to hear the worst. Don't make me wait another moment!"

Sensing that her taut hold on discipline had come to the breaking point, he relented. "As you wish." As he settled back into his chair, his fine dark eyes never left hers, steadying her. "A few months ago, near the border between Nicaragua and Honduras, a mercenary was found, barely alive after being shot and dumped in a ravine. He had been tortured and starved as a guerrilla prisoner for many months. Evidently his condition was too poor to withstand the rigors of a forced march, so when his captors pulled out of the area, they decided to get rid of him."

Keely's gaze never flinched. "And this is the man who had the photograph?"

"Yes. His injuries were so severe that he was in a coma for several days. Since he could not tell us anything about himself, all we could do was trace the photograph."

Keely was filled with a strange impatience. What was he getting at, she wondered. Had the mercenary stumbled across the wreckage of Bryan's plane and found not only the photograph, but the grisly remains of Bryan's body as well? Or had he actually known Bryan before he died? She was not really interested in the saga of this nameless stranger; she wanted to hear only the hard facts, collect her husband's body, and go home to deal with the emotional aspects of telling Helen. But Castillo would not be rushed.

"While his condition was being stabilized at the U.S. army base, preliminary attempts to identify him through government bulletins of missing persons were unsuccessful. At first, all we could be sure of was that he was American. The photograph was traced to the wedding chapel, but unfortunately the freelance photographer or his files could not be located. Meanwhile, Amnesty arranged with the Red Cross to fly the injured man to Mexico City for surgery."

"Couldn't you trace his fingerprints?"

"Unfortunately, he had no fingerprints. They were burned away with cigarettes."

The brutal words, emphasized by his quiet delivery, were met with a level glance from Keely and a tone as dispassionate as his. "Then perhaps a relative would recognize a photo of him in U.S. newspapers?"

Castillo shook his head. "I'm afraid his own mother would not recognize him."

"No? Why not?"

Their gazes met, and she was acutely aware of his eyes on her, as if measuring the tensile strength of the woman behind the fragile exterior.

"When they dumped him, they took steps to ensure he would not be readily identified." He paused. "His face was smashed—obliterated, with a rifle butt."

Keely blanched, no longer able to pretend equanimity. She stared a moment at her companion, then pushed her coffee away quickly. "My God." Gone now was the cool composure that had protected her at the start of their conversation, and for the moment the unlucky mercenary had her full attention.

Even in her shock, Castillo could admire her poise. He leaned forward with concern on his lean features. "I'm sorry—it is not a pretty story."

She managed a stricken smile. "I'm in the news business, Mr. Castillo, but I'll never, never get used to man's inhumanity to man."

"Nor I, Mrs. Easton. Amnesty International deals with many atrocities which make me ashamed to be a member of the human race," he agreed. "I have been with the organization for ten of its thirty years, and every day I regret the necessity for its existence. But as long as political imprisonment, torture, and murder continue, we shall persevere."

As he spoke, she noted white, even teeth under the neat mustache, which imparted an air of worldly sophistication. And as he continued, she found herself fascinated by his British intonation flavored with a musical Latin accent. "Fortunately," he said, "some stories have happy endings."

"And this one?"

"I rather think that depends on you."

"Me?"

He paused, his face taking on a curiously penetrating expression as he watched her face for the effect of his words.

"Mrs. Easton, your husband is alive and here in Mexico City."

FOUR

Caught off guard, Keely laughed, two silvery notes that ended on a choke and a gasp. "My husband is dead, *senor!*"

"Perhaps you are afraid to believe after all these years, Mrs. Easton," he said gently. "That is why I asked you to come here in person—"

"To make arrangements!" she cried, profoundly shaken at the error that had culminated in this cruel joke, but he put his hand out and gently covered hers to stop her frantic denial.

"You may be certain our organization would not have asked you to come all the way to Mexico City on a whim, Mrs. Easton," he said. "Although your confirmation is sought to officially close the case, our experts are independently convinced that the man we found half-dead in the ravine is indeed your husband."

She had never once expected to hear anything more from him than confirmation of Bryan's death. Alive—! Her mind refused to make the connection, leaving her disoriented and almost dizzy.

The waiter hovered with refills of coffee, but sensitive to Keely's agitation, Castillo waved him away while he attempted to soften the shock.

"Every aspect of his story and identification was investigated most thoroughly before we contacted you," he went on. "And although his jaw was broken and he could not talk for several weeks, he is now able to confirm what our research had already proven. For all the severity of his injuries, there does not seem to be any brain damage, and after a short period of retrograde amnesia his memory seems to have returned nearly intact." He was persuading her, cajoling her, reassuring her. "As his wife, of course, you will surely recognize the man you married beneath the stranger's face, and with time his physical differences will ño longer matter."

"Physical differences?" she managed.

"Yes. Our best surgeons have performed a miracle in reconstructing his face, but because of the extensive damage and subsequent plastic repair, he no longer resembles your husband as you remember him. You must be prepared to accept this small price." He smiled patiently as if convincing a frightened, recalcitrant child. "In every way except his face, this man is Bryan Easton. His dental records, unfortunately, are somewhat compromised due to the damage to his jaws and teeth; even without them, however, there is enough other evidence to establish identification."

"Such as?"

"He is still six feet tall, his eyes are still blue. He has many new scars, but the appendix scar has been there since childhood . . ."

"There must be thousands of American men who fit that physical description!" Keely hedged desperately, her golden eyes blazing with tears.

"Surely, Mrs. Easton—"

"Don't you understand?" Struggling mightily to regain her composure and sensibilities, her mind scrambled to organize a defense. "His mother and I have been hoaxed and huckstered and lied to so many times that I refuse to be railroaded into accepting this man as my husband. What if you people are wrong? Can you repair the damage it would do to Mrs. Easton after she's finally reconciled herself to Bryan's death? Now to suggest that he cold-bloodedly abandoned her for seven years while he played war in Nicaragua would kill her, can't you see that?''

She seemed unaware of his flicker of interest in her vehement resistance. It only just occurred to him that she might be less than eager to find her missing husband alive. This sudden knowledge whetted his curiosity about her on an entirely different level.

He said quietly, ''Our discussion is entirely academic, is it not? There is only one way for you to be convinced that this man's claims are true or false.'' His black eyes were serious as they held hers. ''I charge you with caution, Mrs. Easton, before you deny this man his birthright without even a hearing.''

For a long moment she observed him across the table, weighing his subtle challenge, then rose, suddenly in a hurry to end this nightmare. ''Then by all means, let's get it over with.''

As they traced the route northeastward along the Paseo de la Reforma, past the central plaza known as El Zocalo, there was no pretense of conversation, and there was nothing to take her mind off the coming ordeal. They passed impressive monuments and historical buildings along the way, but Keely was lost in fragmented thought, remembering the Bryan she had met and fallen in love with at a fund-raising gala that summer so long ago.

At first she had been intrigued, then strongly attracted to the barely leashed, smoldering energy that seemed ready to erupt from Bryan at any moment. He had a dark spirit of restlessness and anger, accompanied by a cocksure sense of his mission in life. He was a rich man's son who hated his inherited station with all its unearned privileges and stagnant responsibilities. Keely never really understood what he saw in her—perhaps she had been just another rebellion against his rigid establishment father.

By the time they entered the University Hospital, she was almost panicky. Castillo had the attending physician paged and, after what seemed an interminable wait, they were ushered into a spartan office. Dr. Horacio Villarde held out his hand to Keely.

"I am glad to meet you on such a happy occasion, senora," Dr. Villarde beamed. "I have heard much about you from your husband, but he neglected to mention how very exquisite you are."

Keely smiled thinly, less at the Latin gallantry than at the doubtful flattery from her "husband."

The doctor sobered to the business at hand. "Your husband is a lucky man, senora—lucky to be alive. We were able to give him a face—not his original face, but a human face at least, and I think you will be pleased with the result." He began tacking charts and X-rays to the wall board. "As the preoperative photographs graphically demonstrate, the damage to the face was obviously a deliberate attempt to thwart identification. Perhaps you should refrain from viewing the 'before' file, they are not pretty pictures."

"I want to examine every one of them." Keely took the chart and as she thumbed through the sheaf of eight-by-ten black-and-white glossies, the two men exchanged glances.

When she paused at one particularly gruesome photograph, the doctor explained, "It is a wonder he was not blinded, though he suffered a detached retina. See this? Here is the point of impact where the mandible and maxilla were in-fractured—"

They could not see Keely's struggle to keep nausea at bay as the plastic surgeon warmed to his subject. With charts, he showed the miracle of reconstruction; how the team of surgeons had entered through the mouth and nose to pin together splintered bone and to insert grafts, much of it done without cutting into the skin. "To avoid as much facial scarring as possible, senora," he explained with modest pride. "As you can see, many of the facial bones were comminuted—that means crushed, including the zygomatic processes and the left orbit. But see the results!"

He produced the final photographs with a flourish. If Keely had expected to see a monster, she was in for a surprise. Though the man looking up at her from the glossy black-and-white photographs could not be mistaken for even a distorted version of Bryan, he was a fairly normal-appearing male with a strong, though very lean, face due to excessive weight loss. Whether or not he had the bone structure of good looks to begin with, his features now had an arresting asymmetry that gave him that intriguing, ugly-handsome ruggedness that fascinates women far more than pretty-boy looks. His nose was far from classic; the internal bone and cartilage had been rearranged until it was now fairly straight, but shorter than Bryan's aristocratic one. Yet its lack of prominence had been well balanced by the contrasting strength of jaw and chin. Several well-healed scars were visible, but most of the surgical ones were skillfully tucked into the natural creases of his face.

Whereas Bryan had been a brooder who knew how to use a dead stare and a slight curl of the lips to advantage, there was nothing here of his heavy-lidded, sensual presence or his potential for violence that had both fascinated and repelled her. This man's facial planes were still somewhat obscured with residual swelling, but it was his eyes that were the dead giveaway. Forthright and open, they crinkled at the corners, staring up at her from a face that seemed slightly amused to find himself alive, but determined to enjoy the joke. Though she studied each view carefully, trying not to be influenced by the puffiness and discoloration, she could not see even the slightest resemblance to Bryan in this unfortunate man.

Until she exhaled, she was unaware she had been literally holding her breath. She couldn't quite put her finger on what bothered her about this man, but she knew intuitively that he wasn't who he claimed to be. She handed the photographs back to the doctor, shaking her head. "No. I'm really quite sure of it now. This man is not my husband."

Castillo's head swiveled around, surprised, and the doctor blinked in protest. "But surely you may not make that determination on photographs alone, senora. Of course, he does not look the same! I have explained that his face has been surgically altered, inside and out. You must speak with him, question him, listen to his voice and his answers. Only then will you know."

Keely had already made up her mind, but Castillo took her arm firmly. "Come. This is necessary," he said. "You are afraid to be disappointed, and that is understandable. But how can you in good conscience deny his claim unless you have interviewed him? And if he is an impostor, only you can expose him."

Somehow they were standing in the corridor in front of Room 211. "Go," urged Castillo softly, coaxing her with a little shooing motion. "I shall wait here should you need me."

Keely waited a moment, took a deep breath, and opened the door.

FIVE

The room was dark. She stood in the doorway, marshalling her courage. The man in the bed moved his head in her direction, and she realized all he could see was her silhouette from the backlighted door.

"Keely?" he called. "Is it you?"

Her heart did a kettledrum roll at the sound of her name on a stranger's tongue. His voice was low pitched, much more resonant than Bryan's, with a husky timbre to the tones that sent a shiver up her spine. She came all the way in, letting the door close behind her.

"Why is it so dark in here?" she hedged, unable to see him clearly.

"The light still bothers my eyes. Come to the window." When she hesitated, he said with self-mockery, "Don't worry, you're in for a treat—the nurses say I'm a dead ringer for Tom Selleck."

Caught off guard by his self-deprecating humor, she responded lightly, "But you have no mustache."

"Well, nobody's perfect," he grinned. Moving toward the bed, she saw the flash of irregular but intact teeth with a band of wire across the surface, unlike Bryan's cosmetically perfect ones. She closed her mind to the sudden image of a rifle butt smashing against them.

He saw her wince, and ran a rueful finger over the surface of his teeth. "My old orthodontist would turn over in his grave. Fortunately, I lost only two—the others were able to be wired back into place."

Against her will she found herself admiring the man's humor and acceptance of his injuries. How could this pleasant, easy-smiling man claim to be her smoldering husband, even considering he was on his best behavior? Standing next to the bed, she studied him intently—in much the same way Delilah must have examined Samson for signs of unguarded weakness when she would point a finger in accusation and pronounce, "The Philistines be upon you, Samson!"

Castillo was right—there was a superficial physical resemblance to Bryan, but this first impression was offset by the aura of the man himself, a quiet composure rather than the barely contained volcano beneath Bryan's surface.

Staring while trying not to stare, she could only barely see the thin pink scars just inside his hairline and under the jaw where his face had been reconstructed.

She said coolly, "Considering what you've been through, you're lucky to be alive."

"Are you glad?" he asked softly.

She was startled. "Of course—why wouldn't I be?"

He lay back against his pillows and smiled. "You have every reason not to be. Come over here where we can both get a better look at each other."

She obeyed reluctantly, making an effort to study the face beneath the residual swelling and faint shadows of bruises still in evidence. To her chagrin, she had difficulty looking him in the eyes—there was something too direct, too unsettling about them. In the darkened room, they seemed a deeper, warmer color, unlike Bryan's icy-blue eyes. You could change a man's face, but you couldn't change his eyes, could you? And his hair. Cropped surgically short, it had grown out enough to see it was a crisp salt and pepper, entirely different from Bryan's brown, rampant curls. Had Bryan had a widow's peak, too? Or would it have been hidden by all that hair in vogue at the time of his disappearance? Oh, why was she having such trouble disregarding the obvious physical differences and concentrating only on the man beneath the facade?

Her thoughts were interrupted by a suck of breath from him, and he blinked and squeezed his eyes shut for a moment.

Realizing he was in pain, she asked in alarm, "Are you all right? Shall I call the nurse?"

"No, no. I'll be all right in a moment," he said, pressing his fingers to his temples. "The doctor tells me that the stabbing pains mean that the ruptured nerves are knitting together." His smile was tentative, as if afraid to trust that the pain had subsided. "I still get killer headaches, though less frequently now. At first they were so bad I thought I'd die, but when they worsened I was afraid I wouldn't." She waited a moment until he looked up at her. "But dying would have meant I'd never see you again, Keely."

Ignoring the implications in his remark, Keely asked polite, noncommittal questions and listened carefully to his replies. Whoever he was, he was obviously intelligent and well educated, and though she listened for traces of the slight Harvard accent Bryan had affected during his years at school, there was no detectable similarity in cadence or inflection. Had she been prepared, she could have come up with some test questions, but she could think of nothing but generalities. For the next half hour they skirted around the sensitive central issue of his bogus claim. It was his job to convince her, not the other way around, wasn't it? She deliberately made no mention of what her life was like since Bryan had left it so abruptly, or of Helen, or the vicissitudes of the magazine. Out of tact, she refrained from asking about his ordeal in the Central American jungle, not because it might be painful for him to remember, but because she did not want to care.

Occasionally their glances would meet, and she was increasingly annoyed that hers seemed to drop away first from the compelling blue of his eyes, but gradually the panicky sensation inside her chest began to dissipate. Now that she was satisfied he really wasn't Bryan, she was brave enough to question his future plans.

"Dr. Villarde says you're to be released from the hospital soon," she ventured, wondering who would pay the enormous hospital bill.

"Yes. After so many months in this place, I'll be glad to get home."

"And where is home?" Keely asked smoothly, hoping to catch him off guard.

"With you, where else?" he said, pinning her with his bold cerulean gaze. "Wherever that may be."

A rush of sensation akin to fear assailed her, but she managed to reply calmly, "I'm afraid that isn't possible."

"No? Why not?"

Both were oh, so casual, as if discussing where to go for dinner.

With a deep breath she took the plunge. "Because, quite frankly, I don't believe you are my husband."

"You don't." The monks-hood eyes narrowed a bit.

"I'm sorry, I don't."

He leaned forward, his lower lip jutting out like a teaspoon. "Well, we're finally down to brass tacks. You're repudiating me. I don't have to guess why."

"And I don't have to tell you why, but I will. You're nothing like him."

His casual tone now changed to one of impatience. "And what do you base this miraculous divination on? Your womanly intuition? You haven't asked one question a wife would ask a missing-and-presumed dead husband."

"As far as I'm concerned, there's nothing to ask."

"Surely you're not rejecting me on the basis of my altered looks and a few minutes of small talk?"

She bristled. "Certainly not." If she had hoped to avoid a confrontation, she knew now she had been too optimistic when millions in Easton money were at stake.

"Then what?" he exploded, and for a moment she had a glimpse of a Bryan-like temper. "Dammit, Keely, you know damned well it's me. I let you play pattycake for the past quarter hour because I thought you needed the time to get used to the idea that I'm even alive, much less adjust to my new face. Well, enough's enough. You're checking me out of this hospital today and I'm going home with you." He threw the coverlet aside, swinging long, bare muscular legs over the side of the bed without a care for his modesty.

Keely jumped up in alarm. "Not with me, you're not!" Adrenaline shot through her, and her temper rose at his audacity. "I don't know who you are, but you're not my husband. For all I know, you and Bryan might have met in some Mexican cantina, got drunk together, and swapped sad stories. Maybe he gave you our wedding picture as a souvenir. To me and in the eyes of the law, my husband is dead!"

"I can't believe this." He seemed almost dazed with convincing incredulity. "My own wife . . ."

Keely pressed her momentary advantage. "I've no doubt you can stir up trouble if that's what you have on your mind. I'm sure you've done your homework—an afternoon in the library with *Who's Who in America,* just chock-full of Easton trivia. But let me remind you that the penalties are severe for blackmail and fraud, and I have friends in high places."

He said softly, sadly, "You have every right to be bitter, Keely, but don't do this to me."

"To you? What about what you're doing to me, to Bryan's family?" she cried. "Do you honestly think you're the first con artist trying to weasel in on the Easton money? Let me tell you, Mr. Whoever-you-are, I'm an expert on crank claims, false trails, and phony leads."

"But my mother? I can't believe she wouldn't at least investigate—"

"I'm doing the investigating," she interrupted. "And

I'll thank you not to call her 'mother'!'' The knowledge
that even after her warning, he might try to move in on
Helen in her weakened condition filled her with fear and
anger. She must nip this in the bud—now. ''Mrs. Easton
is a very sick woman, and if preying on her is on your
mind, I'll make you the sorriest con man in the western
hemisphere.''

Keely fumbled with her handbag, nearly dropping it in
her haste. She took out her checkbook and flipped out a
pen. There was strained silence as she quickly scrawled
out a check and signed it with a decisive flourish. ''I warn
you not to construe this check as a first installment in
extortion. It is strictly a humanitarian donation toward
your hospital expenses. There will be no more.''

Their eyes clashed as she held out the check to him,
determined to expose his intentions at the outset. Would he
play the role to the bitter end, or could he be bought off
with a lump sum? He never allowed his expression to
waver as his eyes flicked derisively down her body, insulting her all the way, until Keely felt the color flooding up
from her throat in a hot tide.

''I get the picture.'' His lip curled. ''A woman with
your looks must have men stashed away like cordwood
just waiting for a chance with the beautiful widow. It must
be very awkward to have a prodigal husband drop in out of
the blue.''

''I find your remark only slightly less offensive than the
scam you're trying to pull,'' she snapped. When he made
no move to take the check, she rose with as much hauteur
as she could muster and let it flutter contemptuously from
her fingers to the bedcover.

His temper snapped. Without warning, and with surprising
strength for a sick man, his hand shot out to grab her wrist.
She lost her balance and half fell across him on the bed.

''What do you think you're doing?'' Struggling to maintain some semblance of dignity, she projected as much
cold outrage in her voice as she could.

His face was just inches from hers. "If you came to test me, then by God, finish the job," he gritted.

"Let . . . me . . . go!" She wrenched around, but his grip was like steel. "Damn you. Get your hands off me!"

But she was held fast, their faces just inches apart. His dangerous male proximity and power over her were never more frightening than when she glimpsed the anger and frustration that darkened those ultramarine eyes. She knew that words and persuasion, a woman's only strength in dealing with men in a man's world, were no help to her now. Their battle had been reduced to its basest component, the brute strength of man over woman. With her feminine power stripped away, she was defenseless.

"Under the circumstances, I could hardly expect you to be faithful to me while I was off to the wars," he jeered. "I'm sure you didn't mourn long. But I'm betting you'll remember the last time we made love."

Again she struggled, and again he subdued her by force. As she lay over his lap, his eyes smoldered over her heaving bosom under the white silk blouse. In the privacy of this hospital room, she suddenly realized he was a stranger, a madman obviously deranged by brain-damaging blows to the head. What would stop him from doing with her as he pleased? She fought with renewed frenzy to free herself.

"I'll scream," she trembled.

"You were never a screamer, Keely." His eyes were enormous, filling the world. "Think back. Remember our first time together?"

A hundred conflicting memories flashed through her mind like pages in a book, all of them unwelcome. Keely was shaken less by the ineluctable force of his will and the strange sensations zigzagging along her nerves than by his knowledge of their first time together. Time was suspended as the memory she'd buried years ago rose like a specter from the grave.

She had told no one about the day ten years ago when a

younger, impetuous Bryan had brought an even younger, hopelessly romantic Keely from her college dorm to the Easton mansion in Westerby to meet his family.

His parents had not been home, and the housekeeper was away doing the marketing. To Keely, it was a deliberate snub; the Eastons obviously thought her "not quite good enough" for the scion of a publishing fortune.

"I don't care what they think of you, I'm going to marry you," he had sworn. "And someday you'll be mistress of this house."

She had pressed her tearstained face against his shoulder. "Oh, Bry, I love you so," she breathed.

His lips hunted for her mouth, then rather roughly, in an excess of exhilarating emotion, he had kissed the curve of her throat down into the vee of her blouse, and it parted. He caught his breath, and suddenly he scooped her up into his arms and headed for the stairs.

When she realized his destination, she became alarmed and struggled to free herself. "No, Bry, we shouldn't, Bryan—"

"Why not?" his voice sounded strange, almost angry, muffled against her hair. "We're going to be spending a lot of time in my bedroom after we're married, so you'd better get used to it."

"Not like this, not here," she said faintly. "Your parents might come home and find us—"

"They're at Cape Cod for the weekend."

"You mean—you lied to me about meeting them today?"

"So what? Wouldn't you rather be with me?" He set her on her feet on the landing, bending her back over his arm, kissing her protests furiously away, daring her to deny him. When she realized he was nearly out of control, she tried to break away.

"Don't, Bry," she gasped. "You're hurting me."

"Then stop fighting me."

It was as if her struggles inflamed him, making up his mind to act out his rebellion against his parents on the battleground of her body. He whisked her into his arms and rushed the stairs two at a time, whirled her into his room and onto the bed, oblivious now to her frantic hands and protests as if they were only token maidenly objections to be overcome with ardor. In his storm of angry passion, he didn't take the time to fully undress her or even himself. It was rip, tear, shock as his body violently invaded hers. She wanted to scream, but she couldn't when he clamped his mouth over hers to muffle her fear and pain. When he was finished, he rearranged their clothing as almost an afterthought, scarcely breathing hard, while Keely lay trembling in shock, disbelief, and shame.

After a moment he leaned over on his elbow to look down into her tear-glazed eyes and dipped his head to kiss her lips. She canted her head aside, her face crumpling.

He looked dumbfounded. "Well, I'll be damned. What's the matter with you?"

"You hurt me, Bry."

He looked puzzled, then laughed gently. "What did you expect, silly girl? It's supposed to hurt the first time."

Her eyes grew enormous in her white face. "I don't mean that kind of hurt. You really don't understand, do you?" she whispered. "You just took what you wanted and you never even cared if it was what I wanted, too. It was our first time, and I wanted it to be special. But it was ugly, ugly, ugly!"

She tore his hands away and flung herself off the bed to limp to the bathroom. She sobbed out loud at her reflection in the mirror. Her hair, so carefully arranged for the meeting with his parents, was wild, her makeup smeared, her skin and clothes sticky. She felt incredibly bruised, inside and out.

Bryan pounded on the locked door. "Honey, I'm sorry. Come on, I thought we were being spontaneous. It won't happen again, I promise. Keely, do you hear me? I said I was sorry . . . ahhhhh, hell!" He kicked the door and swore. "All right, stay in there, you little prude. When you get over your tantrum, I'll be waiting in the car!"

In the years afterward, Keely managed to bury the memory. Bryan was gone, dead these many years, but now another rapacious man wanted something from his widow far more valuable than her virginity had been. He wanted her dead husband's inheritance.

The man who would be Bryan slipped his arm under and around her body, under the expensive linen jacket, and she was pulled so firmly against him she could feel the hard bone and muscle thrusting through his hospital gown. Keely opened her mouth to scream, but no sound came out. The silence was long, breathless, and deafening. She struggled, but she could control neither her desperate breathing nor the thunder of blood in her veins. She felt like a hapless pheasant impaled on the talons of a hawk.

His low intimate laugh jolted her back to reality. "I have a feeling this is one test I'm going to pass with flying colors."

There was no haste in anything he did and, though he gripped her firmly to prevent escape, he was gentle. His head moved to search for her lips, and at the first touch of his mouth her breath left her in a sudden gasp, flaming her cheeks and heating her throat. Oh, the shivery sensation of that feathery kiss! It was the way she'd often wished Bryan would kiss her, not eating a woman alive, choked by a thrusting tongue! She tried to stiffen her lips but she couldn't, so caught up was she in the sheer outrageousness of what he was doing to her, what he was making her feel. Slow, sensuous, languid . . . every movement he made laid bare the long dormant core inside her body until Keely found herself momentarily giving way to the force of this stranger's embrace. The moment was electric, as if all the anger had exploded into hot consuming passion that was all too real.

She realized then that by her passivity she was allowing this stranger, this imposter, to do as he wished with her.

She was appalled, mortified, and before she consciously knew what she was doing she had jerked backward and her hand flew out and connected with his face in a wicked slap that rocked his head sideways. Without a word, she rolled away from him and off the bed and fled.

Panting, heels clattering on the tile floor, stomach in full rebellion, Keely rushed headlong down the corridor. She found the ladies room just in time to retch over the sink. Afterward, she rinsed her mouth with tap water and leaned shakily against the lavatory with her eyes closed for a long time. Then she clamped her hands over her mouth to stifle the incoherent sounds that fought to escape. She had to get away from this place, this man, these memories.

Twenty minutes later she came out, pale but reasonably calm. At the elevator, before she could even push the buzzer, the door slid open and Castillo stepped out.

"There you are, I've been looking everywhere for you." After one glance at her unnatural pallor, he caught her by the arms. "Mrs. Easton—are you all right?"

Dr. Villarde emerged from Room 211, clutching her handbag which she had left behind in her haste. He looked outraged. "You struck him! Why did you strike him, Mrs. Easton? You could have damaged his face!"

Keely was too shaken to be insulted by the doctor's misplaced sympathy. "That man is nothing—nothing like my husband. And when I refused him, he tried to force himself on me—"

The doctor was holding his temper in check. "I hardly think a man in his condition—"

Keely felt the edge of hysteria creeping into her voice. "I don't care what you think. Just keep that man away from me!"

Castillo moved between the distraught Keely and the blustering doctor as if to shield them from each other, and his voice was soothing. "You're understandably upset, Mrs. Easton. This has been very difficult for you, but it is over now. Come. We will return to the hotel."

With a meaningful glance at the physician over her head, he gripped her arm and steered her toward the elevator. From that moment of rescue, Ricardo Castillo became Keely's white knight. Gratefully she committed herself to his care as Dr. Villarde excised himself with poor grace and hurried away to assess the damage done to his prize patient by the loco *americana*.

SIX

That evening Keely accepted Ricardo Castillo's invitation to dinner with gratitude. She appreciated his courtesy, tact, and understanding after being roughed up and insulted by the would-be rapist in Room 211, and by evening's end she was determined that he, too, would be convinced that Amnesty had made a mistaken identification.

As the taxi sped down the Pasco de la Reforma toward Chapultepec, the western sky flamed over the low blanket of purple smog, which had lifted just enough to see the smudge where Popocatepetl and Ixtacihuatl should be. For the first time in three days of nightmare, she was determined to throw herself into the evening with all the forced gaiety she could muster.

At dusk they reached a glittering restaurant crowning a forested garden landscape, which Castillo explained had been originally designed for the Empress Carlota during Empire days. Dinner was an elegant affair, and her escort's personable company and the candlelight softened her agitated mood. Keely had dressed with care in a low-buttoned white silk jacket over a soft dirndl skirt—no blouse or jewelry, except for glowing aquamarines in her ears which had been a birthday gift from Vern last year. Ricardo Castillo's admiring glance told her that he liked what he saw, and she was strangely pleased. It was important that he see her as an unmarried woman, unconnected in any way to that man in the hospital or even her late husband.

Soon he was calling her Keely and she was calling him Ric, and during dinner they could faintly hear the sounds of revelry from a nearby trendy discotheque where the music could be felt as well as heard, thumping like a heartbeat on the perfumed night air. The day's happenings could not be ignored forever. Keely was determined that Castillo should see her as the victim in this fiasco; to fail to convince him would place her and Helen in a dangerous position. Should the charlatan in Room 211 press his claim, she would prefer to count Castillo as an ally.

"What will happen to him now, Ric?"

He glanced across the table at her, his face inscrutable in chiaroscuro. "Since you do not claim him, he will probably be returned to your country under some sort of medical arrangement."

"But why can't he stay here? I'm sure he speaks fluent Spanish."

"Because American mercenaries are persona non grata in Mexico. *Turistas, si; contras, no*." Something in his voice made her open her eyes, but all she could see in the candlelight was his classic Spanish profile. He added slowly, "Then you do care . . . a little . . . what happens to him?"

"I feel nothing but contempt for a crook who's trying to capitalize on Bryan's death!"

"How will you feel if you find out later that you were wrong?"

"I'm not wrong. I've never been more sure of anything in my life, and I refuse to conduct myself as if there were any possibility." She was silent then, not knowing exactly how to elaborate. Ric wisely refrained from committing himself one way or another, and she had to respect him for that. In the taxi on the way back to the hotel, replete from good food and far too much wine, Keely allowed her head to loll back languorously on the taxi seat cushion.

"Ric?"

"Mmm?" He glanced over at her in the shadowed interior.

"Thank you for not leaving me alone tonight with my ghosts."

He laughed softly, picked up her hand and kissed it. "I could have sworn my only motive was a selfish one—the pleasure of your company."

Everything about him, from the shared human contact she had needed so desperately tonight, to the faint scent of his cologne mingling with the fragrance of cigar smoke and immaculate linen, symbolized comfort and security. As the taxicab rolled up in front of the hotel portico, an unreasoning fear of being alone overwhelmed her. In the face-saving darkness of the cab, she turned to him impulsively and whispered, "Stay with me tonight, Ric."

The moment her desperate invitation was out of her mouth, he knew she was in psychological crisis. "Keely, you don't mean that."

"God help me, Ric, I do," she cried softly, clinging to him unashamedly.

He pulled her arms from his neck, but she slid them around his waist, under his jacket. "Keely, carissima . . . pull yourself together. Tomorrow you would despise yourself, despise me. I cannot take advantage of you in your vulnerable condition . . ."

He could sense the powerful signal of need emanating from her, and he found himself wanting to do more than comfort her with words. The thought of holding her in his arms made his breath catch and his own self-control weaken. Mesmerized and excited in spite of himself, he could almost taste her trembling, half-parted lips. Almost as if some unseen, giant hand were pressing down on his neck, his head dipped reluctantly, yet compulsively, until his mouth hovered over hers. For a long, agonizing moment, he struggled on the brink of insanity, his ethics warring with a body pulsing with a sexual energy he had not felt for any woman in years.

It was with a superhuman discipline that he put her away from him and tipped her chin so that she was forced to look up into his face. The pupils of his eyes were blacker than night. "Don't do this," he said, shaking her gently. "It is the wine, the moonlight. You are hurting, and your feelings are confused. Tomorrow you will be on a plane back to New York, and I will be but a regret in your heart." He paused, then said softly so that she had to strain to hear his voice, "Do not use me tonight, Keely."

Her face flamed. "Am I using you?"

"You seek to separate yourself from the memory of your husband in the arms of another man." He smiled sadly. "Carissima, I would much rather be your friend tomorrow than your lover tonight."

His words brought her to her senses, and she was flooded with shame. "You're not just any man, Ric."

"I know that." His reply was quick, knowing he had stung her pride with his refusal.

She stumbled out of the cab and walked quickly through the door while Ric paid the driver. All she wanted now was to get away from him before her humiliation was complete.

He caught her at the elevator, grabbing her arm and pulling her around to face him. "Keely, Keely—I cannot let you go like this—"

She managed a smile. "I'm all right, Ric. Really."

At a loss for words, he reached out to break the teardop glistening on her lashes with his thumb, then raised it to his lips. "If we should ever meet again in New York," he said with a hard grin, "you may not count on my being noble a second time."

Then he turned and walked swiftly away.

Keely was appalled at what she had almost done—it was as if someone else had taken possession of her senses. What must Ric think of her? She had not fooled him for a moment, only herself; yet he had let her down tactfully, a gentleman to the end. The elevator door glided open silently and she stepped in, already feeling the familiar black solitude settling around her like a malignant miasma. Over the years, she had learned that loneliness was the price of a woman's independence.

She squared her shoulders and prepared to pay it again.

SEVEN

The dark-haired man in the Pierre Cardin business suit shouldered his way through the crowd toward the baggage checkout. The first glimpse of his angular, familiar figure sent such a leap of gladness through Keely that she dropped her case and flew into his arms, their bitter words forgiven but not forgotten.

Vern Preston's usually taciturn face broke into a tight smile. "Well? The usual wild goose chase?"

"Oh, Vern—" She clung to him, ridiculously close to tears again, hating to let him see how much she needed his support.

"What is it? What went wrong?" he asked, suddenly concerned. He tried to hold her away to see into her face, but she shook her head, afraid he would see how ragged her nerves really were. "I knew I should have gone with you." He took her arm decisively. "Come on. We can talk in the car."

Once there, he left the key dangling in the ignition and turned to her, his fine eyes never leaving her face.

"Out with it," he said softly. "What's upsetting you?"

Everything poured out of her then, the letter from Amnesty International, Ricardo Castillo, the hospital . . . the man who claimed to be her missing husband. Vern sat there unspeaking, apprehension deepening the lines in his face as he listened.

44

When she finished, he said quietly, "Are you sure, one-hundred percent positive, that this man could not be Bryan?"

She looked at him indignantly. "We lived together for six months. I think I'd know my own husband."

"Then what's his angle?"

She responded bitterly, "What else? Helen's money." Then she told him about the check she had given the man in Mexico City.

A soft expletive left his lips as Vern struck the steering wheel with his fist. "My God, Keely, why did you whet his appetite with money? Do you have any idea what the press would do to you if they get wind of this? They'll call it blood money, hush money. Did you really think you could pay him off once and be done with him?"

"It was a gift of charity," she defended. "If he comes after us again, at least I bought Helen a little time until she's physically stronger. It was a gamble, but maybe I scared him off and he'll be satisfied with what he managed to get. And if he dares to make trouble, I'll make him wish he'd never been born!"

Vern grinned then. "In that case, he may need my sympathy."

Keely was in no mood for Vern's needling. "What's that supposed to mean?" she flared.

Vern took her hand impulsively. "Keely, for God's sake, you frustrate the hell out of me. Going to Mexico City hasn't changed anything—Bryan's still legally dead, so what's to be gained by postponing our wedding? And if this man presses his claim, we'll be that much stronger united as man and wife. Marry me now!"

She pulled away and rubbed her temples with her fingertips. "Vern, I'm exhausted. Can't we discuss this another time?"

"We've been discussing it another time for two years now," Vern persisted. He took her hand again and held it firmly, giving it gentle little jerks to keep her attention when she tried to turn aside. "Dammit, all I'm asking is a formal announcement of our engagement. We can wait to get married until after the election. Now stop stalling and say yes."

She closed her eyes. "Yes."

He paused. "Do you mean it, or are you just tired and a yes is the quickest way to shut me up?"

She opened her eyes wearily. "I said yes, Vern." She was too exhausted, too shell-shocked to argue. Without protest, she allowed him to draw her against his chest for a brief embrace, and she wondered where the gladness she'd felt on seeing him at the airport had fled.

Vern started the car, his expression a mixture of aggravation and triumph. "We'll make the engagement announcement at the fund-raiser dinner next month. That will give you time to break the news to Helen."

"Helen!" Keely groaned.

"For God's sake, how surprised can she be? I've been a part of your life three times longer than Bryan ever was." Exasperated, he turned into traffic and the next hour was spent in silence as they drove to Westerby.

Dusk was just creeping over the hills, casting deep pools of shadows under the stately old trees in the exclusive residential community. Vern pulled into the tree-shaded lane leading to the Easton mansion and parked in the circular drive. Hoping to forestall any more conversation, Keely got out of the car and waited until Vern followed to unload her cases out of the trunk and carry them up the sweeping, urn-lined steps into the house.

"Just set them in the foyer," she instructed. "Mrs. Maguire can unpack them later."

After a perfunctory kiss and a promise to call her tomorrow for lunch, Vern took his leave.

On the way to her room, she stopped in to see Helen. Her mother-in-law was asleep in her Empire bed, her apricot hair a flame against the lace pillow. Keely drew up the velvet boudoir chair. Looking down at that delicate, careworn face, Keely wondered how to break the news to Bryan's mother that her beloved son's wife had promised to marry another man.

Over the years, Helen had stubbornly clung to the hope that Bryan might still be alive. Such a fragile shell! Freedom from trouble, unhappiness, and pain should be the solace of old age, not the cruel limbo of uncertainty and bereavement. Keely intended to see that Helen was protected from another emotional upheaval, no matter the cost to herself.

Touching the soft hair tenderly, she could see no trace of the strong, self-sufficient woman who had run the Easton empire after her husband died of lung cancer. Keely pitied Helen and had made the mistake of humoring her delusion that Bryan would return once he sowed his wild oats. She was painfully aware that although Helen loved her, she was only a stand-in for Bryan.

Sitting there watching the gentle rise and fall of Helen's breathing, Keely wondered where she would get the courage to tell Helen she was abandoning the vigil and would marry Vern Preston. Surely Helen could understand that Vern could give her the stability that Bryan never had. The Prestons had handled the lucrative Easton account for years. The two young scions had gone to Harvard together, but were never friends. Bryan was volatile and unconventional, while Vern was conservative by nature and after graduation slipped into his father's law firm without a ripple.

But what counted to Keely was that in the media circus aftermath of Bryan's disappearance, Vern had taken the traumatized Keely under his wing and helped restore her shattered self-esteem as no one else had done. Grateful for his attention and impressed by his innate self-discipline, she found in him a man whose mind, body, and principles were as straight as the clothes he wore with such masculine severity. As she came to know him better, she understood that it was more than just control—he was sexually as cool as she, which enhanced his value in her eyes.

Keely had put that part of her life on hold for the past seven years, and she wanted never to be caught up in an emotional maelstrom where that control was jeopardized.

A gourmet, art collector, and avid theater patron, Vern introduced her to the world that had been snatched from Bryan when his father disinherited him. Though Vern's sophistication and knowledge were worlds beyond her own experience, there was never a trace of patronage. She openly appreciated his intellect and he literally basked in her admiration.

Then he spoiled it all by asking her to marry him. Her wounds were too raw; she turned him down as gracefully as she could and fled to Europe. A freelance newswriter who lectured in her college journalism class offered her a job in Paris. She jumped at the opportunity.

Jeff Blume was forty-two years old, short but built like a fullback. A native New Yorker, he now worked for a world news syndicate as a foreign correspondent. If his journalistic talent was prodigious, his fondness for alcohol and cocaine was legendary. At first, Keely was oblivious to his problems, and Jeff soon realized her potential.

"I've finally found a woman who can read without moving her lips and doesn't look like Pierre Salinger in drag," he exulted.

With London, Paris, and Rome on the menu, Jeff Blume introduced her to a veritable smorgasbord of top writers, producers, businessmen, and politicians, and the very air was charged with intellect and talent. Keely thrived on Jeff's charmed circle of world-class thinkers and leaders, forming many valuable connections that would stand her in good stead in later years.

Jeff discovered Keely's uncanny talent for getting difficult interviews and asking penetrating questions without causing offense. She had a knack for translating even the most arcane governmentese into language the man on the street could understand. Her writing matured rapidly, and she was soon delivering thoughtful treatises on economic and political developments, and doing it on a deadline.

Though she was fiercely loyal to Jeff, she was not so blind she could not see that his cocaine and alcohol habit was affecting his work. He was soon letting her write more of his assignments and then no longer bothered to edit and stamp them with his own journalistic style. When her father began sending her clippings of her own uncut articles from American magazines and newspapers under Jeff Blume's byline, Keely knew he was in serious trouble. Yet he refused to get help. Where she had once been buoyed by her mentor's infallibility, she was now in the uncomfortable position of shoring up his confidence and bailing him out of scrapes. With her there to manage the deadlines, Jeff was free to slide even further into the oblivion of drugs. But she couldn't make herself quit him for his own good. Jeff made the break for her—with an overdose.

She went home to Stamford to lick her wounds over Jeff's untimely death, and scarcely a week later she got a telegram from Easton Publishing. There was an assignment for her if she was interested.

"Guilty as charged," Owen Neal admitted cheerfully when she accused her father of setting it up. "So I sent Mrs. Easton a few clippings. Why shouldn't I look out for my daughter? I'm damn proud of you, honey."

"She probably wants me to do an article on 'Drugs and Journalism,' so she can make a million at Jeff's expense," said Keely bitterly.

"Go see what she wants," her father urged. "If the assignment doesn't suit you, spit in the old bag's eye."

Keely was still very sensitive to the fact that Alfred Easton, and therefore Helen Easton in marital solidarity, had considered her an upstart fortune hunter and the direct cause of Bryan's fall from grace. But with a living to make, a job was a job.

When she called for an appointment, she was surprised and suspicious when Mrs. Easton sent her chauffered limousine to pick her up. For some reason, the interview was to take place in the Easton apartment in the fashionable Dakota.

Helen Easton seemed strangely cordial and complimentary about her journalistic credits, then quickly gave up any pretense of discussing business. "I've always regretted the way we parted, Keely. We were both caught between our men and their power struggle with each other. I realize now that you were as much a victim as I, and I hope you'll find it in your heart to forgive me."

Keely was amazed. For the first time she realized how much Helen had been torn between her irascible, conservative husband and their bohemian son.

As if reading her thoughts, Helen went on softly. "Alfred was hard—too hard—on Bryan, of course, but at times it seemed that Bryan went out of his way to annoy his father."

"And marrying me certainly annoyed his father," Keely observed with more rancor than she intended. "Because of me, Bryan was disinherited."

"Not actually disinherited," Helen defended quickly. "Money was Alfred's misguided way to control Bryan. If you had really known my husband . . . the two of you would have admired each other." Her eyes grew misty as she fidgeted with a lace handkerchief, and Keely saw that she still wore a plain gold wedding band on her left hand. "Our son's political positions were a bitter disappointment to Alfred, and the thought of someday turning responsibility for the magazines over to Bryan, who openly mocked his values, made him frantic. Their goals were basically the same, but where Alfred believed that change must be wrought by law, Bryan felt physical action and force were the answer. And he was willing to back up his beliefs in Central America."

The friendship between the two women had been unbreakably forged from that meeting.

One day, while having coffee in the elegant yet comfortable living room of her Dakota apartment, Helen broached another subject to Keely.

"I'm planning to start a new magazine," she announced. "And I want you to be a part of it."

As Helen unveiled her ideas, Keely could hardly contain her rising excitement. The new magazine would diverge widely from the stodgy, intellectual viewpoint of both *World Forum* and *Business Forum* magazines, while following a total news format. Helen wanted something fresh and exciting to appeal to the "yuppie" segment of the population.

"Sensationalism sells magazines, and we want all the staples that feed the reading appetites of Americans—sex, crime, and scandal, but I don't want a tabloid," Helen explained. "And I'm not handing this to you on a silver platter because of your connection with the Eastons. Your ideas must compete anonymously with other unsigned prospectuses, and the winner will be chosen by an objective panel. To win, you must make it on your own talent." She didn't need to add that if her idea was chosen, Keely would become a very rich young woman.

Outwardly Keely sipped her coffee sedately, as if thinking over an ordinary assignment offer, but inwardly she was exulting. Helen's protestations notwithstanding, Keely knew she certainly would never have had a chance at this incredible opportunity had she not been married to Helen's son, but she was not inclined to quibble. She wanted to run to the window, throw it open, and shout the news to the people below. But of course she didn't; instead, the offer was accepted with modest thanks.

Keely plunged into the prospectus for the project. To make up the dummy, she used her own stories, digging out a veritable treasure trove of unused articles written for Jeff Blume which he had rejected as not suited to his milieu. She combed through staff files for show-and-tell photographs.

After a month of preparation, the prospectuses were ready for the panel's decision. When Keely saw some of the other entries, her heart sank. Her own dummy, with its oversize photos, simplified line drawings and satirical cartoons, somehow seemed amateurish beside the slick, low-key layouts of more experienced journalistic teams. But it was too late to withdraw.

Keely retreated home to Connecticut to await the verdict. She had no illusions about her chances of winning the competition. But she had done her best, her father consoled her, and she gained valuable experience in the process. What Keely regretted most about losing was that the brilliant name she had chosen for the magazine, *EastonWest*, would fall by the wayside.

When the telegram arrived, Keely could not bring herself to look. It lay on the kitchen table until her father came home from work, and when he opened it she knew how actors must feel on opening the envelope at the Academy Awards ceremony. Even when her father threw the telegram into the air with a shout and grabbed her in a whirling bear hug, she couldn't believe she'd won. Even now the memory of that heady moment of victory brought a bittersweet smile to her lips.

If Keely had thought composing the prospectus was difficult, she soon learned it was child's play compared to the grueling months of preparation for a new magazine. Most terrifying of all was the knowledge that the ultimate responsibility for the magazine's success or failure rested entirely on her untried shoulders. All the experts openly doubted her ability to carry it off, and predicted that the new magazine would fall flat on its face.

But it did not fall flat. Not only did the public embrace *EastonWest*, but they did so with a passion. Instant success was an unexpected phenomenon and a circumstance that ended up costing Helen a few million more than she had planned to get the fledgling enterprise off the ground.

When public demand skyrocketed, giving advertisers four times the circulation they were paying for, rates had to be hastily readjusted. Helen was delighted with the meteoric success of *EastonWest* and unwilling to let the bonanza fizzle with too few magazines to meet the demand, so the print order was doubled, then tripled, and new subscriptions poured in.

From that moment on, Keely's touch was pure gold.

She was a woman of Camelot, the darling of the business world, a baby tycoon. Helen's gamble on her daughter-in-law to keep the family business in family hands succeeded beyond her wildest dreams.

Five years later, after Helen's devastating stroke, it fell to Keely to take over the rest of the publishing empire and hold it together. With Bryan gone and her mother-in-law in ill health, everyone recognized Keely as the heir apparent, and she was courted like a crown princess.

Meanwhile, she and Vern resumed their friendship. In the intervening years, their positions had shifted dramatically. At one time, Keely stood to gain most from a liaison—socially, she had been a nobody, deserted by her husband and ignored by her in-laws, while Vern was from a good family with old money, already on the rise with a sky's-the-limit career ahead of him in law and politics. But now the pluses had shifted to her side; Bryan's celebrity disappearance and her success with *EastonWest* had conferred a Jackie Kennedy star status on her, and any connection with the powerful Easton empire was bound to reflect glory and benefits on the man who wed her. When the beautiful young widow did not marry again, the public admired her for being "true" to her late husband's memory. No one seemed to take Vern Preston's quest for her hand very seriously.

Rousing herself back to the present, Keely stood up and gazed down at Helen who was breathing fitfully. She had made wonderful progress after her stroke, but she tired so easily now and her speech was slow and halting. A physical therapist came twice a day, and she could now walk with a quad cane. With loving fingers, Keely brushed the soft, thinning hair back from the lined forehead. Tonight, in the semi-shadow of the room looking down at the fine old face, she was never more conscious of the pain Helen had suffered in losing a son in the prime of his life.

Unbidden, a mental picture of the mysterious man in Mexico City flashed through her thoughts. To have her hopes raised then dashed down again had been hard enough on her when she was healthy. In her present condition, the shock could be fatal. Keely vowed anew to prevent that from ever happening.

Returning to her room in plenty of time to catch Vern's new campaign spot on television, Keely flicked the remote control to the right channel, the sound muted during the commercial. A news bulletin flashed on to a scene of pandemonium at JFK airport, a jumbo jet in the background. Her news interest piqued, she fumbled for the remote control, wondering if any of her people were covering—a foreign dignitary? A hijacking? A reporter squinted into the camera lights, and gestured behind him at an ambulance whose red lights cast an eerie glow over his face.

The camera panned to the open doors of the jetliner, its portable stairs in place. Passengers streamed down the steps, and Keely watched with heightened interest until the last passenger, evidently the person everyone was waiting for, appeared in the doorway.

The camera telescoped in. A man in a wheelchair, wearing dark glasses, paused at the head of the steps as if surprised at the reception. Keely's eyes riveted on him in recognition, every nerve in her body tingling.

It was the man she'd left behind just hours ago in Mexico City—the man who claimed to be Bryan Easton.

EIGHT

Darkly silvered hair ruffling in the evening breeze, the familiar stranger paused, glancing down at the waiting throng below. He waved and smiled for the cameras, almost courting them. Even the television cameras could not dilute the relaxed confidence and male presence that had so fascinated and frightened her in Mexico City. It was almost as if—he truly believed his own grandiose claims.

As Keely watched in mesmerized shock, the lift rose and his wheelchair was anchored in place for the brief ride to the ground. In moments, he had been whisked away in an ambulance, leaving a milling crowd of reporters and the curious behind to speculate on the significance of the event.

The awful spell into which she had fallen was broken, and Keely realized she had watched the entire scene with the volume turned too low to hear. She leaped up, spilling several letters onto the carpet in her haste to turn up the sound.

A blast of wind, roaring engines and the cacophony of voices were overridden by the terse, high-pitched commentary of the reporter. "There he goes, ladies and gentlemen, apparently the scion of an American publishing family, shot down in Central America seven years ago and presumed dead . . . but he's alive and looking quite well tonight in New York City considering his ordeal. Back to you, Dan.''

The studio anchorman turned from the screen and with utmost gravity addressed the unseen audience. "Thank you, Bill. There you have it, folks, Bryan Easton, alive to tell the tale of capture, torture, and imprisonment. We'll have a special report at eleven.''

The telephone began to ring.

From the depths of the house, there was a scream, and Keely rushed into the corridor in time to see Mrs. Maguire running toward Helen's room.

With superhuman strength, Keely lunged and caught her.

"Oh, ma'am, ma'am, have you heard the news?'' The housekeeper was crying and breathless at the same time.

"I've heard. Calm yourself,'' Keely said, not letting go her grip on the woman's arm.

"I must tell Miss Helen—''

"You'll do nothing of the kind,'' Keely interrupted firmly. "Not until we discuss it with Dr. Houten. Do you understand, Mrs. Maguire? Do you want her to have another stroke? I'm going to call the doctor right now. No one—and I mean no one—tells Mrs. Easton until I give the word, or I'll hold you responsible. Do you understand?''

The housekeeper was reduced to teary babbling. "Oh, ma'am, to think our sweet boy is alive and come home! Did you see his poor face, all different, like a stranger's! Oh, what those animals did to him—'' Her face crumpled and she threw her apron up over her head and began to sob.

Keely encircled her shoulders with an arm and walked her back to her room. "Calm yourself, Mrs. Maguire. You mustn't get your hopes up before this man's claim can be thoroughly investigated— ''

"Claim? Whatever are you saying, ma'am?'' Mrs. Maguire pulled up short, aghast.

"I'm saying you should remember two years ago when

Helen got that chopped-off finger in the mail with a demand for money in exchange for Bryan's body. It was a hoax, but do you want to put her through that again?''

"But this is different," Mrs. Maguire argued. "Miss Helen would know in a minute if it's Bryan—"

"And as his wife, so would I, wouldn't I?" Keely reasoned. "I checked this man out myself in Mexico City, and he isn't Bryan. He's a clever impostor who thinks he's going to cash in on a juicy fortune."

But searching the woman's obdurate expression, Keely saw only resentment and disbelief, and her heart contracted with foreboding.

From then on, Keely lived in a state of siege, running gauntlets of shouting reporters every time she stepped out on the street. The house opposite her bedroom at home sprouted telephoto lenses at every window and her telephone was bugged. The next morning Vern and Dr. Houten had to wade through television news crews blocking the driveway and lawn, to be ushered in by Sikes through a side entrance. On Vern's advice, Keely told the doctor the whole story. The doctor's face grew grave, and he immediately agreed that until the man's identity was verified beyond a doubt, Helen was not to be told.

Finally, Keely decided she'd better give some sort of statement to the press to relieve the pressure. Looking far more composed and businesslike than she felt in a gray wool suit over an open-necked cranberry blouse, Keely had never been so grateful to Vern as she was now. He fielded the questions and shielded her from the scuffle around the front door. Reporters and cameramen shoved and pushed to get a view of her as she stationed herself in front of a makeshift lectern bristling with dozens of bound microphones. Flashpaks popped everywhere, making her blink. Her glance caught the headlines of two papers held aloft in the melee—MISSING PUBLISHER FOUND ALIVE? and EASTON HEIR RETURNS!

Vern waved his arms for silence. "Here! Here! Mrs.

Easton will make a brief statement and answer some of your questions. But only if you behave in an orderly fashion. Now, fall back and let her breathe!''

Keely looked around at them all, waiting for silence. When she spoke it was in a low, steady tone to force their close attention. Her words were chosen carefully. ''Ladies and gentlemen of the press, seven years ago Bryan Easton was shot down in a helicopter over the Central American jungle and was declared legally dead. I will not go into the many cruel hoax attempts that followed, or the carnival atmosphere that attended his death, or the trauma that Helen Easton suffered as a result.'' She paused and looked directly into the television camera, as if challenging the impostor face to face. ''Two days ago, after being contacted by Amnesty International, I flew to Mexico City for a meeting with a man claiming to be my husband. After our interview, I concluded that he was not. I stop short of calling this man a liar; he may well be, but it is also possible that as a result of head injuries suffered during his ordeal he is the unfortunate victim of delusions. Regardless of speculation, the fact remains: He is not Bryan Easton.'' There was a rushing hum from the press at her strong statement, and Keely waited a moment to continue. ''Within the next week, I understand he will remain hospitalized for tests and further investigations into his identity. And when these studies are done and his intent is discovered to be a deliberate attempt at fraud, I shall prosecute him to the full extent of the law.''

Pandemonium broke out, and Keely saw Vern's worried lawyer-look over her inflammatory language. But she meant every word she said. Nothing could be strong enough. Then, her lovely eyes softened to eloquence as she beseeched them on Helen's behalf. ''I would like to remind you that I am in the business of reporting news. But I hope you will resist the temptation to print rumor and scandal, and stick to the truth. You must know that having my husband's tragic death periodically exhumed in the press is very traumatic to both me and to his mother. Now that Mrs. Easton is recovering from a stroke, it could be deadly. So please, I ask you—beg you—to use restraint. Thank you all.''

There was a moment's pause as they digested that. Then the barrage of questions began, all shouted and mixed together in a meaningless stew of human voices.

"One at a time!'' Vern called out over the din. "Raise your hands or she walks!''

Hands waved frantically and Keely picked one.

"Does Helen Easton know about this? When do you plan to tell her?''

"Since I fully expect this matter to be resolved within a few days, there will be no need to inform Mrs. Easton of yet another dead end,'' Keely replied.

"Are you making all of Mrs. Easton's decisions?''

Keely's eyes flashed dangerously. "While she is ill, it is my decision, based on her doctor's instructions.''

Keely had never deluded herself that she was exempt from grilling by the press. But these reporters skewered her with questions she would have fired her own people for asking.

"Is it true that you are financing a team of psychiatrists at Bellevue to test the claimant?''

"No, it is not true.''

"Is the CIA involved?''

"You'll have to ask them.''

"Can you tell us, in light of your husband's complete facial plastic surgery, your criteria for positive identification?''

"No comment. I'd like to remind you to precede the word 'husband' with alleged,'' Keely warned sharply.

"Is it true you paid his hospital bill in Mexico City, and how much was it?''

"I did not pay his hospital bill. The man was indigent, and I impulsively donated a small sum to help him when he left the hospital.''

"If the claimant can prove his identity, will you divorce or reconcile?"

"No comment!"

"Does this change your plans to marry Vern Preston?"

Mercifully, Vern called a halt, and to the accompaniment of camera flashes exploding in her face, she was hustled back in the house. Keely was shaken from her ordeal, more from anger than anything else. How dare they ask questions like that, with Helen upstairs in her sickbed? While Vern wrapped up the impromptu news conference and attended to some of his own pressing business, Keely got on the phone, pacing, shaking her fist, snapping orders left and right to her assembled staff.

"I want a twenty-four hour guard around this house to keep those ghouls off the grounds," she seethed. "One of them actually stuck mountain-climbing pitons in an upstairs windowsill! And I want a restraining order slapped on that—phony excuse for a man. If he as much as shows his artificial nose around Helen, I want him arrested!"

The bogus "Bryan Easton" was hot news. Every newspaper and magazine ran headline stories, and even Vern's run for the Senate, rather than being eclipsed, vaulted him into national attention. The switchboards of both Easton Enterprises and Vern's campaign headquarters were inundated with calls. At home, Keely had the phone temporarily disconnected, then the number changed and unlisted. Political gossip columnists were having a field day, speculating on who was the real villain of the piece—an impostor out to cash in on a famous name, or a spiteful wife who had moved in and grabbed her husband's rightful inheritance.

The ersatz Bryan's new face was plastered over every magazine cover, as was Keely's. Photographs were clipped and doctored to show them nose to nose in angry confrontation or billing and cooing. The stranger had become almost a national hero, and his guerrilla exploits, prison ordeal, and subsequent plastic surgery were recounted ad nauseam in the papers. Even Congress was moved to approve more aid to the region. There was a Senate investigation into American mercenaries and gunrunning sponsored by the CIA in Central America. Stories detailed the investigation into the claimant's identity, and several people came forward who said they knew who he really was, but they were all eventually discounted as sensation seekers. All was mass confusion.

While extensive physical examinations and tests were being made, her nemesis lived in a suite in a private hospital, and periodic reports were issued to Keely. So far, all polygraphs and medical records were inconclusive or in his favor. There were adherents to both sides. The claimant's grave injuries and subsequent plastic reconstruction conveniently camouflaged his physical differences, and inconsistencies in his story could be attributed to "memory lapses."

But the days passed and no real evidence one way or the other was forthcoming. Keely lived on tenterhooks. How long could she keep Helen from getting involved while this mess dragged on interminably?

She was puzzled, too, that not once did the man make any attempt to contact Keely or Helen personally. He granted no interviews. He seemed content to let public opinion build his case for credibility. Every newspaper, magazine, and yellow tabloid ran lurid daily headline stories. Strung together, they almost had a plot:

NOT MY HUSBAND! WIFE DECLARES.
AMA AND CIA TO QUESTION EASTON CLAIMANT.
CLAIMANT TESTED BY PANEL OF DOCTORS.
EASTON PASSES LIE DETECTOR.
CLAIMANT FLUNKS LIE DETECTOR.
FAMILY FRIENDS RECOGNIZE EASTON.
BRYAN FATHERED MY CHILD, STARLET CLAIMS.
COULD BE FAKING, ADMITS PSYCHIATRIST.
CLAIMANT EASTON REINCARNATED, SAYS PSYCHIC.

EASTON CASE CIA PLOT?

KEELY LONE HOLDOUT!

KEELY SECRETLY WEDS ATTORNEY IN BIGA-
MOUS MARRIAGE.

HELEN EASTON: RECLUSE OR PRISONER?

With Vern's election just a few weeks away, the furor over the ersatz Bryan Easton was reaching crisis proportions. Yet the claimant still had not come out of seclusion. He was clever; he knew that if he waited, public pressure for a juicy confrontation would mount until Keely was forced to acknowledge him as public opinion tilted first this way and that.

Every day Keely found herself more on the defensive with not only frankly hostile factions, but with her own friends and supporters. Some thought she was subconsciously rejecting him either for his past transgressions or fear that he would usurp her position in the Easton enclave; while others urged her to wage war with the man in the press, bringing her considerable power and clout to bear. This she adamantly refused to do. She had made her statement; nothing had changed since then, and the ball was in his court.

The Eastons were mercilessly parodied on late night talk shows and lampooned in every comedian's standup routine. A political comic strip ran a continuing segment, and several thinly veiled melodramas were aired on television. An editorial cartoon in the *Times* cast Keely as "Hard-hearted Hannah," poised with a bucket of water over a drowning Bryan Easton. Subtly the tide of public sentiment and sympathy began to ebb away from Keely, flowing instead toward the underdog.

Even at work she met opposition.

At her first weekly planning meeting since the bombshell fell, Keely was determined to settle the future handling of the matter in the Easton publications once and for all.

As she swept into the conference room, Keely hoped

she looked more in control and decisive than she felt. All heads swiveled to look at her, lovely yet businesslike in a wide-belted safari-style suit with leopardskin patterned pumps.

Everyone on staff was eager to hear firsthand how Keely planned to handle the hot story they had been ordered to ignore in their own publications. Keely whipped through the routine business with her customary elan before coming to the part that interested them most.

Frank Cabell, the editor-in-chief, was vocally unhappy with her decision to ignore the Bryan Easton story in the pages of *EastonWest* magazine. When he attempted to introduce an article on the subject, Keely quickly cut him short.

"But it's news. You can't ignore it just because it happens to touch you personally," Frank argued. "Every other news agency in the world is making millions off the story, while our circulation is suffering because you won't use it. The public is hungry for Bryan Easton stories. They're even digging up old stuff on the disappearance of Michael Rockefeller in New Guinea back in the early sixties, for chrissakes, and comparing it with that! Keely, we look like a bunch of jackasses for letting everyone else cash in on a story that by rights is our exclusive. It makes people wonder if you have something to hide."

"I've never sunk to muckraking for a story yet, and I'm not starting now," she snapped. "I've refuted this man's lies in public already and that's my final word on the subject." Although her voice was quiet, there was a hard edge to it. "We'll run a factual report as we always do, when there's something factual to report. But I will not—repeat, will not—stoop to using this publication to lend credence to scuttlebut and blatant speculation just to titillate the scandalmongers. And I will not have Helen Easton dragged into it, period. I want to see every word written on the subject emanating from this office. Do I make myself clear?"

She stared them all down, willing them into submission, and when every eye had dropped away, she turned to go. Just as she closed the door behind her, somebody started humming "Hard-hearted Hannah."

Keely walked briskly to her secretary's office to instruct her before leaving for lunch, when she heard a male voice behind her.

"Keely."

She turned around, politely inquiring. When she recognized the man walking toward her, the blood stood still in her veins.

NINE

Silence fell as everyone in the outer office stopped what they were doing to watch the drama unfold. It was the moment the world had anticipated for weeks. Keely felt rooted to the spot as the man who claimed to be her husband covered the distance between them with a curiously graceful economy of movement.

He was a different man from the pale rack of bones she had seen a month ago in a Mexican hospital bed. His flesh and muscle were nearly back to what they must have been before his ordeal in the jungle. She hadn't realized then how tall he was—he seemed taller than Bryan, and though still lean in comparison, it made him seem more powerfully built. Not even the light jacket over slacks could disguise the enormous energy contained in a body honed in the jungle instead of a boardroom. She wondered if he had used her money to pay for the clothes on his back.

Keely knew very well why he was here, and it wasn't a social call. Tension rippled through her. She would have been less than honest if she didn't admit that the sight of this magnetic man stirred her pulses, as it would any woman with eyes in her head. And he made it plain he liked what he saw, too, looking her over from the top of her stylishly cut, glossy black hair to the feminine curves above and below her slim waist. There was a slight smile on his artificially enhanced face, and Keely had the sensation she was being dissected as neatly as a frog in a laboratory.

After her momentary lapse in poise, her face shut down, leaving only cold inquiry in her expression. "How did you get in here?" she demanded. "Get out before I have you thrown out."

There was an indolent flick of one dark brow to punctuate the amusement in his blue gaze. "Is all this rancor really necessary? I'm merely making a bread-and-butter call—to thank you personally for your generosity in Mexico City."

She wasn't quite sure whether or not he was being facetious, but she took no chances in letting down her guard. "No doubt you were hoping my philanthropy would extend to New York," she rejoined caustically. "I was wondering when you'd show up to put the bite on me."

He laughed softly at her choice of words and let his eyes stray to her neck. "If that's an invitation, I accept. Actually, I came to repay the money you loaned me." She looked startled when he brought out an envelope from his inside jacket pocket. "My own funds were transferred from my bank in Panama," he explained. "I'm not really destitute."

"I don't want it." She couldn't make herself touch the envelope.

After a moment he put it away. "Then it seems we have a problem—what to do with the money. Shall we discuss our favorite charities over lunch?" His voice, low-pitched and husky, added to the impression of intimacy and familiarity he conveyed with his banter, and in that moment she remembered why and how much she hated him.

"I could suggest what you can do with the money, but I'm a lady," she retorted. "And I have nothing to say to you, over lunch or anywhere else. Now please leave."

He said admiringly, "Such fire. You used to be a passive little thing. But then maybe I've mellowed—"

She hissed at him, "You have your nerve, coming here

like this, stirring up more cheap publicity, playing on public sympathy to convince people you're someone you're not.'' She was panting with angry passion. ''You phony! You cheat . . .''

Two security guards appeared at the door. ''Trouble, Mrs. Easton?''

With supreme effort Keely controlled her wrath. ''Yes. Will you escort this—person out of the building?''

''I was just leaving,'' her unwelcome guest soothed them. Flanked on both sides by the uniformed men, he raised his hands, palms downward in warning, and they did not touch him. Though their faces were impassive, they must have wondered what would happen to their jobs if he turned out to be Bryan Easton after all.

Keely couldn't resist a parting shot. ''From now on, if you have something to say to me, I suggest you contact my attorney.''

''Your attorney—or your lover?'' With a riveting look of contempt, he turned on his heel and walked rapidly away.

When the guards made a move to intercept him, Keely interrupted, ''No. Let him go.''

She went into her office and phoned Vern, annoyed to discover that her hands were shaking. He listened, and his voice was grim. ''So, he's come out of the woodwork at last. Darling, meet me at Zelda's for lunch at two and we'll map our strategy. I may be a bit late, but wait for me.''

Somehow Keely didn't feel reassured.

The restaurant in the East Fifties was one of those chic little basement places done beautifully in Art Deco. After being seated in a private booth, Keely started to ask for coffee, then changed her mind and ordered a carafe of wine, something she rarely did at lunch. It was then she realized the state of her shattered nerves. She was too fragmented to even concentrate on the *Wall Street Journal* as she waited for Vern's arrival. If she was a smoker she'd be chain smoking right now, she thought wryly.

A shadow moved between her and the lamp glow, and she looked up, expecting Vern. Instead, her erstwhile tormenter slid into the seat opposite her, then reached up and closed the curtain.

"How dare you follow me! Get out!" Her hand flew up to grab the curtain away from him and she knocked over her wine glass.

He reached over to right the glass and dab the stained tablecloth. "Relax. It's a public restaurant, and I can hardly compromise your virtue here. Besides, you're going to have to talk to me sooner or later."

"We have nothing to talk about, least of all my virtue. If you don't leave immediately, I'm going to call the captain."

"What, and risk a photo-opportunity riot among the paparazzi gathered at the bar? Whatever would they say if we were seen together?"

She was trapped and he knew it. She couldn't even call his bluff and demand that the captain throw him out on his bogus ear for fear of a scene that would end up in every newspaper in the country. He sat back, watching in amusement as she wrestled with her dilemma. Keely choked back an overwhelming desire to slap that maddening smirk off his phony face.

"Vern is meeting me here for lunch any minute," she blustered. "You'll leave now if you know what's good for you."

He shrugged and said blandly, "I don't mind at all. It'll be like old times. Until then, why not have a drink and some civilized conversation? I know you're feeling threatened, Keely, but I'm not your enemy."

"Don't you patronize me." Her bosom heaved in impotent fury.

"Sorry. I'm trying to be considerate of your feelings, but you're making it damned difficult."

"If that were true, you'd get back on that plane and never show your face here again."

"Granted, you think I'm some con man out to rob you blind, but I'm curious . . . on a more personal level, if you knew for sure I was Bryan, would your reaction to my return be any different?"

"But you're not, and I don't speculate on horror stories."

"Well, I can see this line of conversation is going nowhere fast." He helped himself to Vern's glass and poured himself some wine, saluted her, and took a drink. "So, let's try a more neutral subject—and what could be more neutral than Vern Preston?" He laughed in appreciation of his own joke.

She flushed to her hairline. "I don't intend to discuss Vern with you."

"Don't you think that a real man would have married you before now?" He was looking at her intently.

"Are you forgetting there's a seven-year wait to declare a missing spouse legally dead?" She met his eyes squarely, irked as much by his equanimity as his mockery.

"Come off it, Keely. You could have shed me easily enough, you and your lapdog lawyer. Admit it, an undissolved marriage strengthens your ties to Mother and your claim to the Easton empire when she dies. It's also an excuse to fob off Preston, because deep down in your heart you don't really want to marry him. And you're using the sorry excuse of an 'engagement' to him to fob me off."

Keely was shaking with anger, but an underlying shock of recognition of how her position must look to others disturbed her far more than his cutting words. "You have a talent for twisting the truth."

"Until you stop using Preston as a smokescreen and see me clearly for what I am today, instead of what I was seven years ago, you're still the insecure little mouse I married. And when you finally decide there's no future in sulking about the past, maybe you'll admit you still have feelings for me."

"Oh, I have feelings. Hate, disgust, outrage—"

"But not indifference," he said softly. "That's how I

know I'm still under your skin." He leaned back carelessly in his chair and looked into her tense face, and his own expression was inscrutable. "But I digress. We were discussing how you're letting lover boy cash in on the reflected glory of the Easton name. You don't think he would have made it this far in the Senate race without it, do you?"

She was stung. "That happens to be a lie. Vern is a very successful attorney in his own right."

"He's a mediocre attorney and he'll make a mediocre senator."

"I refuse to discuss Vern with you," she fumed. "And as soon as we expose you for the fraud you are, I'm going to marry him."

Where was Vern? she wondered, looking restlessly at her watch.

"Well, since you're so touchy about Preston," he said with a quizzical grin, "you're welcome to ask me questions about my personal life."

"Your personal life doesn't interest me in the least."

He shrugged. "It should. You could be missing an opportunity to expose me for the fraud you think I am."

"That would be redundant," she said sarcastically. "However, speaking strictly as a reporter, maybe you'd like to tell me what you were doing in Nicaragua and for whom."

His eyes narrowed and he pursed his lips before answering. "Sorry—no can do. I've been debriefed by the CIA, but I'm not giving out free interviews on U.S. business in Nicaragua to anybody but the U.S. government."

"Since you were technically listed as a mercenary, I assume you got money for killing people, unless you did it for fun." Her sarcasm was blatant now.

His low, impatient voice overrode hers. "I only did what I had to do to stay alive and still keep my self-respect."

"I'm sure everything you did was sanctioned, but that doesn't necessarily make you one of the good guys," she shot back.

A flash of restive anger marred his features for an instant, though when he spoke his voice was calm. "Whether you're a good guy or a terrorist depends on whose side you're on, now doesn't it?" He paused, then went on thoughtfully, "Look, I made a deal with myself that if I ever got out of that prison camp I wasn't going to flagellate myself for the rest of my life. And how meaningful is moral introspection while somebody's burning your fingertips off with cigarettes?"

"Sounds like moral doubletalk to me," she said flippantly.

He regarded her intently across the table. "I don't claim to be a hero, but I'm no villain, either. I got a bellyful of adventure, if you can call it that, and far from warping me, the experience made me realize what I'd thrown away. I'm damned if I'm going to muff this second chance." He leaned back in his chair and observed her through eyes lowered to half-mast and a different note in his voice.

Keely shivered. This man radiated sex, mystery, even danger. She ought to have her head examined for allowing him within a hundred miles of her. She let her eyes drop away to the table, to his hands, next to hers on the cloth but not touching. They were extraordinary hands, powerful. A controlled force about them was suggested by long but very strong fingers, large knuckles, heavy bones, big wrists. Hands that had been cruel. Could they be tender as well? She couldn't really remember Bryan's hands . . . And then she remembered.

In their tiny first apartment after they were married, the bathroom window had been nailed shut, and Bryan used a claw hammer to remove the nail. He opened the sash and, like a harbinger of spring, a large, green praying mantis flew in, lighting on the sill.

"Oh Bryan, look!" Keely had cried, fascinated.

Without missing a beat, the hammer swung down and smashed the unlucky insect into a million pieces, spattering the remains over her blouse.

Keely squelched the disturbing memory with difficulty.

Tearing her eyes away from his hands up to his face, she shook herself back to the present and found a stranger once more. "Pardon, what did you say?"

"I asked about my mother. How is she?"

Resentment immediately flared in her eyes as all her protective instincts rose to the surface once more. "Helen is none of your business!"

"She's my mother and her health certainly is my business," he contradicted, dangerously quiet now. "Why else do you think I haven't tried to contact her before now?"

"I'll tell you exactly why. I had a restraining order slapped on you!"

"It's not worth the paper it's written on once she finds out I'm back. Obviously, you have to keep us apart because you know she'll recognize me." His eyes gleamed like blue vitriol. "I can't blame you for feeling insecure about your cushy position with Easton Publishing, but spare me the daughterly routine. As I remember it, there was no love lost between you and my mother."

"That was a lifetime ago, before I really knew her. I love her, and no fortune-hunting opportunist is going to hurt her again with false hopes while I have breath in my body! Why can't you admit what you really want? I'd have a lot more respect for you!"

"I'll worry about your respect once you recognize a couple of facts about me." He leaned forward, his big hands in a death grip on his glass, and she could almost feel them around her neck. "One, I don't want your money and two, I couldn't care less about your fancy magazine."

"Really. Then what do you want?" She was trembling.

"I want to come home."

"To Westerby?" She regarded him in stony disbelief as their gazes met and clashed. "You're joking, of course."

"Haven't you punished me long enough?"

She threw up her hands. "Stop. Stop! You're making me crazy. Is that what you think this is all about? Getting even with Bryan for deserting me?"

"Isn't it?" He picked up his wineglass, swirled the contents, and set it down again with a bang of finality. "Come on, Keely, your fit of pique and martyrdom has worn thin. The experts have poked and prodded, the CIA has checked me out, and I've passed every harebrained test you've thrown at me. Yet you're the lone holdout, and people are asking why."

"If I ran my affairs on public opinion I'd be out of business in a week," she snapped. "Bryan doesn't even figure in this. You're not my husband, you're a crook. And I don't need the CIA and a panel of psychiatrists to tell me that!"

His eyes hardened. "Just how long do you think you can keep me away from my own mother?"

Before she could retort, the curtains of their booth were flung aside. But instead of a rescue by Vern at long last, flashbulbs popped in their faces, and with them the dawn of truth. Her temper flared in a killing rage.

"You twenty-four carat fraud," she hissed. "You set this up to make it look like a reconciliation for the tabloids, didn't you?"

He looked startled at her accusation, but she was too incensed to notice. She motioned to the photographer. "Want a picture of the happy couple? How's this?" She snatched up her glass of wine and flung it into her table partner's face.

"There," she said, noting with malicious satisfaction as the wine dripped off his nose and stained his shirt front. "We just made all the papers." Turning on her heel, she strode from the restaurant, heedless of the clamor behind her.

Not until she was safely ensconced in the plush backseat of the limousine on the way back to the office did Keely wonder about repercussions from her loss of control in the restaurant. She regretted that Vern would be walking in on a hornet's nest in a few minutes. He could ill afford the back splash of mud from Keely's personal problems in his campaign for Senate. But it couldn't be helped. She and Vern could take care of themselves; Helen could not.

The night of the one thousand dollar-a-plate election campaign fund-raising dinner ball at Easton House arrived all too soon. Keely was late getting home from the office, and the stately home was already ablaze with lights as she drove down the service drive toward the loading area near the kitchen. The florist and catering trucks were still parked outside unloading their wares into the kitchen under the eagle eye of Sikes, who pocketed her keys to put the car away.

With everything under control, Keely hurried upstairs to bathe and dress. At the top landing, she almost collided with Mrs. Maguire, who stepped aside looking smug and almost shifty.

"Why aren't you downstairs with the caterer?" Keely asked, instantly alert. "Is everything all right with Mrs. Easton— ?"

"Oh, she's feeling fine, ma'am," the housekeeper assured her. "Dr. Houten says she can come to the party tonight for a few minutes if she stays in her wheelchair and doesn't overdo."

"That's wonderful!" Keely enthused. "Seeing old friends will do her a world of good. I'll just pop in to see her."

"I wouldn't do that, ma'am. She's—resting."

Keely paused, irritated as always by the woman's take-charge attitude. "Well, I'll get ready first and then drop by. Is my dress back from alterations?"

"Yes, ma'am, and laid out for you."

"Thank you."

Within an hour she had taken a bath, followed by a spirited rub scented with sandalwood. She was dreading the evening to come. Having too much of it in her own business, she hated big parties, receiving lines, dancing with portly old men, the politics of sprightly conversation, the protocol of the political pecking order. And as Vern's wife, there would be even more of it.

But tonight the specter of the false stranger who had invaded their lives overshadowed the election festivities. She was determined to avoid the subject tonight at all costs. However she really felt, she must appear the perfect hostess—gracious, smiling, beautifully gowned.

She glided down the corridor toward Helen's suite and was surprised to meet Mrs. Maguire hovering outside the double doors. "Shouldn't you be downstairs seeing to last minute details?"

"Oh, ma'am, you won't wake Miss Helen now, will you? I thought we could let her nap until eight-thirty, and then I'll dress her myself, and Sikes can bring her down in the chair lift."

Keely looked at the woman closely. "I'm not sure she's feeling up to this—"

"Oh excuse me, ma'am—you must have a word with the electrician. He says he might have to move the dais to get more electrical outlets—"

"What now?" Distracted, Keely moved away, making a mental note to come up and check on Helen herself a little later. Her fleeting premonition was quickly forgotten.

"You're a knockout, darling," Vern declared enthusiastically as Keely swept downstairs and forward to peck his cheek. "Mmmm. All this feminine pulchritude and brains, too."

"If your feminist constituents heard that remark, you'd be in big trouble at the polls," she said fondly. "You look rather a hunk yourself in that dinner jacket."

After the banquet and before the speeches began, Keely wondered if she should slip upstairs to check on Helen when Senator Eakins leaned over, drink in hand.

"Vern is a shoo-in, my dear," he confided to Keely, his alcoholic breath turning her head. "Yes, indeed. Now this is what I call a fund-raiser! Senator Fulton held a cheapie the other day at a Chinese restaurant—a hundred bucks a head for a little moo goo gai pan and soy sauce. And a congressman from the Midwest had a sock hop for God's sake and charged ten bucks a dance. No class, but that's Democrats for you.''

Keely smiled coolly. She disliked most of Vern's pork barrel cronies. How would she ever survive as his wife?

Vern's campaign manager interrupted to address the senator. ''Almost time to introduce the candidate, Alf. Will ten minutes do it?''

''Good heavens, I won't take that long. With an eyeful like Miz Keely as the next speaker, who wants to listen to an old goat like me?'' He chortled and jabbed Vern in the ribs with his elbow and winked at Keely, who smiled back wanly.

After Senator Alf Eakins's gravelly voice at the rostrum, Keely's, by comparison, was clear and well modulated.

''My friends,'' she began, looking around to include everyone. ''We've come a long way in this campaign because we need men like Vernon Preston in government. Tonight I'd like to tell you something about the man behind the public face—''

At that moment there was a buzz of excitement that began at the back of the room and rolled forward like a tidal wave. The huge, carved double doors opened and Helen Easton was being wheeled into the ballroom. Wearing a Dior dress of blue crepe with pearls at her ears and throat, she looked her old vibrant self again, and Keely's heart swelled with pride.

She froze when she saw who was pushing the wheelchair.

TEN

As impeccably turned out as any man in the room, the compelling presence of her tormenter eclipsed even Helen's first public appearance since her stroke. Of significance was that one of Helen's favorite tiny floribunda roses was pinned to the lapel of the pretender's handsomely tailored tuxedo. Every head craned around in the hush, then swiveled back to Keely as they watched the unfolding drama, and before the excited whispering began, the silence was palpable. With the roaring inside her head, Keely felt in danger of suffocating. Her glance raced wildly from Helen, to her escort, to Vern, and she saw that her fiance's grim face was as white as her own.

But Helen bloomed with happiness as the imposing stranger gently guided the wheelchair to the place of honor next to Vern on the dais. Her delicate face crinkled into a thousand smiles, her eyes brilliant with tears of joy.

Keely's mind whirled in a thousand directions, unable to alight. Well and truly usurped, she stood rooted to the spot, not knowing if she should stand there and choke down the bitter gall at the back of her throat, smile sweetly and pretend that she, too, had been in on the secret; or to throw a scene and insist on his arrest for violation of the restraining order. Mrs. Maguire's duplicity did not come as a surprise, as obviously Keely's antagonist had been upstairs with his appropriated "mother" all along. She felt helpless and betrayed by everyone.

But what could she do now that the damage was done? Denunciation of him not only would cause embarrassment with Vern's campaign at stake, but might also trigger another stroke for Helen.

How clever, how diabolical he was! The smile on the impostor's face as he watched her kaleidoscopic expressions proved he had planned it all. How could she have underestimated him as an adversary or counted on his honor? And how could she explain to Helen that she had known of the existence of this pretender for weeks and never said a word? She closed her eyes to block out the thought and forestall panic.

An ice cube clinked. There was a tentative cough here and there as a microphone was lowered to Helen's level and adjusted. As in a dream, Keely's nemesis walked up to her as the assembly held its collective breath. He reached out and took her hand, and like a mindless zombie Keely was led to the dais where they all stood shoulder to shoulder like one big happy family posing for a newsworthy reunion! He looked down at her but she could not meet his mocking gaze for the furious thumping of her heart.

"My friends." Helen's voice quivered with emotion. "Tonight you share in the happiest day of my life. My son, my prodigal son, who was lost these past seven years, is found. With all the joy and thanksgiving in a mother's heart, please join me in welcoming home my dear, dear son, Bryan Easton."

She turned then and held out her hand to Keely, who felt as if a piece of wood were on the end of her arm. Helen tugged at her hand until Keely bent stiffly to kiss the withered cheek. Her mother-in-law whispered, "Oh, my dear, please be happy that our dear one is home! Promise that you'll work to make everything right again between you so I can die in peace." She reached for their two hands and joined them while the man-who-would-be Bryan looked down at Keely with a knowing smile on his lips. How he must be laughing at her! When he was ready to make his move, all her threats, blustering, guards, and court orders had been brushed aside like so many bothersome flies. He had gone straight to his source of strength and Keely's weakness: Helen.

Oh, Vern, help me, Keely cried silently.

A smattering of applause broke out, then swelled until the sound of it was like ocean waves crashing in her ears. The press, with the exception of a selected few, had been banned, yet flashes popped for unauthorized photographs before Keely could disentangle her hand. What a cozy little family group they would make for the morning editions!

Senator and Mrs. Eakins came forward first.

"Welcome home, Bryan," Mrs. Eakins gushed. "We're so very, very happy for your dear mother. And Keely, too, of course!"

"You can fool some of the people some of the time, but you can't fool a mother, eh, son?" the senator said, wringing the hand of the most devious charlatan ever born on the face of the earth.

Like sheep blindly following the leader, the other guests surged forward, and Keely knew it was too late to withdraw herself in protest. She was committed now, committed by her enforced silence and the shining expression on Helen's face. The conversation, laughter, questions eddied around her, but she felt lightheaded and strangely disconnected. Once he leaned down and whispered in her ear, "Smile. You look like death warmed over."

Roused momentarily, her eyes glittered with hate, but she held her tongue.

He laughed and squeezed her waist appreciatively. "I can see it's going to be a fun reconciliation."

Even after the clock struck midnight, Helen, flushed and animated, refused to go upstairs, unable to let go of Bryan's hand, as if afraid by magic he would turn into a pumpkin and disappear. If only that were true, and this evening a nightmare that would be banished with tomorrow's reality!

Finally, Helen consented to go upstairs only if her dear

Bryan went with her and, amid enthusiastic farewells, they disappeared. Keely was on the verge of following, to have it out with him, have him arrested, something, when Vern caught up to her.

"Let them go," he urged. "We need a minute to talk." He guided her to the adjoining study. "I was afraid you were going to throw a plate of caviar in his face."

"Well, it wasn't because of your campaign that I restrained myself, I was thinking of Helen. Oh, Vern, what are we going to do?"

"It's a damned sticky situation. My first inclination is to call the police and have him arrested for trespassing and breaking your injunction, but we're dead on that one if he's here tonight at Helen's invitation."

"Vern, she's moved him in already!"

"Here? Into the mansion?" Vern stared at her, then swore and began pacing. Every muscle was rigid, his mouth taut. "I knew it, I knew it! The minute I saw that oily bastard, I knew what he was really after. Keely, I forbid my future wife to live under the same roof with that—that—"

"Vern, what choice do I have?" she asked helplessly.

"Move out! Marry me now, dammit!"

Every hair on the back of her neck rose up in alarm that this normally cool attorney was saying these wild things in utter disregard of the legalities and consequences.

"Vern, if I marry you now that Helen's accepted him, he could charge us with bigamy! Think of your campaign, your career mired down in a lawsuit! And can you seriously expect me to leave Helen alone in his clutches? Like a piranha, he'd strip her to the bone in a week!"

"We've got to stay calm and think this thing through," he agreed, running agitated fingers over his temples. "Maybe you'd better go back to the ball while I make some inquiries."

She nodded, relieved that he had pulled himself together enough to take charge. In the ballroom, she fielded well-meaning and malicious questions alike, keeping the focus on Vern's campaign as best she could, trying to put the pieces of the stolen evening back together again. But time stretched out interminably and her head was now pounding with the effort.

A strong male hand clamped itself around her waist and she looked up into the challenging, glittering blue eyes of the man she was now expected to call Bryan. "I think a dance is in order for the newly reunited couple," he said smoothly. "I hope you've improved your tango since our last attempt."

She was too startled to hide her reaction. Her tango had been a private joke between Bryan and herself on the night they met, but how could this man have known? His uncanny guess sent a prickle of *deja vu* up her back.

"Get your hands off me."

"Now, don't be mean to me or I'll have to tell Mother on you." The remark was meant to be teasing, but stated the case with chilling clarity. He shifted his hold from her wrist to the curve of her waist in one fluid motion. "The talk will get back to her if we don't dance at least once this evening, so we might as well sacrifice this tango for her sake."

With a sound of smothered rage, Keely allowed herself to be drawn onto the dance floor. The other couples were dancing closely to the sexy beat, but Keely held herself stiffly away from contact with the leanly muscled body of her partner. His steps formed a basic pattern that was easy to follow, and the hand at her waist firmly directed her movements to match his. When the dance ended, he did not relinquish his hold on her, moving instead to a sedate rhythm in a more conservative dance position.

"Not bad," he mocked softly. "But I remember when you used to slow dance with both arms around my neck. Tonight you're so far away I can feel the draft between us."

"I hope you catch pneumonia and die," she retorted.

He laughed and forced her closer. To resist would end in a public brawl on the dance floor, so Keely suffered his will. Since she was forced to dance with him, she decided to use the experience to good advantage and compare him with Bryan, but being this close to a man of his magnetism made it difficult. She was conscious of his slanted jawline and strong chin on a level somewhere near her forehead, and although he was supposedly the same height as Bryan had been, the feel of him was different as he held her.

When the orchestra moved into another syncopated Latin beat, Keely couldn't help but melt into the novel sensation of dancing with him. This man moved as easily as Bryan had done, but with a power and grace that transformed their mutual rhythm into exquisite awareness of a leg sliding against leg, hip bumping hip in a sensuous contact that implied an intimacy that was all too misleading to everyone on the crowded floor. If Keely couldn't avoid breathing the clean-smelling fragrance he wore, or feeling his muscular body moving against hers, at least she could speak and reassert the antagonistic footing of their relationship.

"I must really congratulate you on your tactics, gate-crashing my party for Vern." She lifted her chin defiantly.

His low laughter fanned her hair. "Gate-crashing, hell. I lived here before you were ever born."

"Taking advantage of a sick old woman is nothing less than contemptible," she flung back, her voice deepened by a curiously breathless anger. "I hope you know I'm going to tell Helen the truth about you."

"As long as we're issuing ultimatums, hear mine," he countered, and their noses were only inches apart, their teeth bared now in open battle. "I'm home to stay. And if you do or say anything to upset my mother about it, you'll answer to me."

She laughed incredulously. "That's my line you've stolen, among other things. I've been more a daughter to Helen than Bryan ever was a son!"

He held her away from him so that he could look down

at her with that intent gaze that had such power to unsettle her. "Since our common goal now is her health and happiness, why don't you stop fighting me? She's had little enough peace in her life."

"And whose fault is that?" Keely fumed, her golden eyes spitting sparks.

His reply was to slam her against him for a series of whirls around the dance floor that left her too surprised and breathless for another riposte. From the corner of her eye, Keely saw Vern wading toward them through the other couples with fire in his eyes. Her dance partner saw him, too, and perversely whirled her away and out of his reach until they all ended up on the terrace.

"Are you planning to monopolize the hostess all evening?" Vern demanded belligerently when he caught up to them.

"I'm not dancing with the hostess, Preston," he responded coolly. "I'm dancing with my wife."

Vern's face darkened. "She happens to be engaged to me."

"Vern, let's go inside and dance," Keely interrupted. She had no doubt that this powerful stranger, whose arm and shoulder muscles she had felt bunching under the tailored jacket, could break the slim candidate for the Senate in half. An altercation between them would do irreparable damage to his campaign, yet she had never seen Vern so reckless and impulsive as he was tonight. Someone's cool head had to prevail. She tried to disengage herself from the unwanted dance partner, but he held her fast.

"Just a moment," he commanded softly. "Another time I might challenge your fantastic claim, Preston. You'd think that a hot-shot lawyer like yourself would know that until Keely and I divorce, we're still husband and wife."

Keely watched, paralyzed, as Vern took another step toward his antagonist. "She was married to Bryan Easton, friend, not you. And he's dead. She has a piece of paper from the court that says so. Now, in anybody's book, that means she's a widow and free to marry again."

The men were as stiff legged as two dogs sniffing for a fight.

"My mother might argue with you about that, friend." The other voice was edged in smooth steel.

"Until the courts decide, keep your hands off Keely," Vern bit out. His fists were clenched at his sides.

When he spoke again, the pretender's voice was curiously conversational. "Now, we can settle that issue in one of two ways. We can bloody each other up, or we can be gentlemen with the understanding that the only time a man has to share his wife is at a dance. Take your pick, Preston."

"Oh, please, Vern," Keely begged. "Can't you see what he's trying to do? Don't let him push you into a fight!"

"There you are, Bryan, you naughty man," trilled Mrs. Eakins, waving her handkerchief and mincing over to catch hold of his arm. "I've saved this dance especially for you."

The interloper relaxed, and with a sideways look at Keely, his mouth quirked into a mocking smile. "Well, Preston, have we settled the ground rules, or shall we hammer out the details? It's up to you."

With the advent of the senator's wife, Vern's sense of political expediency reasserted itself, and his eyes dropped away from his challenger's.

Mrs. Eakins danced away with her prize, oblivious to the storm narrowly averted. As they whirled away into the mainstream of dancers, Keely heard him say, "You're as lovely as ever, Ilsa."

Vern was still fuming and it was a few minutes more before Keely was able to coax him into returning to the ballroom. Keely was sick to think how close the two men had come to a public brawl at Vern's campaign fund-raising party.

"I don't like the way he muscled in on you tonight." His movements were automatic, jerky, stiff as they moved onto the floor. "I don't like the way he looks at you or dances with you. I felt like knocking his damned teeth down his throat. Why did you dance with him?"

"Vern, I was trying not to cause a scene by refusing. Somebody has to think of your campaign image!"

"I don't want that man living under the same roof with you," he gritted, as if she hadn't spoken.

"You saw Helen tonight," Keely said helplessly. "It's her house."

"I don't care, he's not your husband! And as for dear, sweet, loyal Helen, at a crook of a finger from that devil, she'll cut you out of her life and her will with a dull knife. That's what you'll get for being a good steward all these years!"

"Vern, stop it. I don't care about the money—I don't need it. But if you'll just calm down, we can see that that flimflam man never gets a penny."

"Oh, God, Keely," Vern groaned, holding her tighter and almost stopping in the middle of the floor. "When I think about you being alone with him tonight, I—"

Her face flamed at the implication. "Don't be ridiculous," she said, but just the thought of the stranger claiming marital rights sent the same odd feelings through her that she had felt in his embrace in Mexico City.

"Marry me," Vern whispered urgently. "I feel you slipping away from me already. United, we stand a chance against him."

Keely was alarmed at his loss of poise. She had counted on him to be the strong one. "Vern, it will only make a bad situation worse. Now, here comes that congressman I was telling you about earlier. We'll talk about our strategy tomorrow."

At long last the party began to break up and guests said their goodbyes. As hostess, Keely stationed herself in the foyer. From nowhere, the bogus Bryan appeared to deliberately foster the impression of a united farewell committee at the door. Keely masked her anger as best she could, reminding the leave-takers of Vern's campaign. But Vern was largely forgotten tonight as the impostor basked in his stolen limelight.

"Well, Bryan," a guest exclaimed with a goodnatured slap on his shoulder. "Now that you're home, what are your plans?"

Keely forced herself to stare blankly in front of her, ignoring his raking gaze. "The first thing I'm going to do is get reacquainted with my family," he announced. "I think it's high time my wife took a few days off."

The other man laughed suggestively, catching the undercurrent of meaning and missing Keely's gasp of anger. "Sort of a second honeymoon, eh, Mrs. Easton?"

Color suffused Keely's face as she met the arrogant and amused smile on the gadfly's satirical features. "I think not," she smiled thinly. "I'm married to my schedules."

"I guess I'll have to remind her where her priorities lie," he declared with a proprietary gleam in his eye that set the blood steaming through her veins. There might be a truce of necessity between them, but lovers they would never be! The unsettled mood created an odd constraint, and she felt poised on the edge of something from which she could not withdraw.

The orchestra finally signaled an end to the party, stopped playing, and began to pack up their instruments. A general exodus of the remaining guests began. As she repeated the polite words of parting, Keely kept glancing toward the doors, looking for Vern. But he was gone.

The cleaning crew moved in.

Too keyed up to go upstairs and chance another encounter with the enemy, she busied herself seeing to the crystal glassware and silver, straightening pillows on the sofas, and wiping out the ashtrays. She needed to think.

When the house was quiet at last, she wandered out on the terrace. Not a breeze stirred the evergreen shrubbery.

The air was crisp, the stars were hard and brilliant, presaging a light frost before dawn. The leaves from the trees had nearly completed their autumn fall.

Keely paused near the far edge, feeling the warmth of the embedded electric coils under the flagstones, yet shivering. The only sound to be heard was the distant bark of a dog.

Finally, she turned reluctantly toward the house. A dark form separated itself from the shadows, and Keely stiffened when the moonlight outlined the now familiar planes of the intruder's face. A crackle of tension charged the empty space between them.

"I brought you a nightcap."

"No, thanks."

There was no way past him without physically touching, and she would rather touch a snake, so she turned away to shut him out.

His voice was subdued, faintly conciliatory. "Can't we even talk, Keely? We need to reach an understanding."

"Understanding? I think you've made your intentions abundantly clear." Events had swept her along in a floodtide she was powerless to control. She hadn't felt so powerless in a long time, and it was a bad, bad feeling.

"I didn't plan tonight's little public reconciliation. That was Mother's doing. She called me at the hospital. Should I have refused when she begged me to see her? 'Sorry, Mother, not until you have permission from Keely.' I'm her son, dammit."

She whirled on him then. "Liar! Why did you have to come here and reopen all the old, healing wounds?"

"I'm not lying. And why shouldn't I come here? I was born here. I grew up here. I fell out of that hickory tree right over there when I was six years old and broke my nose. I played cowboys and Indians in the box-hedge maze." He paused, not bothering to hide the plea in his voice. "Keely, my mother needs me. Let me make it up to you both."

Keely took refuge in a mantle of ice. "Your timing is impeccable. With Helen so ill, maybe you'll have to humor her only a little while before you inherit her money."

"Obviously, her money is the big issue with you. Oh, I can understand why you're worried. If I play my cards right, I know I could easily persuade my mother to sign over everything to me lock, stock, and barrel. I could even have you kicked out of this house—just like that." He snapped his fingers.

She was trembling. "Then what's stopping you?"

"You." He lifted his forefinger to trace the line of her cheekbone and the sensitive edge of her lower lip.

His touch set off a physical reaction so deeply through her that it was almost a shock wave. She turned her face away, trying desperately not to be caught up in the tenderness of the gesture. "I don't understand."

His head cocked slightly so that his eyes could play over the enticing shadow between her breasts in the low-cut gown. "Because I want the whole package, Keely. And that includes my wife. I want you back."

She shook her head in a quick gesture of denial. "You may have fooled Helen, but never me."

For the first time she glimpsed his temper. "Goddamn it, Keely, how much longer are you going to punish me? How much more prodding and probing from doctors and headshrinkers am I going to have to endure to satisfy you? And after they've proved I'm Bryan Easton right down to my genetic pool and DNA, you still won't accept the truth because down deep in your heart, you truly wish me dead!"

"That's a lie."

"Is it, Keely? With me dead, you're free to marry Vern Preston. With me dead, you stand to inherit the Easton fortune—"

She had to stop his words. She raised her hand to slap him, but he grabbed her wrist in mid-arc, twisting it until her body bent into his. His head swooped down to take her mouth with a savagery that crushed all breath and resistance from her, stunning her into submission. The kiss went on and on with desperation in it for both of them, and finally when he held her away, she was breathless with his raw power and her consuming emotion.

His eyes smoked over her, lingering on her mouth, parted and trembling from his onslaught. "Don't get physical, Keely. You're no match for me."

Keely's face was deathly white in the moonlight as their eyes caught and held, and a peculiar pulsing started deep inside her. He didn't move for a moment, holding her, and Keely began to shake as his arm went around her neck, his thumb tilting her chin up. Her glance dropped to his firm yet sensitively molded lips, remembering the first warm taste of them, and for the first time doubts forced their way into her darkened, swaying mind.

He kissed her slowly this time, his hands sliding sensuously down her arms, then up again before he released her. "Who am I, Keely?" he asked thickly.

She stared up at him, dazed and flushed.

He gave her a little shake. "Tell me."

Her eyes closed again, helpless in anticipation.

He released her arms abruptly. Her eyes flew open, questioning. "You'd better get off to bed now."

Her wits came back with a humiliating rush. With a little cry, she whirled and ran into the silent mansion, and up the stairs to her suite, where she slammed the door and leaned against it, panting with rage and humiliation and, most of all, fear.

Correspondents covering local politics arrived early to take reserved seats in the Easton Building auditorium. Metal nameplates on the first rows spelled prestige—AP, UPI, the big three television networks, and all the prominent newspapers. It was an unusually large turnout because the news at hand was a juicy, national-scale story fraught with foreign intrigue, missing persons, fraud, and a beautiful widow who stood to win or lose all. Speculation had boiled to a froth after the campaign fund-raiser three days ago when Helen Easton made her first public appearance since her stroke to acknowledge a man her daughter-in-law had openly repudiated and privately despised.

Keely's position was further compromised the very next day when the CIA investigation verified the original report of Amnesty International, supporting the man's "probable" identity as Bryan Easton. Then the psychiatric report from Bellevue Hospital came out in his favor, though it stopped short of positive endorsement. Handwriting experts were divided because of tendon injuries which affected writing patterns. Interviews with many personal acquaintances of Bryan's, including former teachers, were mixed, but with enough positive IDs that they could not be dismissed out of hand. Yet Keely continued to dismiss them all, confident that Vern's private investigation and connections would turn something up. Most damaging of all to Keely's stand was that every single Easton household member, from servants to the mistress, was unhesitatingly certain that Bryan had returned. Keely found herself in the uncomfortable position of being the lone dissenter in, not only her own home, but in the office and the world at large.

Besieged on all sides, Keely remained adamant in her own mind, even though Helen's wishes in the matter could not be ignored so easily. After all, she had welcomed this stranger into her home, treating him as her long-lost son; short of an open break with her, there was nothing Keely could do about it. She was not about to abandon a vulnerable woman to the clutches of this clever fortune hunter.

Five minutes before the press conference, now moved up to ten-thirty, Keely was being briefed by Vern Preston on the latest developments of their private investigation. At the end of his report, he asked sotto voce, "Has he tried anything with you yet?"

Her lips tightened in annoyance at a question that did

not merit a reply, and stood up to signal the start of the press conference. The crowd hushed as Keely Easton picked her way among the cables that snaked underfoot to arrive at a podium bristling with microphones. Her no-nonsense tan gabardine suit, sedate paisley neck scarf, and alligator pumps were duly recorded in a blizzard of flashbulbs. She waited while they popped nonstop for two full minutes, her smile strained but confident.

"Thank you for coming, ladies and gentlemen." She looked around at the men and women of the press, most of whom she knew on a first-name basis. "I've called this conference today hoping to set the record straight and to head off yet another round of rumors which are already much too rampant." She stopped to allow the buzz of anticipation to subside. "As you know, a man has come forward with the fantastic claim that he is the missing-and-presumed dead heir of Helen Easton. Obviously, a bereaved mother with new hope is dangerously vulnerable prey. Just as obviously, accepting such a claim at face value would be the height of folly, especially in a family of this prominence and with so much at stake. Everyone has had his say on the validity of this man's claim; now it is up to Bryan Easton's wife and Bryan Easton's mother to make the final determination. This has been all but impossible to do since Mrs. Easton's illness has rendered her relatively housebound. For the sake of access, Mrs. Easton has invited the claimant to be her guest at Easton Manor. Although she approaches the project with optimism and I with skepticism, we anticipate that our final conclusion will be the same."

Again she paused until the audience quieted, her knuckles white with strain on the lectern as she plunged to the finish. "Let me make myself perfectly clear: His presence at Easton Manor may in no way be construed as acceptance of his claims by either myself or Helen Easton, and official investigations by medical and legal teams will be ongoing during his stay. Meanwhile, I repeat what I have said many times already so that there is no misunderstanding as to my position, and I hope you will quote me verbatim. If, at the end of the investigation it is determined that this man willfully sought to perpetrate a fraud on Helen Easton or myself, he will pay dearly for it in a court of law.''

There was a roar of questions from the reporters as soon as they realized the conference had just ended, but Keely declined and disappeared into the front door.

A new atmosphere came to Easton Manor. The old estate absorbed its exotic resident in a remarkably short time until it seemed he had always been there. Too soon his presence pervaded every aspect of their lives.

At first Keely had attempted to ensconce the interloper in a far wing of the house with separate meals and no contact with the rest of the household, but she soon discovered she was the one cut off; she quickly abandoned this tack. With Lida Maguire his staunch ally, he now took his meals at the table when Helen could come downstairs or in her suite when she was indisposed. Keely's place at the head of the table somehow became reversed as he cheerfully sat at the other end, and Mrs. Maguire positively hovered over him, spoiling him with all of Bryan's favorite dishes.

Whether he was enthusiastically discussing a new recipe with "Lida" (Keely couldn't imagine calling her by her first name) or carburetor adjustments on the Bentley with Sikes, he seemed totally at ease and was accepted at face value by everyone, which filled Keely with dismay. Bob the gardener, usually so taciturn and jealous of his prerogatives that he resented even simple suggestions from Keely, gladly discussed compost and tree-spraying schedules with "Bryan." Couldn't they see that everything he said was superficial and geared to impress them? He had a prodigious memory for detail for someone whose recall had convenient gaps whenever he couldn't remember the faces or names of old family friends. Everyone eagerly filled him in. His knowledge of the whole history of the house and family and servants was just too pat. Whoever he was, he'd done his homework very well, playing to his gullible audience like a magician pulling rabbits out of a hat.

It became increasingly clear to Vern that "Bryan" 's presence took Keely's time away from him, and he was livid with resentment. He redoubled his investigations to dislodge the interloper and took to calling Keely at the office during the day to harangue her about him.

"If I want to see you these days I've almost got to get an appointment with him," he complained. "Can't you see what he's doing to us?"

It was true, but Keely was helpless to stop what was happening to them all. She was irritated to discover that even she wasn't entirely immune to the man's charm. A couple of times she caught herself responding to an intelligent question about the magazine or a practical suggestion for Helen's comfort. His easy manner and complaisance made it increasingly difficult to give him the cold shoulder. He deferred to her in everything except access to Helen, and otherwise was an unobtrusive, well-mannered houseguest. And after that first night in the garden, he never again tried to push himself on her, which in a way secretly disappointed her. If ever he did, she told herself fiercely . . . wouldn't he regret it!

A week after he moved in, Keely was halfway through the soup course at dinner when her nemesis arrived home from a doctor's appointment. Mrs. Maguire fussed behind him, taking his coat, sending looks of reproach at Keely, which she pointedly ignored.

"Sorry, am I late?" He glanced good-naturedly at his watch while taking his place on the other side of the table. "Since when do we eat before eight?" Mrs. Maguire placed his soup in front of him with a disapproving sniff.

Keely arranged her face into a polite expression. "Since I changed the dinner hour two years ago," she replied stiffly. "Eight is too late for me."

"I see," he returned, his eyes probing hers for a long instant. "Then the eight o'clock dinner hour since I've been home was for auld lang syne? I hope your digestion didn't suffer on my account."

"Not at all. With Helen visiting friends tonight I thought you might prefer to have dinner in the city."

"And miss Lida's linguini? Not a chance." Cheerfully he arranged his napkin on his lap. "Where did Mother go?"

"Mother? Oh, you mean Helen."

His expression was sardonic. "Let me rephrase the question. Do I know the friend?"

"How could you? The Harley McTavishes—something like that."

His eyes took on a derisive gleam. "I think you mean Farley Cavendish. Grace is Mother's old school chum from Edinburgh, I believe."

She shrugged, refusing to let him ruffle her composure. Helen, for all she knew, might have filled him in on the entire Cavendish family tree.

A sensuous smile tugged at the corners of his mouth as he appraised her caftan, as if the slow, downward flicker of his lashes could unravel it at will. "That's a hot little number." He was mocking her, the frank nature of his inspection quite deliberate. "Did you wear it just for me?"

Keely's gaze assessed him coolly. "I don't wear anything just for you."

His laugh was full of dark mischief. "Well, there's a Freudian slip if ever I've heard one."

Keely glared.

Fortunately, Mrs. Maguire chose the moment to serve the linguini. She was as flustered as a young girl around her "Bryan," which also angered Keely. And he didn't help matters any, buttering up the woman outrageously amid her twitters of pleasure.

"The best clam sauce this side of Ireland!" he grinned up at her. "Liberally laced with our secret ingredient, eh Lida?"

Mrs. Maguire flushed with pleasure, sending a stab of something ridiculously akin to jealousy through Keely. "Oh, you bet, sir! Sikes went out special."

"Shhhh! A tot of Irish whisky," Bryan told Keely in a loud stage whisper. "Mother never knew, and we never told her, did we, Lida?"

Keely felt like snapping that alcohol was forbidden to Helen on her high blood pressure diet, but she bit her tongue; after all, Helen wasn't here tonight to partake of forbidden spirits. And tasting the clam sauce, she had to admit it was delicious. She couldn't remember the last time pasta had been served at the Manor.

After dinner they moved into the salon for coffee so that Mrs. Maguire could clear the table and go home to the gatehouse where she and her husband Bob, the gardener-maintenance man, lived.

"Amaretto with your coffee?" the self-appointed man of the house inquired, opening the armoire housing the liquors as if he did it every day. She watched as he unstoppered the crystal decanter, grudging the smooth fit of his English tweed jacket over wide shoulders and long tapered back. Even standing still one could sense the dynamism harnessed inside that masculine body. But unlike volatile Bryan Easton, this man had all the kinetic energy under control, doing nothing by impulse but instead by deliberate action. For some reason, Keely found that even more alarming.

"No, thank you." She took a sip of her own plain coffee.

"Still straight as an arrow," he mocked. "The only problem with perfection is that you can never have any fun."

"Maybe that depends on your definition of perfection and my definition of fun."

He grinned appreciatively and took off his jacket, slinging it casually over the back of the barstool. He hadn't lost any time getting to the tailor, Keely noticed with scorn. He was as impeccably turned out as if he already owned the company. The thought that Helen was now probably supporting this gigolo made her mouth twist.

"Actually, I'm watching my own alcohol intake," he confided, restoppering the liqueur without sampling it. "I don't want to dull the headaches at the expense of a drinking problem." He sat down next to her and she watched resentfully as he stretched out on the sofa, his long legs draped across the carpet, his arms reaching above his head in a luxurious stretch. She wanted to slap his arrogant face.

"Ahhh, how nice to relax in a real home again instead of a hospital room," he said, closing his eyes.

"Anybody's home, obviously," she said shamelessly.

"And how soothing talking to you," he jibed. "Why, after a conversation with you I feel like I've danced ten rounds with a prizefighter."

"Then don't talk. I'd just as soon go to bed anyway."

"That's the best offer I've had all day," he drawled, amusement in his eyes at her gaffe and, to her annoyance, she flushed. He teased, "Is that a shiver of anticipation, or a polite shudder?"

"Try revulsion."

"I'm crushed." His tie came off, followed by his jacket, draped over the back of the sofa. "Tell me—what has the merry widow been doing for sex all these years?" His expression was no longer amused but curiously intent and questioning.

"That's none of your damn business."

He started undoing his shirt, watching her reaction with a sideways look. "Just curious if you play the field or if you prefer one-on-one—um, pardon the expression?"

He arched his head back and rubbed his neck. "I'm sure you don't lack for offers. You're a good-looking woman, but you really need to loosen up. Speaking of which, would you mind massaging my neck? This spasm is excruciating."

She laughed at the absurdity of his request, though her throat was suddenly dry at the thought. "I will not."

"Still playing the vestal virgin, Keely?" The merest hint of a smile eased the lines of pain around his eyes. "Somewhere beneath that icy shell, we both know there's a woman of passion, don't we?"

She certainly didn't consider herself a prude, but if he meant she'd changed from the wide-eyed child Bryan had married, she certainly had, radically so. After he'd disappeared, she'd grown up all too fast around the vacuum he'd left in her life, like bark around a hollow tree. The shell had continued to function, but the heartwood was gone.

There was a curious vibration in his voice now. "Was coming home such a terrible crime, Keely?" The watchful look from those clear eyes seemed eager, almost puzzled. "If we're lucky, we learn from our mistakes. If we're even luckier, we get a second chance. I'm no longer the callow, inexperienced boy you remember."

"How dare you," she said, her voice was a low tremble. "How dare you brag to me about the new tricks you've learned. I don't give a damn how proficient a lover you are!"

He leaned back, startled. "I must be slipping if that's the impression I gave. Keely, Keely, what am I to do with you . . ." He stood up and her pulse quickened as he came toward her, reaching out to trail warm fingertips down the curve of her cheek, producing a quiver that made her jerk her head away.

"Don't . . ." she stopped short, suddenly horrified at what she'd been about to say.

"Bryan. My God, can't you even say my name?" He dropped his hand abruptly, looking aggrieved. "How long will I have to answer to 'Hey you'?"

"As long as you continue to impersonate my husband," she said coldly. "For the record, you're nothing like him, inside or out. There's not even the faintest similarity, and

I'm not talking about your looks. And I will always hate you for insinuating yourself into this house, into Helen's life, and into mine against my will. And for you to try to insinuate yourself into my bed is the final insult. Good night.''

She rose swiftly and left the room. A glance backward at the door showed him stretched out full length on the sofa, his dark head flung back, eyes fastened somewhere on the ceiling. Then they closed.

In her suite, Keely undressed and showered quickly. She got into bed, put out the bedside lamp, and curled up under the satin quilt, chilled to the core. She was afraid. Afraid of the way she felt around this man. There was something unsettling about him that she couldn't quite put her finger on, and it terrified her. She was a grown, sensible woman, yet tonight's events left her floundering as if she were the same naive, vulnerable girl Bryan married on impulse and so carelessly abandoned all those years ago. It was a long, long time before she slept.

Life settled into a routine of sorts, though the house was an armed camp. He was the enemy within, and Keely never let him forget it. So he spent most of his free time with Helen, consolidating his position. He insisted on driving Helen down to the family cottage on Cape Cod in the Bentley on one blue, sun-kissed Indian summer weekend. "She needs to get out once in a while," he said, and of course, Helen thought it was a wonderful idea—anything "Bryan" wanted was wonderful.

Keely didn't want to go, but no way was she going to entrust the fragile Helen to his care. It was bad enough that she had to stand by while he worked his voodoo on her. No. Keely would be there every minute, watching him. He was bound to slip sometime, and she wanted to be there to point the finger.

The "cottage," called Turtle Cay, was actually a large house nestled in a tangle of wistaria and morning glory vines at the end of a lane outside the little town of Sandwich, just steps from the beach. Helen was carried down the polished mahogany steps to her lower level bedroom while Keely opened all the windows to air out the rooms. She was unloading groceries into the cupboards when he strolled into the kitchen.

"I love this old place." He ran his eyes over everything as sensuously as if he were making love to it. Keely stiffened, waiting for the barrage of historical facts about Cape Cod, the origins of the house, and whatever else he'd no doubt dug out of some library. But he surprised her with his knowledge on a more personal level. "Did you know I sanded these floors myself? It was the summer we bought the cottage, and I was fourteen and taking woodshop in school. I slaved every weekend scraping paint off the floors. It was like magic to watch the bleached beauty of the oak appear from under eighty years of history."

A strange stab of presentiment went through her at his words. Keely too loved the old jerry-built summer house, but had never imagined Bryan here as a boy and caring for it as she did. She had renewed the white paint and added wicker furniture and blue-striped cotton upholstery to represent sand, sea, and sky for a stylish, spare, uncluttered look, and considered the cottage stamped with her own personality.

"Hey, stash that stuff later," he urged impulsively. "Let's head for the beach before it gets too late. I'll show you some of my old haunts." He took her hand with such boyish exuberance that she couldn't take offense; besides, she was itching to dig her toes into the sand herself. "Mother—Helen's napping," he said to her unspoken concern. "We won't stray out of sight of the house."

The beach was sparsely populated, a winter beach, just fishermen and a few lovers strolling on the sand. Somebody's dog went running ahead of them, sidetracking through clumps of tall grasses in search of birds or rabbits, flushing to the chase, then diving out of sight again among the hilly dunes.

They had to laugh at his antics, then for a moment his expression was far away. "I wonder whatever happened to my old dog, Ace."

"Helen said that after Bryan left, Ace pined away and died." The moment the cruel words were out of her mouth, she almost regretted them. He said nothing but turned quickly away toward the ocean as if to hide his pain. Keely hardened her heart at his pretense of mourning an animal he most certainly never knew.

The sea was calm with an unexpected summer blue, and in spite of her companion, Keely's spirits rose like a glad bird at the awesomeness of the New England landscape. She hadn't visited for two years, and she had missed it.

"I always like this time of day best, when the beachgoers have gone and the late sun shines over the water." He scooped up a piece of weathered driftwood and threw it for the dog who cavorted in front of them, begging for a game.

Stripping his shirt off, a well-built physique was revealed to Keely for the first time. Whoever he was, he was obviously in his prime, though his skin was untanned and bore the scars from his sojourn in the prison camp. Bryan's chest had been relatively hairless, but this man had a healthy salt-and-pepper thatch that tapered and disappeared enticingly into the front of his tight jeans as he leaped and chased along the beach with the dog. But didn't masculine body hair increase with age—? Keely fretted.

After a few minutes, the dog's owner whistled and the game ended. A panting male body flung itself at her feet, sprawling on the sand in mock exhaustion. Laughing up at her, he was windblown, sandy, and gorgeous. Disturbed, Keely looked away and slipped off her shoes to let her toes luxuriate in the rapidly cooling sand, refusing to let him see how closely he had touched her thoughts. She didn't have to look at him to know he was watching her or that his eyes were a brilliant reflection of the sea. His intensity unsettled her.

"Why are you staring at me like that?"

"Am I staring?" There was no time to turn away from the smoke in his voice. "Maybe it's because you're so damned beautiful and I can't wait another minute."

He reached up to her, pulled her down on top of him by the shoulders and captured her mouth with his in a hard, hungry kiss. Before she could protest or push against his muscular torso, he broke contact to grin up at her. "I couldn't help myself. So sue me."

"Let's get something straight," she said, when she could speak again. "Don't presume, just because you're here and I'm here, that anything has changed between us. I'm here strictly to keep an eye on you and to protect Helen's interests."

He propped himself up on one elbow and dribbled sand on her leg playfully. "Very commendable, but where is it written that you can't have any fun? And kissing is lots of fun."

She brushed the sand away, and her voice was as icy as she could make it. "May I remind you that I'm very much engaged to Vern Preston?"

His smile disappeared, replaced by a frowning challenge. "Do you really think I'll let you divorce me for him?"

Her manner bristled with affront. "Divorce? Let—? I happen to be a widow. The only reason I haven't already married Vern is because of Helen's health and his campaign."

His brows rushed down toward the bridge of his nose and he sat up. "Is that so? Or is it because you know I'd slap you both with a charge of bigamy so fast it'd make your heads spin?" Immediately his tone became placatory. "Keely, even aside from that obstacle, can't you see that Preston isn't the right man for a woman like you?"

Keely turned on him in a kind of desperate fury. "And I suppose you think you are!"

He got on his knees and placed his hands on either side of her to prevent her from getting up. "Why won't you give us a chance to find out? I don't understand you at all, Keely."

"Bryan never did either," she said bitterly. "When I needed someone, Vern was there for me, while my husband was off playing war in Nicaragua with the CIA."

"People change."

"Do you really flatter yourself that I would dump a loyal friend like Vern for an opportunist like you?"

"How can you marry a man to reward him for loyalty?"

"How can you romance the widow as a sop to Helen?"

"I hardly think of you as a sop. A sap, maybe, if you insist on burying your head in the sand—"

"Stop it." She shaded her eyes to hide sudden tears that blinded her view of the sea.

For long moments nothing was said. Together they breathed in the same scent of verbena and lemon balm and their hair was ruffled in the same sea breeze, but they might as well have been on different planets. Finally they got up and trudged back to the cottage, both lost in their own disturbed thoughts.

That evening after dinner, when the three of them were cozily ensconced in front of an unnecessary but beautiful driftwood fire and sipping hot chocolate, Helen tossed the bomb. She had waited until Keely got up to replenish the popcorn and the conversation turned toward business.

"Bryan has been home almost two weeks now," she said. "When are you going to take him downtown and show him all the changes you've made?"

Keely's eyes were burnished gold in the firelight. "I'm sure Frank Cabell can arrange a tour," she hedged. "I can't spare the time right now."

"My point exactly!" Helen pounced triumphantly. "You need Bryan at the office—the company is simply too big."

"Helen, we discussed a promotion for Frank Cabell."

"Yes, but that was before Bryan came home. Frank's excellent, but he isn't family," Helen pointed out.

"Family business should remain in family hands." How

many times had Keely heard that tired dictum? Yet it was the very reason Keely had been brought into the Easton mansion and made head of Easton Publishing; she was "family," if only by a defunct marriage. It was as useless to try to change Helen's mind as to change the very bedrock of Manhattan Island!

The recipient of Helen's largesse distributed the hot chocolate, his shrewd glance taking in Keely's furious expression, but taking care not to interfere in the discussion.

"Maybe I haven't made myself clear," Helen pursued, and it was then Keely heard the first subtle but unmistakable steel in her tone. "Keely, I expect Bryan to take a more active part in the business."

Keely's heart began pounding. "I see. Does this mean you're asking me to step down?"

"Of course not!" Helen was genuinely astonished, then hurt, that Keely could have thought that for an instant. "Please don't misunderstand me, darling. After my stroke I came to accept my own mortality, yet never once did I worry about leaving it all in your hands. But with Bryan back and the two of you at each other's throats—" she looked worriedly from one of them to the other. "Keely, I couldn't love you any more than my own daughter, but I love my son, too. I want to see things settled between you while I'm still alive, rather than have the State of New York or the divorce courts do it."

"Mother," he interjected quickly seeing Keely's bloodless expression. "I appreciate your intentions. But you can't expect Keely to just move aside after all she's done—"

How despicable he was, pretending to intercede in Keely's behalf! Did he think he was fooling her or that she would be mollified into acquiescence? He knew Helen would insist and prevail because no matter the cost to herself, Keely would not jeopardize Helen's health. He knew that all he had to do was sit back and wait for the plum to fall into his lap with Helen his eager, unwitting accomplice.

"I'm not asking her to move aside, but to accept you as

a business colleague just as she would have accepted someone like Frank Cabell. What I am asking is that you both put aside the past which is interfering with the common goal, and that goal is to keep Easton Publishing intact for our heirs." The unwavering purpose was clear in the elderly woman's voice. "If there is never to be the laughter of your children in this house or in my arms, so be it. But as long as I am alive, the family business must survive. If you can't do it for yourselves, then do it for me."

Keely felt sick as she looked across at her enemy, his face an enigma but his motives all too clear. The challenge was unmistakable—he was daring her to expose him. The words burned her tongue with the need to say them, but Keely wasn't prepared to accept the consequences; they were better never spoken. An eternity passed and with it the opportunity. Her eyes dropped away in defeat.

Having said all there was to say on the subject, Helen went to bed, leaving a shattered and disoriented Keely to sort out the pieces of a decision made by default. She sat on the sofa and dropped her head in her hands, suddenly tired, more tired than she had ever been in all her life. Exhausted in body and spirit, her mind ticked away as mechanically as the clock on the mantel.

A shadow appeared at the doorway. "Why didn't you challenge her ultimatum? I would have backed you up."

Just the sound of her tormentor's voice rendered her speechless with anger. His uncanny ability to play one role to Helen and another to her was something she couldn't cope with. Listening to him, one would think he was on Keely's side and merely placating Helen! It just wasn't fair that he could win any confrontation with her by using Helen as an emotional hostage. Without answering him, she turned on her heel.

"Keely!" But his call was lost in the slamming of the door behind her.

He was right behind her, catching her by the arms until she swung around to face him. "Do you hear or aren't you listening, Keely?" he demanded, his warm baritone resonant with impatience. "You still think I want the company back. Well, I don't and I never did."

"Then why don't you tell Helen you don't want it?" she flung back, trying to twist away from the hands that imprisoned her.

His mouth tightened into a thin line. "For the same reasons you can't. Face it, Keely, we're in this together, and if you'll stop taking offense at everything I say, we could work out a solution."

"The only solution is for you to crawl back under your rock," she answered bitingly.

"You're still not listening. I'm willing to sign a duly executed legal waiver of all rights—property, business, everything."

She stared up at him, all the fight gone out of her. "You—what?"

"You heard me. A contract between you and me seems to be the only way to ease your mind that I can't get my hands on her money or on the publishing company."

"What about Helen?" she asked suspiciously.

He shrugged. "If I go through the motions at the office, she doesn't have to know I'm a figurehead."

"A flimsy contract like that wouldn't stand up in a court," she jeered.

"If I'm really Bryan Easton, my quit claim would protect Helen's—and your—interests," he pointed out. "And if I'm the fake you think I am, I have no legal claim anyway."

"So what's in it for you?"

He sighed in exasperation. "Keely, you're so damned scared somebody is going to take your candy away from you." Though his expression was neutral, Keely caught a fleeting trace of something else she couldn't quite put her finger on—anger, maybe. "I'm sure your boyfriend can draw up some airtight papers. At this point, I'll sign anything to end this eternal, destructive bickering between us."

To execute the legal waiver, Vern Preston was summoned to Easton Manor on a weekday evening. On the surface it seemed a straightforward business transaction, but Keely later realized it was a devilishly effective way to needle Vern with a firsthand demonstration of the new resident's remarkable impact on the Easton household.

Vern noted with dismay the fresh flowers adorning every table and breakfront, and the subtle transformation of a home occupied by women into an unmistakably male domain. The greatest changes were in the women themselves, from Mrs. Maguire's beaming countenance to Keely's flowing dresses with swirling hemlines. But the most astounding difference was in Helen Easton herself, startlingly youthful during her brief appearance downstairs in her wheelchair to greet Vern. There was new animation in her fine old face, and her hair was restored to the apricot shade she had made famous.

Alarmed by what he saw, he took Keely aside while his adversary read over the legal documents presented earlier. "What the hell is happening around here? You've changed the furniture around, and isn't that a new dress? I don't like it, Keely." His voice dropped to a harsh whisper.

"Don't be ridiculous. Let's get these papers signed," she whispered back. "Has your private investigator turned up anything new?"

"No, but something had better break soon—" he gave her a significant look, "—before my fiancée starts to believe the charade she's playing for Helen's benefit."

When Vern left with the duly signed papers shortly afterward, the whole evening loomed ahead for Keely and her unwelcome houseguest. No doubt he now expected her to show gratitude for his "sacrifice" of an inheritance that was never his to begin with. Keely considered retreating to the safety of her suite, but why should she let him chase her out of her own parlor?

"Well?" The voice made her blink up at him. Strolling toward her, hands in trouser pockets, jacket and shirt collar open, his impressive height and lean muscularity immediately put her at a disadvantage from her rather vulnerable position on the sofa. When he smiled that conspiratorial smile, he was far too sexy and much too disturbing. Maybe that's why I dislike him so much, she surprised herself by realizing.

"Well what?" she asked shortly, embarrassed at her unseemly thoughts and irritated anew at seeing Alfred Easton's gold watch chain glittering against his closely fitted vest.

"I've surrendered to you body and soul tonight, but will you respect me in the morning?" He was smiling, but he was watching her carefully to gauge the effect of every word.

She sat forward and slipped her shoes on for protection. "If you're looking for a medal for not stealing Helen blind, forget it."

"Just remember that I signed away only tangible assets, not my name or my right to use it."

"And you remember that I accepted only the tangible assets, not you."

"Then this calls for a toast—sort of." His blue eyes were hooded as he moved over to the decanter and poured himself a whisky, and she knew he had a headache. "As I recall, you're not much of a whisky drinker, but have some Campari and soda."

After the strain of tonight, she would actually have preferred the whisky, but she accepted the offer of the milder drink with murmured thanks. The mellow splash of liquid followed, and before he sat down, he lifted his glass. "To our first civil encounter, may it be fruitful and multiply."

Acknowledging the toast, she made her smile as noncomittal as possible, but his appreciative scrutiny made her prickle with awareness. When his smoky glance met hers, she reacted with a frosty hauteur that belied her suddenly pink cheeks.

He grinned. "Still cool as the wrong side of a pillow, aren't you? Can't you relax and enjoy a man's compliment?"

"Perhaps it's the man, not the compliment," she retorted. She wished now she hadn't accepted the drink. She didn't want to be obligated to another minute of his baiting, biting attempts to break down her defenses.

Sensing her impending flight, he changed tack. "So, how's Vern's campaign doing in the polls?"

"We don't pay much attention to the polls." She took a calm sip of her drink, grateful for this neutral ground. "He's pounding hard on the crowding and safety conditions at all the metropolitan airports."

His brow lifted at that, and a cynical grin touched his lips. "That old political chestnut? Twenty years of noise and overcrowding, and all they can come up with is limiting the number of airlines allowed to operate out of each airport."

"What would you know about it?" she bristled. "Landing light planes on jungle airstrips hardly qualifies you as an expert on New York air traffic control."

His eyes were fixed on her with that same odd mixture of goading fascination that set her nerve endings afire. "Maybe Ms. Keely Easton should stop supporting other people's politics and run for office herself."

"It's been suggested," she couldn't resist saying.

His grin grew broader. "Of course! What could be more apropos than you and Vern riding each other's coattails to victory?"

"What's that supposed to mean?"

He shrugged. "It's a time-honored tradition in prominent 'political' families. The Kennedys have been doing it for years." At her angry stare, he teased, "Now that I'm out of a job at Easton Publishing, maybe I should take advantage of the coattail effect and run for office myself."

"You!"

"Sure, why not? I'm the guy who provided the coattails in the first place, remember? Since the public loves to elect dashing war heroes, I'd be in select company."

"You're insufferable!"

The wicked grin was in place again. "And that's only one of my faults. Would you care to discuss the others over dinner tonight?"

"Sorry. I just remembered I brought work home tonight."

"Too bad. Well, liver has less cholesterol than a nice, juicy steak anyway."

"Liver?"

"Yep. That's what Lida has planned for tonight."

Keely grimaced. "I know Dr. Houten said Helen should get more iron in her diet, but once a week is a bit much."

He set his glass down. "Then get your coat."

"I never said I'd go," she amended quickly. "Besides, the liver has no strings attached."

He rose, and this time his amused air was laced with impatience. "Keely, stop being such a hellion. This is a simple dinner invitation. I'm not putting the make on you."

Still she hesitated until he took her cashmere wrap from the closet. Draping it around her shoulders, he murmured into her hair, "Live dangerously—what have you got to lose?"

You, Mr. Whoever-you-are, Keely thought grimly. And for my own good, the sooner the better.

The River Cafe was an anchored barge across the East River in Brooklyn Heights. The attraction was not the cuisine, but a most spectacular view of lower Manhattan and midtown framed by the arch of the Brooklyn Bridge. The dark water was as shiny as wet blacktop under city lights and river traffic. Keely blew out the candle on the table to enhance the twinkling illusion of tugs and coastal freighters passing so close they could be touched.

"The baby beef liver looks good. Or maybe you'd prefer the foie gras," he observed with a twinkling look at her over the menu, and for the first time she could smile at him without rancor.

"A rose by any other name still tastes like liver," she returned in the same light tone.

He was just too easy to be with, Keely fretted inwardly. How unreal to be sitting here with a man she truly despised but was perversely attracted to! He was such a familiar presence in her life now that the memory of the real Bryan was becoming blurred and faded. The thought upset her visibly and she turned her head to banish it by looking out the window, a reaction not missed by her companion.

"I have the requisite penny if you'll share your thoughts."

She shrugged and shook her head, at a loss for words.

"A million dollars then, and that's my final offer."

She lifted one shoulder noncommittally and played with the stem of her wineglass. "I was just wondering . . . if your face ever bothers you," she temporized, observing him as his head swiveled up in astonishment. Had she read a glimmer of satisfaction in that look? If so, he was in for a surprise.

One dark eyebrow cocked up in question. "Do you realize that's the first personal thing you've ever asked me?" The dig was subtle but unmistakable, matched by the sardonic glimmer in his eyes. "But to answer your question, I still get headaches—bone pain, nerve pain, muscle pain—who knows?" He held her gaze, as if trying to gage the reason for her sudden interest. "That's not what you meant, is it?"

"Actually no," she said, but there was no mistaking the meaning underlying the noncomittal words. "I just wondered if it seemed strange to walk around with a face you weren't born with."

He refused to grant her any satisfaction and grinned instead. "I've startled myself a few times in the mirror. At first it was like shaving a stranger in the morning. Even now, when I catch a glimpse of myself in reflection, I can understand why you have such trouble seeing past the facade. Maybe what bothers you is that I'm not as—um—handsome as I was before." His eyes glimmered engagingly as he offered his new profile for her inspection.

"Not having known you before," she replied archly, "I wouldn't know."

"Ouch." There was a warm, dancing malice in his eyes as he surveyed her. "You never give an inch, do you? I feel like I'm traversing a mine field."

"Eventually you'll make a misstep that will blow you out of the water," she said sweetly. "Until then, you're still a long way from where you want to be with me."

"By that, I assume you mean in your bed." His eyes raked her. "You bring sex into the conversation so often I wonder if you're sexually frustrated or attracted to me and just won't admit it."

She willed herself to resist rising to the bait but couldn't. "Hardly," she retorted, her cheeks hot. "You're not my type."

"Ah, yes. The manly Vern." His tone was deliberately insulting. Something flickered behind his eyes. "I'm trying to understand the attraction. Does he just look effete, or is he that good in bed?"

Scarlet swept into her face. "Now who's always bringing sex into the conversation?" Goaded beyond endurance, she got up so quickly that the glass of wine rocked precariously close to the edge and people looked around at them.

He half rose and drew her down again by the wrist. "For God's sake, take it easy. You're as prickly as barbed wire. I was teasing and I apologize."

"Why do you torment me?" she cried in a strangled voice.

"Because you torment me," he countered. "Keely, how else can I penetrate your defenses? Why won't you believe me?"

She shook her head in desperate denial.

He leaned forward with such intensity that she drew back, almost overcome by an irrational dizzying wave of fear. "Keely, if it would convince you I am who I say I am, I would tear this face off with my bare hands. It's me in here, dammit!" Then, "How can you discount all the evidence?"

"You're so smart, you figure it out. If we'd met under different circumstances, I might have liked you. But not with a relationship built on a basically dishonest premise."

He laughed a little wildly. "It's tempting to abandon my claim just to see if you mean that."

"Why not? You've tried everything else!"

He had little to say during the rest of the meal, sunk in self-absorption, and Keely, too, had great difficulty pretending interest in the food. Yet she found she was strangely reluctant to end the evening when they finally rose to go. When he helped her on with her wrap, she thought his fingers lingered on her shoulders an instant longer than necessary before dropping casually away.

"Intriguing thought, though."

"What?"

"That if I were somebody other than Bryan you might be . . . receptive to me."

She looked at him narrowly, sensing a trap. "I said, if you didn't claim to be Bryan."

"Did you mean it?" he persisted.

She shrugged.

He took her shoulder and swung her around to look at him. "You started this, now answer the question, dammit."

For the first time she realized how much her reply mattered to him, and it intrigued her. "How could I know?" She twisted away. "You aren't and I'm not and we'll never find out, will we?"

What she did not see was the twitch of his jaw muscle, and to her bemusement he dropped the subject.

ELEVEN

Balanced on the knife-edge intensity of her ambivalent emotions, Keely stayed as far away from him as she could after that encounter. It would be too easy to fall under the spell of this flimflam man. But total avoidance and denial of her attraction to him was next to impossible, and she was annoyed— no, terrified—at her growing acceptance of him as a man in his own right. Even though she felt swept along by circumstances beyond her control, she knew that to succumb to either his claim or his charm would lead to a wild downhill ride that could only end in tragedy for them all. Keely took pride in her self-discipline—over the difficult years, it was all that had carried her through.

Her dilemma intensified when Helen called her at the office to remind her to be home early for Bryan's birthday celebration. The Easton household had been in a dither for a week planning for the surprise party. Keely was tempted to refuse participating, but she couldn't bring herself to upset Helen just to spite him.

She settled for being late, arriving after seven. Mrs. Maguire informed her that Mr. Bryan had been sent on an errand to delay his arrival, and that dinner had been re-scheduled for nine. It was a reprieve of sorts, and Keely went upstairs to dawdle in the bath. Emerging from the scented water, she treated herself to an all-over perfumed emollient, which made her feel sinfully pampered and feminine, washed and blow-dried her black hair into a gleaming, upswept halo.

In the dressing room before she put her clothes on, she inspected herself for the first time in a long time. Over the years she had slept with Vern a few times, nothing regular or routine, usually at particularly lonely times and after a few drinks. Neither of them set the world on fire sexually, and since the advent of the interloper and Vern's escalating political schedule, there had been nothing at all between them. Yet looking at her reflection, she found herself wondering what another man would think if he could see her now, and that man was not Vern.

It was nearly eight-thirty when the birthday boy arrived. There was the usual commotion of greetings downstairs, followed by an athletic bound up the steps two at a time, the quick knock at Helen's door and a cheery hello and five-minute visit before entering his own suite. Though she couldn't hear him through the adjoining walls, she could not stop herself from imagining his routine—the strip for the shower, the vigorous lathering all over his lean-muscled body, the careless towel draped around the sinewy waist as he shaved. Was he fantasizing about her routine as well?

Her color was high as she donned a clingy peach silk camisole over her bikini panties, secretly pleased at how leggy and sexy she looked; a person totally removed from the carefully tailored outer image that had become her armor. Tentatively her hands wandered lightly over her shoulders, around high, rounded breasts, undulating in at the curve of her waist, and suddenly in the looking glass her imagination traced the route his hands would take, over the subtle flare of the hips, the taut stomach that had never borne a child. She turned sideways, wondering if he'd notice the firm bottom, the slim and shapely legs, the toned resilience of her skin. For long moments she was lost in erotic warmth until the pounding of her heart jerked her awake.

Her face flushed, and she was appalled. Suddenly she

couldn't take off the offending lingerie quickly enough. Tomorrow she would burn it!

She had the camisole up over her head when a brief rap at the door preceded its immediate opening, and the object of her imaginings stepped in. Keely whirled with a cry, covering her bare breasts with crossed arms.

Bryan glanced at her, then without missing a beat, as if his walking into this room were his marital habit and his wife's nakedness the most natural thing in the world, said, "Keely, could you—?"

He had changed into evening clothes, but had not yet donned his jacket. She was too mortified to notice he was working on his cufflinks.

"What do you mean barging into my room like this?" Keely screamed.

He looked up from his cuffs, surprised at her vehemence, scarcely seeming to notice the pink-tipped breasts she was frantically trying to cover while fumbling for her dressing gown, or the tiny bikini panties that concealed next to nothing. "The door was open and I needed help fastening my cufflink." He held his wrists out. "Would you mind . . . ?"

"Can't you see that I'm not dressed?!"

"Now that you mention it."

"Get out," she gritted, tears of rage springing into her eyes.

"Come on, Keely, you haven't got anything I haven't seen before."

"Get out, damn you, get out, get out!"

"Ah, Keely, what a hypocrite you are," he sighed softly.

"—What?"

"If you'd really wanted to keep me out, why didn't you just lock the door? Admit it—you were hoping I'd come in."

Keely squealed in fury. "You have an over inflated opinion of yourself if you think I'm that starved for a man!"

Now his gaze did sweep down her body, touching like a pulse point of fire wherever it lingered. "Really?" he murmured seductively. He took the camisole top off the bed and hooked his finger under one tiny peach-colored strap. "Now tell me. Is this the garment of a celibate?"

Keely snatched it from his hands while trying to maintain her cover with one hand. She turned her back on him and with shaking fingers donned the robe and tied it at the waist with a jerk before whirling to face him. "You're like a wolf circling a wounded deer, waiting for the right moment to rush in for the kill." Keely's cry was bitter. "Do you actually expect me to offer my neck?"

"For a kiss, maybe, not a bite," he said mildly.

"Stop baiting me," she warned. "Because you'll never get what you want from me!"

"If you're so sure, then why are you so worried?" A dark fire glimmered in his eyes as he hammered home his point. "Could it be that I'm melting the ice you've built around yourself over the least seven years?"

"Don't flatter yourself."

"You can't deny the electricity between us. By your own admission, if we were together under different circumstances, you'd be in my arms right now."

"Don't—!" Keely turned her head aside to escape the sensuous web he seemed capable of spinning at will.

"Don't!" he mocked. "Don't do this and don't do that. Someday I'll change that refrain to do, do, do."

"If only—" she bit her lip to stop its trembling, and his eyes glowed like blue fire at her hesitation.

"If only what?"

"If only I knew what you really wanted!" She stared up at him, bemused, perplexed, her gold-bright eyes flashing a thousand questions.

Now his look was openly challenging. "I gave up everything of monetary value when we were in Cape Cod. What do you think I want?"

"I'm not really sure any more," she replied slowly. "If it isn't the business or the house or the money . . ."

His smoky eyes played over her features intimately before settling on her full-lipped mouth. "Perhaps all I want is you," he suggested.

"No," she said thoughtfully. "I don't think it's me. Sex would be easy enough for a man like you to find without going through all the hassles that come with a woman like me." She looked up at him, unaware that his concentration was still fastened on the silken moistness of her mouth. "I wouldn't be easy, you know."

"No, you wouldn't," he agreed equably. "Then what? Do you realize you've run out of possible ulterior motives? So far we've ruled out avarice, revenge, and sex. What's left?"

"Maybe it's the chase," she conjectured gravely. "The challenge of a woman you know doesn't want you."

For a full three seconds he was so quiet she wondered if he was angry at what she'd said. Although he hadn't moved a muscle and his expression hadn't changed, she sensed he was like a tightly coiled spring that had been wound beyond endurance. Then he relaxed with a little laugh. "Well, keep working on it. Maybe you'll figure it out." He crossed to the door, pausing before he turned the handle. He gave his head a little shake and one side of his mouth went up and the other went down. "How truly brutal you are, Keely." Then he was gone.

Helen was carried downstairs and ensconced at the head of the table, which had been set magnificently, as if for a banquet, with crystal Baccarat and gold William Rogers and translucent Limoges. Helen's favorite Schubert piano concerto played softly in the background.

As usual, Helen hung on every word of the wolf in sheep's clothing. How could a mother who had borne a son and raised him to manhood not recognize him? Not once had a word of doubt or a testing question passed her lips. Was she so eager to have an heir in the Easton nest again she would accept any cuckoo who came along?

The birthday dinner began with a fresh fruit cocktail,

followed by succulent roast duckling with tangy orange sauce and crisp vegetables. Bryan's passion for haute cuisine was well remembered, and Mrs. Maguire had pulled out all the stops tonight after such a lean period with Helen's dietary considerations coming first. She and Sikes served the meal with outwardly sober expressions as befitted their dignity, but beneath the surface was a bubbling exhilaration in anticipation of the celebration to come.

Keely withdrew into herself to observe with rancor this farce played to a fare-thee-well by a con artist supreme. It was too galling the way everyone accepted the impostor at face value and blithely dismissed the legitimate doubts of a wife.

Following the duckling came crepes suzette and fresh, sweet strawberries with clotted English cream.

"Mother, Keely's allergic to strawberries." Bryan glanced over at Keely.

"Oh, dear, I asked for them because they were always one of your favorites, Bryan," Helen apologized. "I'm so sorry, darling."

"It doesn't matter," Keely said stiffly, less hurt that Helen could have forgotten than shaken at his knowledge of her allergy. Had Bryan ever known about it or even cared? And would he have remembered? Doubts and questions seeped into her mind, but she shook them away. No. Mrs. Maguire must have mentioned it.

When the meal was over, Helen suggested they adjourn to the parlor for the remainder of the birthday festivities. She had wanted to invite a dozen or so close friends, but Keely's objection had been seconded by Dr. Houten. Not only was her mother-in-law overdoing things as it was, but for Keely to spend an evening pretending to be a devoted wife was impossible, even for Helen's sake. To her relief and annoyance, Bryan had backed her up, promising a big party next year.

Helen wore blue tonight, which seemed to bring out the sparkle in her fading eyes, and her hands fluttered like white doves around him as if she couldn't stop touching his collar, flicking a wayward lock of hair, patting his hand with her own, smiling, flushed and happy as a young girl with her first beau. And him! Reciprocating with such phony affection. Keely's blood boiled. If only the real Bryan had treated his mother so well!

Through the angry haze of her thoughts, Keely was aware of the commotion from the dining room where the servants congregated to light the candles on the obligatory birthday cake. Then Mrs. Maguire, flanked by Sikes, Bob Maguire, their daughter Janelle and her husband Paul, wheeled the cake triumphantly in on a serving cart. It had been a ritual every year even after Bryan had gone to college, Helen confided to Keely, her eyes shiny and soft with memory.

Soon the cake, Bryan's favorite German chocolate, flamed with candles. "Why is it that the older we get and the less wind we have, the more candles there are on the cake?" he complained good-naturedly.

"Be grateful. When you get to my age, you'll get one candle per decade," Helen's mock reproof set off delighted laughter.

All the candles were snuffed in one pass, but after a moment of suspense, one flickered back into life. There was more laughter when he pinched it out with his fingers.

Neapolitan ice cream was served.

"A ghastly combination," he agreed, smiling at Keely's horrified expression. "But anything else just wouldn't be my birthday. Thank you, Mother, everyone. It's wonderful to be home again, surrounded by my loving family!" He was looking straight at her, and Keely flushed.

Amid laughter and applause, the servants crowded around as Bryan served each slice of cake and dollop of ice cream himself, with kisses to the women and hearty handshakes to the men. The room buzzed with talk. Keely watched all their shining faces, marveling that in all the years she had lived in this house she had never witnessed such an outpouring of love and affection. These same people had always treated her with formal correctness. Keely only picked at her cake and ice cream, transfixed at the whole spectacle of Bryan's birthday and feeling like an outsider.

And then it was gift-opening time. Keely noticed that every one of the servants had brought something for "Mr. Bryan." There was a fountain pen, a knit tie, a hand-monogrammed linen handkerchief, a paperback novel. As he tore the paper from each one, he was visibly touched. The last of the gifts from the servants was a large basket with a lid, brought from the kitchen at the last minute by Sikes and presented as a joint gift from the staff.

Bryan opened the lid and, looking inside, was nearly overcome by what he saw. Then smilingly he lifted a fat, brindle puppy from the basket and held him up for all to see. There were cries and coos and laughter, and Bryan's eyes were suspiciously bright as he held the puppy to his face to receive a sleepy lick.

"He's exactly like my old dog Ace," Bryan exclaimed. "And that's just what I'll call him." After more cuddles and licks, the puppy was deposited in Keely's lap. Stroking the velvet ears, she was unable to maintain her lofty distance. She smiled up at him.

"What kind of dog is he?" she asked. The puppy looked something like a cross between a bulldog and a boxer.

"He's a Staffordshire terrier," he told her. "My grandfather used to raise them for show."

"I don't think I've ever heard of them."

"They're sometimes called the American pit bull, though Granddad tried to discourage that name. Earlier in the century, bull baiting in a pit with these dogs used to be a favorite betting sport."

"How cruel," Keely murmured, as the puppy snuggled in her lap. "Will he grow up to have a vicious temperament?"

He was squatting on the carpet beside her chair, fondling the dog's smooth head. "No breed is inherently vicious, although I suspect that Staffordshires may be more territorial than most. For instance, they won't tolerate other dogs near their people or property. But a lot depends on how they're handled and trained." His head was so near she could not avoid the heady scent of him. "Of course, there are always bad individuals."

"How very true," she murmured.

He looked up at her veiled barb and their eyes met and locked. Though he said nothing, she flushed with the feeling that she had gone too far. He rose abruptly and took the puppy from Keely's arms so that Helen could stroke and admire him, then replaced him in the basket where he immediately began to squeak pitifully.

"I'll take him back to the kitchen with me," Mrs. Maguire offered.

It was the signal for everyone to take their leave so the Eastons could finish their party alone. Keely was glad of the respite to break the spell he had worked on everyone, taking the opportunity to arrange the gifts from Helen and herself next to him on the sofa. He opened his mother's first and lifted several sets of underwear from the tissue, briefs and tank tops in rather erotic colors like plum, blue, brown, and even a leopard print by a well-known designer.

Bryan laughed, delighted. "Who but a mother would buy underwear for her son's birthday!"

"Yes, who? Somebody's got to be practical," Helen smiled sagely. "Actually, as unmentionables go, they're rather whimsical, don't you think, Keely?"

Keely was rather discomfited that Helen would solicit her opinion on the provocative underwear, especially knowing the strained state of affairs between them.

"Thanks, Mom." Bryan kissed her and Helen glowed. "I'll model them for Keely later."

Keely squirmed in annoyance, but said nothing.

He opened Keely's last-minute gift, exclaiming over the handsome topcoat. He did look wonderful in it. "Thank you, darling. The sleeves are just the right length. I'm surprised you remembered I'm a 44-long.'' He then insisted she arrange the scarf around his neck. "Try not to strangle me,'' he gibed, and self-consciously she was aware of his rapt attention to her lips as she busied herself tucking and tugging until the scarf looked right. Before she could turn away, he pulled her against him and kissed her on the lips while Helen beamed. Tingling and angry from the stolen kiss, Keely managed to pull away and busy herself folding tissue and gathering ribbons.

"One more present,'' Helen announced over the rattle. She held up a small box with an oversized gold bow. Bryan's eyes met his mother's as he slowly accepted the box and untied the ribbon. Inside was a set of car keys. Even from where she stood, Keely could see the Jaguar insignia on the gold chain.

"Look out in the driveway,'' Helen instructed mischievously. "Happy birthday, son.''

Instead, Bryan scooped Helen up in his arms and whirled her around and around before setting her down in front of the window to look at the luxurious silver automobile parked in the circle drive. A proudly uniformed Sikes stood at attention beside it. Keely felt physically ill.

"It's still your birthday. Take Keely somewhere nice tonight, son,'' Helen urged.

"Oh, Helen, no,'' Keely protested. "You should go.''

"Nonsense. I'm tired and it's long past my bedtime. You two young people go and have fun so I can hear all about it in the morning.'' She held up her cheek, which Keely dutifully kissed, distinctly unhappy about the turn of events.

"I'll carry Mother upstairs,'' Bryan told her. "Then we'll go.''

Over Helen's head she glared her refusal.

She waited until they had disappeared up the lighted staircase before she followed. This time she locked the door to her room. Avoiding the new lingerie, she laid out a flannelette nightie before undressing quickly.

At the tap on the door she stopped, all breathing suspended, waiting for him to try the door handle, then go away. Nothing. She felt almost disappointed. She sat down at the dressing table with her pots of cream, preparing to take her makeup off when the long-unused door adjoining the next suite opened and her tormentor strode in.

Her hand stopped in midair, her eyes wide. Dangling the door key, he let his eyes rove in malicious male appreciation over her half-clad body, her long legs still encased in sheer stockings and high-heeled sandals.

"Get dressed," he commanded. "I'm not going to let you spoil Mother's pleasure with your childish tantrums."

She had underestimated him again, but this time she would not be bullied. "I won't be a party to your gulling a heartbroken woman," Keely shot back. "You're worse than a gigolo if you accept that car!"

"Watch your mouth and keep your voice down." His tone was tense with scarcely veiled anger. "You can call me any name you like in the car. Now get some clothes on."

"I'm not going anywhere with you."

"Then you'd better be prepared to explain why to Mother."

Once again, she was forced to swallow her rebellion and give in. It was becoming an all-too-familiar pattern, and she hated her helplessness. Soon they were speeding north on FDR Drive alongside the East River. The arc lights illuminated Keely's mutinous face as he glanced over at her.

"I think," he said, as if she hadn't been giving him the silent treatment for the last fifteen minutes, "that we need to talk, really talk to each other, instead of having these knee-jerk arguments that get us nowhere."

Talk won't change a thing, Keely fumed in silence. You'll still be you, whoever that is.

"Maybe the problem is strain and overwork. If you took some time off you might see things in a more reasonable light."

I seriously doubt it, Keely muttered to herself.

"Frank Cabell agrees with me that you're overdue for some serious R&R."

"Where do you get off discussing my vacation time with my employees?" Keely burst aloud, goaded into replying.

"Simmer down. Frank happened to mention you were planning to take four days off this month." Grinning over at her, he added casually, "Since all the official investigations have validated my claim, I was hoping we could declare a cease-fire and celebrate a second honeymoon. What do you think?" She gave him a cold stare as he continued. "This time we'll do better than a $7.95 chicken-dinner special at a Holiday Inn."

Keely felt a chilling tingle down her spine. How had he known where she and Bryan had spent their wedding night, right down to the menu?

"If a honeymoon is too optimistic, we could at least get reacquainted—anywhere you like. You once said you wanted to visit your father's birthplace in Scotland."

Her head jerked up at that. Even had the real Bryan known where her father was born, it wasn't the sort of information one kept on immediate recall. Couldn't he see that his knowledge about obscure facts was suspicious in itself? She had only hazy recall of an expressed wish to visit Scotland, so how could he remember when he had been so wrapped up in himself that he didn't even remember her birthday? All the same, her knuckles went white on the armrest as he continued to lace the conversation with casual references to the past that made the hair stand up on her neck.

"Speaking of Scotland, how is your father? Does he still live in Stamford? We must get up to see Owen—we may not get another chance before Christmas. Did he ever marry that boutique owner he was seeing, what was her name now—?" he snapped his fingers impatiently. "Vera—Vonda—?"

"I don't remember."

"You don't remember if he married that boutique owner—?"

"I don't remember her name," Keely snapped.

"I guess that means he didn't." He looked over at her with another of his charmingly boyish grins. "She wasn't right for him anyway. Why don't we invite him for a visit?"

The possibilities presented by such a meeting had not occurred to her until then, and a slow excitement began to build. "That's a wonderful idea. I'll call him tomorrow."

"Yes? She said yes?" he said incredulously, teasing. "What prompted this sudden capitulation to a suggestion of mine?"

Anticipating her father's alliance with her against this man, she found herself able to respond to his banter with some of her own. "I guess I just can't say no to a begging man."

"Really? I'll have to remember that."

She ignored the erotic implications and smiled a slow, grim smile that deepened the amber glints in her eyes as she anticipated the meeting between her father and a real, live Lazarus.

TWELVE

Keely took only two days off when Owen Neal accepted her invitation to visit and pass judgment on the man he'd read so much about in the papers. Though he had only met his son-in-law a few times before his disappearance, Keely was hoping her father might latch onto something she had missed about the man beneath the new face. She was elated when Bryan offered to pick him up at the airport—the two men would be alone together for the lengthy ride home, plenty of time for her father to catch him in some inconsistency of impersonation.

The first thing Owen Neal said to her after Bryan had disappeared upstairs on an errand was: "Well, honey, if he's a fake, he's a damned clever one." He paused. "He recognized me right away, although I was buying cigars at the tobacco stand instead of where we'd planned to meet at baggage checkout."

"He's probably been through all our photo albums and pumped Helen and all the servants," Keely realized in frustration.

"In the car he asked me if I was still restoring vintage Edsels. I don't think Helen ever knew about my hobby, but I remember discussing it with Bryan years ago." He paused significantly. "But you're right, he's different from the man we knew."

"In what way?" she asked eagerly.

126

"I'd prepared myself for somebody who looked different, but can they do plastic surgery on a personality, too? He's—mellower, not so gungho as Bryan was then. It's as if he had all his rough edges filed off in that prison camp."

"Didn't you notice anything more specific?"

Owen shook his head. "God knows I thought Bryan was a bastard for the way he treated you, but—people do change, honey."

"Daddy! Not you too!"

He hastened to add, "I'm not saying he is or isn't Bryan—you knew him better than I did, and nobody's interested in my opinion anyway because I'm obviously not objective where you're concerned." Owen's expression was wry. "I don't blame you a bit for being careful about accepting him at face value. But you should be fair. Don't reject him just to get even with him for running out on you."

"That's not true, no matter what people say," she declared. "The problem is that I can't fight him openly because of Helen's health, and he knows it. He's weaseled his way into our home and I'm forced into co-existence to keep peace with Helen."

Owen cautioned his indignant daughter. "If Helen believes him, then that's the bottom line, isn't it? Maybe you'd better reassess your own options, because it looks like he's here to stay."

"I can't allow myself to think in those terms yet."

"But when the courts establish his legal claim, you're going to be in a very bad position. If they rule for him, then your only choices are divorce or reconciliation."

"How can I divorce someone I'm not married to? He isn't Bryan, I don't care what the courts decide!"

"What if you're ordered to hand over your Easton holdings to him? Are you prepared to involve Helen in a nasty battle over a man she believes is her own flesh and blood?"

"Oh, Daddy," she wailed. "What shall I do?"

"Honey, you're not thinking with your head right now. Isn't it possible you're overlooking what seems to be obvious to everyone else?" he pointed out reasonably.

"Are you suggesting I accept him for expedience?"

"No, but can't you yield an inch and open your mind to the possibility that you might be wrong? I don't think it's his changed facial features that bother you so much as his apparent change in character. Isn't it just possible that when a man's been through the crucible of imprisonment, it could change him for the better? Do what you have to do, honey, but don't throw the baby out with the bath water."

"What do you mean?"

"The man is obviously in love with you."

"He's in love with the idea of being an Easton."

Although she scoffed, her father's words unnerved Keely. In love with her! Had her father been taken in by this con man, too, believing she was playing the wronged wife punishing a wayward husband? This swindler was after the big prize, and if he had to pretend at being "in love" with her, he would play the part convincingly, just as he played the part of the prodigal son. Couldn't anyone but her see that if it weren't for her lone resistance, he would already have wrested control of Easton Enterprises from a frail, vulnerable Helen, booted Keely out on her ear, and systematically stripped a company he openly admitted not having the slightest interest in? She shuddered at the implications. If she were going to err, she would rather err on the side of caution. And if she were wrong? It would serve Bryan right, she consoled herself grimly. After all, he had thrown her over like so much garbage.

At dinner that night, Helen, so vibrant now, was a gracious hostess; she'd always liked Keely's father. As hard as Keely tried to prevent the ersatz Bryan from learning any more about her than he already knew, the two doting parents kept a steady stream of anecdotes flowing, a veritable treasure trove of priceless information about the Easton and Neal families for someone whose ears were always open. Keely had the feeling that instead of solidifying her position against the impostor, her father had weakened it. Chalk up one more defection to the enemy camp!

It was painful to watch her father falling into the web. Before the evening was over, the two men were smoking Owen's cigars like lifelong friends, discussing politics and sport fishing over brandy. When his purported son-in-law asked for Owen's advice on a tax matter in deference to the older man's profession as a CPA, her father was hooked.

Finally, when the smoking began to blue the air, Helen excused herself for her usual early retirement. Keely stayed, perversely wanting to feel every stabbing wound as the counterfeit Bryan made further inroads on her father's gullibility.

Owen, subterfuge as alien to his nature as to a newborn baby's, assumed the role of peacemaker, oblivious to the sizzling undercurrents between the two antagonists. Well into his third after-dinner drink, he was also feeling no pain. Bryan controlled the conversation, taking every opportunity to direct it in a clever, covert game conducted entirely for the benefit of his new convert.

"I'm proud of my little girl for her brains, but sometimes I wish for the good old days when women were content to stay home and have babies," Owen confided expansively, flicking a cigar ash into the travertine marble ashtray on the Sheraton table beside the sofa where the three of them sat. "I keep reminding Keely that her biological clock is ticking away and I may never be a grandfather."

Bryan winked at Keely, whose cheeks had turned pink. "Well, it hasn't been on my account, sir," he said.

Owen leaned forward, patting Keely's hand, maudlin after his last refill of brandy. "I keep thinking that if the first little fella had lived, we'd be going fishing next summer in the Finger Lakes. He'd have been just old enough to bait his own hook . . . "

Keely's eyes flew involuntarily to Bryan's, who sat thunderstruck. "You lost a baby?" he demanded, eyes flashing between father and daughter like chain lightning. "When?"

"By that, I suppose you mean whose?" Keely bridled.

He drew his breath in sharply at the implication, and Owen Neal intervened. "Honey, I'm sorry! Did I—"

"It doesn't matter, Daddy."

"It damn well does matter!" What an act, she thought, almost admiring as Bryan's eyes scorched over her. She let him see nothing in her expression but hostility, lifting her chin defiantly.

Owen Neal, completely sober now in the middle of a hornet's nest, cleared his throat. "Uh—maybe I'd better turn in now . . . or maybe I should stay, honey?" He looked anxiously at his daughter, whose lovely face was altogether too cool and composed. There was strained silence until Owen rose with an uncertain, "Good night, then."

Bryan sprang up, too, and stalked to the window to stare blindly out into the night. Minutes passed, then he turned and viciously stubbed his cigar out in the ashtray. They glared at each other as he poured himself another brandy and tossed it off.

"Want to tell me about it?"

"You're the expert historian, you tell me."

"Was it mine?"

"Certainly not! I've never slept with you."

"Your gambit wears thin, Keely." His tone was caustic. "Did you abort my child in retaliation when I left?"

His accusation on Bryan's behalf was worse than a slap in the face, but she refused to either confirm or deny. Watching in satisfaction as he struggled in the dark undercurrent of emotion, she thought in wonderment, *Why, I've hurt him!* As if he really cared about that unborn, unsung, unwanted bit of tissue that Bryan had implanted so carelessly and even more blithely abandoned so long ago!

His voice now was dry as sand. "Damn you . . . then was it Vern's?"

She laughed, but with no real mirth. "May I remind you that I've been a widow for seven years? That I'm free to do as I please with whom I please, and if I choose to fornicate with a one-toed Episcopalian platypus, it's none of your business!"

He grabbed her by the upper arms and slammed her against his chest. "Don't push me too far, Keely. I don't give a damn who you've slept with over the past seven years, but for God's sake tell me the truth about the child!"

It suddenly occurred to her, staring into his eyes—she really didn't know this man or his capacity for violence, but she knew Bryan's, and when he gave her a little shake, she was worried enough to relent. "All right! I miscarried before I even knew I was pregnant. Afterward, I went to Europe."

"Didn't Mother know?"

"I'd lost the baby. There was no reason to tell her."

"My God. If I'd only known—" The stricken look on his face nearly dissolved her. "Did you—want the baby?" He choked on the question.

Keely was horrified to feel tears welling up in her eyes, tears she thought dried up long ago. Why, when she needed all her cool reserve, should it abandon her now? And he had no mercy, holding to her upper arms with hands of steel, scrutinizing her face for the answer to that question until her lips began to tremble and she collapsed against him in uncontrollable weeping.

It was a long time before she had calmed down enough to realize she was no longer imprisoned in his arms but tightly embraced, and that she was not the only one with tears for what might have been. All the pain she had kept bottled up so long had finally been released, and they swayed and grieved together, he taking as much comfort from her as she from him. Through his shirt she could feel the rapid beat of his heart against the tumult of her own, felt the warmth of his body, the strength of his arms. His hands moved over her back and shoulders in a half-massage, half-caress, until comfort turned to something else, then—oh, God, his lips were dropping kisses in her hair!

She knew she should push away from his chest, but her strength had fled, and in the absence of resistance he tilted her chin up with a gentle thumb and, dipping his head, he tasted her tears with his tongue, tracing the salty rivulets to the confluence of her mouth.

Keely's hands curled helplessly as warmth turned to electricity through her veins, igniting flickering sparks that set her whole body afire until she was vibrating against him, acutely aware of his lean muscularity in every nerve, every cell, every fiber of her body. She could not break free, either physically or emotionally; she was caught up in a spiral of need she could no longer control, didn't want to control.

His hands were never still. Tenderly they framed her face to draw her mouth slowly to his so that his lips could dip and taste with languid ease. Firmly he lifted her arms around his neck, then swiftly slid his hands down her body to pull her hips against his hardening frame.

And his mouth! Oh, the delicious pressure of it as he explored her chin, the velvet contours of her neck, each sensitive hollow alive to his tongue! She was frightened, but thrilled by an intensity of feeling akin to pain, by the throbbing in places of her body that had never throbbed before, by the heat that suffused her fingers and toes like a rosy fever.

When she opened drowsy golden eyes to his, he knew she was lost and his for the taking. From the tender, parted curve of her mouth to the convulsive swallow in her throat, he knew she had surrendered to his will at last.

"Say you want me tonight, Keely," he commanded in a voice husky with emotion.

". . . yes. Oh yes."

"Say, 'Yes, Bry.' " His cheeks were flushed as they stared at each other.

"I said yes," she trembled, clinging to him.

His hold tightened. "Yes . . . Bry," he repeated. His eyes were glittering now.

Almost at once Keely felt the hectic rush of her passion begin to ebb and common sense return. For a moment, it had been beautiful, a man and a woman about to discover each other, and he had spoiled it with an ill-timed condition as the price for his lovemaking. In another instant, passion had turned into overwhelming realization that she had almost made the greatest mistake of her life.

In a convulsive movement, she tore herself from his arms so violently she hit the wall behind her with bruising force and never even felt the jolt. She had to get away from him—anywhere, anywhere away from him. He reached out to break her headlong rush, his hand on her shoulder, but she jerked away, holding her hands up in a curt halting gesture. "Don't . . . touch me."

She waited a moment until his own hands dropped away before she turned and fled to her room.

On the landing, over the pounding of her heart, she thought she heard a low, bitter laugh from the darkness below.

On election day Keely voted in her precinct at the YMCA, culminating a three-day last-minute whirlwind campaign for Vern. She had never been so exhausted or her fingers so sore from handshaking, and not even the exhilaration of the vigil could relieve the bone tiredness. On election night everybody sat together in Vern's headquarters in a downtown Manhattan hotel. Late in the evening, when most of the major races had been decided, hundreds of balloons were released and champagne was passed around in Styrofoam cups. With everyone high on the adrenaline of a job well done, victory was in the air.

Toward midnight, television coverage of the outlying county races announced Vern Preston the winner. He had been ahead all evening by a comfortable margin, but it wasn't a landslide. Keely was secretly uneasy now that Vern would be going to Washington—in effect he had offered her some protection against her increasing attraction to the man who called himself Bryan Easton.

"Tremendous performance," boomed Senator Eakins in a personal telephone call to Vern at eleven when victory appeared imminent.

"Congratulations to you, Mr. Senator," cooed the amplified voice of a well-known film star in a parody of Marilyn Monroe's song to a past U.S. president. Amid the noisy revelry, balloons soared overhead in bubbled confusion to the ceiling. When Vern arrived at the hotel, he looked tired but elated as he grasped dozens of outstretched hands on his way to the dais. Corks popped and champagne poured, confetti flew everywhere. A cracked recording of "Stars and Stripes Forever" blared over the PA system.

Unannounced and uninvited, Bryan had driven down from Westerby to bring Keely home, and she was too tired to demur. Vern was tightlipped with anger, avoiding his "rival" so that he would not have to shake hands with him or in any way acknowledge him. With mixed feelings, she could not blame Vern, who believed that by not confronting Helen openly, Keely was contributing to the legitimacy of the interloper's claim. She did not know how to combat his growing frustration or her own, so she did nothing.

Outside, reporters with TV minicams crowded Keely for pictures and statements, seemingly more interested in Bryan's newsworthy presence than in Vern's apparent victory. Taking charge without compromising Keely's position, he held them off with good-humored replies, giving her time to escape into his new Jaguar sedan idling at the curb. Tomorrow's papers would have a field day, but tonight she was too tired to care.

In the car, she crumpled in exhaustion, dizzy from champagne, smoke, and elation. Every bone and muscle in her body ached and her right hand was sore and swollen from shaking hands. All she wanted to do when they finally arrived home was crawl among the pillows in her bed and sleep forever. The prospect of climbing the mountain of stairs from the foyer seemed overwhelming.

After a token protest, Bryan swept her up in his arms, and she allowed him to carry her upstairs. He deposited her on the bed and deftly slipped off her shoes. When he started to undress her, she had the presence of mind to object, but she lay back fully clothed, already sunk in torpor. She was only peripherally aware of his presence from that moment on; then she was gone, unknowing, uncaring about anything but the blessedness of sleep.

During the night she awoke in timeless shadows. Her skin felt hot. In a fit of free-floating anxiety she kicked the blankets aside to let the cooling air flood over her body. Just as she was about to drift off again, something, a stirring, nudged her into semiconsciousness. Dimly she was aware she should wake up, but the drugging effect of the wine and her exhaustion, combined with the comfort of the wide bed, made her unable to struggle free from sleep. She dreamed somebody slid alongside her under the sheet, but it was only a dream, and she slept on. When next she opened her eyes, the room was still in darkness, but it was cooler now. The bed creaked a little as she shifted position, and she thought she heard the sound of quiet breathing, but it must have been her own. She closed her eyes and was lost once more to oblivion.

Sunlight was streaming over the bed when Keely slowly returned to consciousness. There was a little tug on her tousled hair, then a teasing finger outlined the curve of her lip until it twitched. When she opened sleepy eyes, all she could see were blue, blue eyes with sun crinkles at the corners. For a moment she wasn't sure where she was, who he was.

"A good morning to you, sleepyhead," he whispered, and leaned down to brush her cheek with his lips.

Her heart did a crazy series of beats, and she bolted up on one elbow, drawing the sheet up under her chin, suddenly aware that all she had on was a satin teddy. "You!" she said.

"Is that all you can say on such a beautiful morning with your candidate going to Washington and everything right with the world?" he complained good-naturedly. She noted he had already showered and shaved and smelled of clean linen. He was wearing a white karate-style kimono with a red sash around the waist, and the vee-neck exposed crisp, dark chest hair lightly frosted with gray. He looked critically at his watch. "It's nearly noon, but I've ordered breakfast anyway."

Keely's face burned. "You undressed me!"

"Guilty as charged. And you, my darling, have no head for champagne."

"I want you out of my room before somebody finds you here!"

"A moot point since we slept together last night." At her gasp he laughed reassuringly. "The operative word is 'slept.' I like my women conscious."

"You're lying!"

"No, you really were out like a light."

"I mean—sleeping here—"

"In the same bed, yet. Is that skepticism I detect on your lovely face? Ask Mother if you don't believe me. She's been up here twice already, but I wouldn't let her wake you."

Hardly had the words left his mouth when there was a knock on the door. Keely gasped, looking around wildly.

"Too late," Bryan grinned, tossing her a bedjacket. "Caught *in flagrante delicto* by the breakfast committee. What are you so worried about? We're married."

She was still frantically buttoning the jacket when he opened the door. Ace bounded joyfully on the bed, whip-

ping his tail in Keely's face as he sought Bryan's undi-
vided attention. There were doggy kisses all around, then
Bryan set him firmly on the floor and told him to lie down.
He crouched, head on paws, watching Bryan's every move
in tail-thumping adoration.

Helen entered still in her dressing gown, followed by
Mrs. Maguire who wheeled in a breakfast tray, and Bob,
who was loaded with newspapers and telegrams. Sikes
busily carted in floral arrangements until the room began
to look and smell like a funeral parlor.

A sob caught in Keely's throat to think he had arranged
this intimate boudoir tableau. Not only had they been in
bed together, but they were neither wearing enough to
maintain any illusion of propriety.

"Good morning, darling," Helen cried, dropping her
cane against the bed to lean over to kiss Keely warmly.
She seemed more excited than was probably good for her.
"Dr. Houten was an old party pooper, but I watched the
returns on television until Vern was the clear winner last
night. Poor baby, you look exhausted!"

"I am," Keely admitted, keeping her eyes carefully
averted from Bryan's dancing gaze. "I could use another
ten hours of sleep."

There was nothing she could do to set things straight
with Helen, who was pretending there was nothing unusual
in finding her daughter-in-law in bed with her estranged
husband.

She beamed at them both. "Well, we've fobbed off the
thundering herd of press for the rest of the morning, but
poor Vern, bless his heart, called three times. You were
both still asleep and I didn't have the heart to wake you."

The pseudo-Bryan was enjoying himself immensely, taking full advantage of the compromising situation with
Helen as his misguided accomplice. Oh yes, he had planned
this little charade from start to finish, knowing Helen
would gladly collaborate to break up Keely's romance with
Vern. Only with Vern out of the picture in Washington

would her recalcitrant daughter-in-law reconcile with her son. Keely held her tongue and tried to respond to Helen's bubbly spirits. Now was not the time to take a stand.

The election news was read aloud from the newspapers. In the middle of the festivities, the phone rang out of reach on the table. Keely knew it was Vern before Mrs. Maguire even picked it up. Bryan got off the bed and took the receiver, his legs bare, hinting at the rest of him which was obviously just as bare, his long feet shoved into corduroy slippers.

"Congratulations again, Preston. Yes, we're going over all the dailies now. It was a trouncing after all. Yes, she's here but she's not dressed. We were just having a leisurely breakfast in bed. What? Oh, I don't think so, but I'll ask her. Any message? Fine. Yes, of course. I'll tell her."

Keely choked down her anger in front of Helen, but he couldn't have missed the murderous daggers shooting from her eyes. Helen had the presence of mind to see them, too, along with the tears welling up.

"Bryan," she chided mildly, the very first words of criticism that had passed her lips since the prodigal's return. "You might have let Keely speak with Vern herself . . ."

"Sorry," he apologized silkily. "He seemed in a hurry, and I did tell him you'd call him later, darling."

Keely was too agitated to be good company, but it was an hour before everyone left, with Helen patting Keely's hand once more. "You've made me very, very happy, my dear."

Keely squeezed her eyes tightly to hide the tears, but the moment the door closed, she rounded on him. "Damn you! Get out of this bed. Get out of my life. I don't care what it costs, name your price, I want you gone! You're nothing but a dirty blackmailer, with Helen as the hostage!"

As she raged, he strolled to the bedside table and picked up a silver lid, found a triangle of toast and buttered it. Then he looked around. "You're getting yourself all worked up over nothing, darling," he said mildly.

"I'm not your darling! Oh, what will it take to get rid of you?" she almost wept. "Haven't you any conscience?"

"Conscience is such a relative term," he chided, opening the jam.

"You've used Helen to keep me 'in line' for the last time. I'm going to tell her the truth about her precious son!"

"Assuming she believes you, which she won't, I have a few other options, so don't threaten me, Keely. Taking you to court might drag on for years, but I have the rest of my life to devote to the noble cause of regaining my birthright. Because of Mother's health, I've taken it easy on you."

"Easy!"

"I think it's safe to say I've taken the high road through this whole thing."

"High road!"

"Is there an echo in here? I could have taken my claims to the American public . . . newspapers, talk shows, magazines, et cetera, for some cheap, messy, but highly effective publicity, but I haven't."

"For my sake?" she jeered.

"For Mother's sake. But I also recognize that I wronged you seven years ago, and you were entitled to vent your feelings on me. But isn't it time for you to let the past go?"

"And winner take all?"

"Even if we should divorce, which I'll fight tooth and nail, you wouldn't exactly leave empty-handed. But for Mother's sake, this personal vendetta of yours against me must stop."

Keely seemed incapable of coherent reply, of any action drastic enough. "Or what?"

"I warn you, Keely. If this thing ends badly with my mother having another attack, you'll regret it."

"Is that a threat?"

"I don't make threats. Only promises." For the first

time he allowed his own anger to show. "Maybe you'd better examine your own motives before you go slinging mud at me. It takes a hard cookie to deprive a grieving mother of her own flesh and blood just to feather her own nest."

A tidal wave of intense rage rolled over Keely, and for the first time she understood how a person could kill. She wanted to rip and claw him, gouge and hurt him. Instead, she got up from the bed, totally oblivious of the short bedjacket that revealed bikini panties and long legs. She flung herself toward the bathroom.

In three strides, he had intercepted her. "Dammit, Keely, why are you so stubborn? You're my wife!"

Her voice rippled with vehemence. "Then prove it!"

"By God, I will!"

Despite her anger, Keely laughed in scorn.

"That tears it," he said thickly. Lightning quick, one hand shot out to grip her wrist while the other imprisoned her waist. In one swoop, he picked her up and dumped her on the bed. He came down beside her. She bucked and flailed, but the struggle was brief when he immobilized her under his heavy body. She tried to scream.

"Shut up," he said tightly. "If you scream I'll stuff your panties in your mouth."

Glaring up at him with hate, she panted, "What now, big boy? Rape?"

He laughed harshly. "Oh, you're doing your best to provoke me into it, aren't you? Forget it, sweetheart, I'm neither that desperate nor that stupid."

She lay still, breast rising and falling, fear subsiding into suspicion.

"Haven't you noticed," he said softly, "how everybody concentrates on identifying me? It can't be proved physically—my old face is gone and my wife pretends she doesn't recognize the man inside. So where does that leave us?"

"It leaves me being squashed to death," Keely said sharply. "Get off."

He obligingly shifted his weight to the side, but one muscular leg, thick and immovable as a log, pinned her to the bed. "Perhaps we should be looking for another kind of proof." She feigned indifference, but her eyes were like gimlets as he looked down at her. "Maybe you can't identify my body, but I sure as hell can identify yours."

Keely began to struggle again.

"Stop it, you'll only hurt yourself." His large hands gripped her wrists determinedly beside her head on the pillow as he eased his body back over hers to smother resistance. "What's the matter, Keely? Afraid to face the truth?"

"Don't . . . you . . . dare touch me!" she trembled.

"Then be reasonable and lie quietly. I hope you'll have the grace to admit the truth when I prove it to you." He waited a moment until convinced she had settled down. He ignored her blazing eyes. "Now. Shall we start at the top and work our way down?"

Keely made a strangled sound in her throat.

"Figuratively speaking, of course," he grinned, eyes dancing. "You once showed me a little moon-shaped scar on your scalp where a cookie jar fell off the refrigerator when you were five years old. I presume it's still there?"

Keely gasped. She'd forgotten that scar. She lay still as an eerie feeling invaded her mind.

"Close your mouth," he drawled. "Or you'll accuse me of cheating when I mention the filling in your third molar, left side, bottom."

She relaxed. Dental records were easy to check.

He watched her with hooded eyes. "That filling fell out while we were eating popcorn at the movies on our honeymoon in Atlantic City."

"I'd be more impressed if you remembered the name of the movie," she said caustically, trying to hide her shock.

"As I recollect, neither of us were paying much attention to the movie." His grin was wolfish. "Remember the drill-happy dentist who wanted to do a root canal on your tooth the next day?'' She could not hide her stunned expression, and he was merciless as he forced her to listen to his deliberate recital of every distinctive anatomical detail of her body from the tiny fishhook scar on her knee that had become infected, to a mole behind her ear she had never even seen with her own eyes. He even described the twin dimples on her lower back and claimed to know the color of her nipples.

That last was too much. Her whole body exuded fury, humiliation, violation. ''You haven't told me one thing you couldn't have got from undressing me last night.''

''I proved my case, Keely,'' he said quietly. ''Now it's time to admit it.''

''I admit nothing,'' she said with as much brittle hauteur in her voice as she could muster. ''Are you quite finished?''

''I guess not.''

Only too late did she realize what he meant, the lengths he would go to ''prove'' his claim. In a moment, he had pinned her flat on her back, and with one heavy-handed stroke he ripped the bedjacket and teddy from her body. She struggled wildly, forgetting to scream while tearing at him with her nails. He took his time because he knew he would win, and all Keely could do was moan in impotent fury.

He waited until the fight went out of her, covering her mouth with his only when she tried to scream. When she went limp in exhaustion, his imprisoning hands no longer hurt but stroked away the red marks his fingers had made on her tender flesh.

''Making love is the last barrier between us, Keely.'' His mouth rasped the silken skin of her neck in a brush stroke whisper, and Keely was galvanized once more by the fibrillations that vibrated through her body. ''How else can I prove it's me?''

''All you've proved is that I can't stop you physically, nothing more.'' She was trembling now. ''You can't make love by force. It's a contradiction in terms.''

"I won't have to force you, Keely, because I already know you want me."

"Oh, please! Spare me the male fantasy flight!"

"You told me so that night your father visited."

"Well, I've changed my mind!"

"And you'll change it back again before I'm through. I'll promise you this—before we reach the point of no return, if you still say no, I'll stop."

Without waiting for her reply, his mouth covered hers, nipping with tiny kisses, rocking over her lips before settling in full, enveloping warmth. One hand tangled itself in the midnight silk of her hair. Could this really be happening? As she would have with Bryan, she steeled herself for a brutal onslaught, but it never came; instead, his lips and tongue wrought a gossamer magic that caught her unaware until a lovely madness forced her body muscles to arch and twist in appalling response. Nothing in her stunted experience had prepared her for this over-mastering feeling. When he pulled her on top of him, it was a tacit last-minute reprieve to her own free will; she could stop what was happening now if she wanted to. But by then she knew that when he made love to her, she was going to let him.

Once she had admitted to her own willing acquiescence, surrender erupted into passion and she was lost in a bombardment of sensation she had not dreamed existed. He was neither slow nor tender as he stroked her, touched her, kissed her, until to her shame she was unable to stifle the inarticulate whimperings in her throat. He was making her forget who he was, who he claimed to be, making her forget to even care. All she cared about was the way her body felt and reacted as she arched into him, gave herself to him. She clung and matched his fiery demands with her own, gasping at the magic he called forth until she was moving, wanting, needing.

When she couldn't stand it any longer, when she thought she would die of wanting him, he was there, in deep, quieting her cries with his mouth. Not content for quick satisfaction, he let a crescendo build until they hung on the edge, then fell back, let it build again and again, until everything merged, blurred, exploded. The end, when it came, was a violent internal cataclysm that left her devastated like a bomb crater after the moment of glory, leaving havoc in its wake. Keely's head fell back, her mouth contorted, tears streaking her face, her hair a black cloud against the pillow, still in the throes of pulsing, contracting, shuddering, long after it was finished.

He lay back, too, and minutes later drew her head onto his chest as their breathing slowed. Under her cheek she could feel the residual quivering of his pectoral muscles, the beating of his heart, and she wondered if it had been as powerful an emotional experience for him as it had been for her. She wondered if he could have stopped as he had promised. He had been only too confident that she would not want to stop.

Inevitably, sanity returned in full, ugly force, and with it the burden of consequences. Keely couldn't believe that she had let it happen, had wanted it to happen. Oh, he had her now! It couldn't be undone. She would pay and pay and pay for this split-second descent into madness. The full enormity of her surrender came flooding into consciousness.

He felt her tears scalding the bare skin of his chest like hot diamonds. After a moment, he raised himself on one elbow to look down into her face. A puzzled frown creased his forehead. "I've made you cry." His voice was husky, his cheekbones still flushed.

She bit her lip and turned her face away.

He raised the corner of the sheet to wipe her eyes. "Was I rough?"

"No, you weren't rough." She buried her face in her hands. "I knew what it would be like, and I didn't want to feel like this."

"And how do you feel?"

Her sob was at once perplexed and full of pain. "Invaded. Possessed and dispossessed . . ."

Her obvious unhappiness bothered him and he lay back to stare at the ceiling. His strong, thick-wristed hand caressed her upraised knee as they lay thigh to thigh, sending another erotic shiver so deeply through her body that she knew he felt it too. "Didn't I please you at all, Keely?"

"Maybe too much," she whispered, tears glistening between shuttered lashes.

His low laugh rippled intimately between them as he turned and propped himself over her on one elbow. "Too much?" He sounded relieved. "I think I've waited forever to hear those words from your lips." He pressed warm little kisses on her breast, then down over her stomach. Complacent in his bigness, his maleness, his virility, he took delight in her femininity. He was like a starving man in a candy store, unable to decide where to touch first. He splayed his hand possessively over her stomach. "With any luck we've planted a little bit of me right here under your heart to reaffirm my survival and this second chance with you."

Keely stiffened, chilled at his words and suddenly aware of the unprotected danger of what they'd done. Could this be his ultimate diabolic plot to compromise her, embarrass her, discredit her public rejection of him?

Sensing the subtle shift and tensing of her body under his hands, he pulled her chin around and the expression in his eyes pleaded with her. "Keely, don't freeze up on me—the war between us is over. I love you and you love me."

She drew back, stung out of lethargy at last. "Love? I never said I loved you!"

He actually flinched. "Then what—"

"You're a man and I'm a woman, and we just had sex. Don't make any more out of it than that!"

The muscle in his jaw worked. "I could have sworn I passed the big test just now."

"Test! If this was a test, then you flunked it. You're nothing like him, do you hear? Nothing!" Her tone was scathing. "You had your way with me, isn't that enough? Or did you flatter yourself that afterwards the widow would be so grateful for a little attention she'd overlook the fact that you're still not Bryan Easton?"

He canted his head to the side as if from a blow. She continued, her voice low with venom. "For Helen's sake I'll be civil to you until I get the evidence to blow you out of the water. But don't you dare ever touch me again!"

His eyes blazed for the first time. "Or what? You're forgetting, this is my house, Helen is my mother, and you, dear wife, are still married to me." He stood up, nude, magnificent, gloriously angry now, and reached for his kimono, jabbing his arms into it, jerking the sash around his waist. Their warring gazes met and clashed. "Since we're laying down the ground rules, let me inform you that, also for Helen's sake, I plan to move into this room with you tonight. We will sleep together in this very bed as man and wife from now on. Then if you can, by day you can play the icicle, but alone with me in the dark of night you can indulge your wildest fantasies . . . the way you did just now."

He stomped to his own room.

Keely fell back against the pillows, her body still tingling from his lovemaking. In her mind she went over every moment of it, every detail. No. She knew it now. He was nothing like Bryan.

Whoever he was, he was wonderful.

THIRTEEN

The interloper carried out his threat to move into the bedroom with Keely. At night, with him lying next to her, so near and yet so far, her sleep suffered. She knew she should move into another room away from him, but Helen's health was deteriorating and she was uncertain how much of an imbroglio she could endure. Perversely, she wanted him to make a move so she could rip his male ego to shreds, but so far he had been smart enough to keep his distance in the bed. Yet between them was a growing volcanic sexual tension that kept Keely constantly on edge. Even going about her daily business, unsummoned thoughts of him too frequently drifted into consciousness, and too much time was wasted with a lot of blank staring into space and loss of comprehension.

She struggled to give words to what she felt for this man. Hate? Not any more. Hate had worn itself out. Liking? How could you like a thief? Wanting? She didn't know. She only knew that she was obsessed day and night by restless thoughts, images of remembered, forbidden sensations. It continued to intrigue her that this man had the power to drive an irreparable wedge between Helen and herself. But he never used that power. Uneasily she wondered why.

After the election, Vern had until January to take his seat in the Senate. The hiatus gave him a chance to wind up campaign matters and his New York law practice, and precious little time to rout the enemy from his fiancée's life. Ever since his rival had moved into the mansion, Keely's objectives had become blurred in her mania to protect Helen, and if something wasn't done soon, she might succumb to the pressure. It was so clear to him that Helen was the problem. Remove her objections and the dilemma would solve itself, and he could hold Keely to her promise to marry him.

Vern finally decided on a plan of action and phoned her at the office. "I need to see you tonight. Can you spare a minute to drop by my apartment before you go home?"

She sighed. "Vern, I really can't. I promised Bryan I'd pick up the dog at the vet's."

"So now it's 'Bryan,' " he noted bitterly.

"What do you suggest I call him?" she retorted. "John Doe?"

"I have a few choice names in mind after he inveigled his way into your bed after election morning." She could hear the suppressed rage in his voice. "He did trick you, didn't he? Or am I going to be the last to find out what everyone else already seems to know?"

"I resent your tone and implication, Vern, and I'm tired of explaining it to you."

"Then why am I hearing rumors that you've reconciled?"

"And why are you reading the gossip tabloids!"

"Have you slept with him?"

"Goodbye, Vern."

"No—wait. I apologize, Keely. Please. Pick up the damned dog and stop by my place on your way home. It's important or I wouldn't ask." Sensing her reluctance over the wire, he tried and failed to keep the edge of hysteria from his voice. "If I ever meant anything at all to you, you'll come."

Keely was silent a long moment before she capitulated. "All right. But I can't stay long."

"Yes, we mustn't do anything to upset Helen." Keely

heard the sneer, the desperation. Vern was hurting. It was the least she could do.

She had not been in Vern's penthouse apartment since Bryan—well, what else could she call him, after all? —had come. He greeted her with a light kiss at the door and took her coat in the foyer while she juggled the heavy, wriggling puppy from one arm to the other as Little Ace scratched at the bandage wrapped around his head.

"How did you manage to get stuck with the little beast?" Vern did not bother to hide his distaste as the puppy whined and tried to lick the nearest face.

Keely set him on the floor. "He developed an infection of one of his ears after cropping—oh, look out!" Huge footed and boisterous, Little Ace skidded on the polished floor and knocked over a yellow, potted chrysanthemum at the base of the spiral, iron stairway leading to the library loft before Keely managed to capture him by the scruff of his neck.

"Sorry about the plant, Vern. And I really can't stay— Sikes is driving down from Westerby to collect Helen and me from the Dakota at six."

"Surely you have time for a glass of white wine." Vern seemed preoccupied and agitated, and the dog definitely cramped his style. Without waiting for her assent, he moved to the fluted glass bar whose smoked-gray panel slid back at a touch to reveal a well-stocked, professionally chosen array of bottles.

"I don't want any wine, Vern. What was it you wanted to see me about?"

Vern glanced over his shoulder at her. "Not even the smallest civilities between us any more, Keely?" His eyes glittered. "I can remember a time when we never had enough time to say it all."

"I'm sorry." She was contrite. "It's the puppy."

"Here then, give him to me. I'll put him in the kitchen. I don't care if he wets the floor in there." He reached out for the scruff of the dog's neck and received a yelp and a growl for his pains. Keely laughed at the grown-up noise issuing from the baby throat. "Maybe I'd better do it. He's very protective of me."

"Then he and I have a lot in common," Vern murmured wryly. An ardent fire darkened his eyes. "Do you realize how long it's been since we've even been alone together?"

He walked up behind her and dropped a kiss on her neck as she straightened from depositing the puppy.

"Vern . . . I only came today because you said it was important. Is it about Bryan?"

"It's about us."

"Vern." She tried to keep her voice gentle. "How can I say this? There is no us. There hasn't been for a long time."

"What?" A stunned disbelief underlined his words.

"I'm sorry, I don't know how to make this easy. It's just that I have too many personal problems, and now that you're a United States senator it isn't fair to keep you hanging. Surely you can see that."

Vern's anger exploded around her. "Damn it, you promised that after the election you'd marry me!" He leaned forward, controlling himself with obvious difficulty. "Now it's dump me and he gets a clear field?"

"I am not a field," she objected indignantly. "Vern, it's been months since he came. Your investigation didn't turn up one single thing I could use to get rid of him. Helen insists he stay at the house. What can I do?"

"If he won't move out, then you move out!"

She replied tensely, "I'll tell you again—I'm not ready to risk a confrontation with Helen over him yet."

"Helen." His voice echoed accusingly between them. "Helen, Helen, always Helen! For Helen you'll sacrifice yourself to this—this reject guerrilla and it's over for us. I tell you I won't stand for it any longer."

Keely lifted her head. "There's nothing you can do about it, Vern."

"Oh, but there is. I've already taken matters into my own hands, something I should have done from the very beginning." He spoke so quietly that there was a faint air of menace about the words.

Before she could get an explanation, the telephone rang and Vern swore under his breath. From the kitchen the puppy began to howl dismally, and Keely gathered her coat and purse to leave.

Vern picked up the phone and snapped into the receiver. "Yes?" She watched a hard, dark mask descend over his features and knew it was Bryan on the other end. "Yes, she's with me. So what?" He looked over at Keely with smug satisfaction. "What the hell do you think she's doing here? Use your imagination, man."

Keely snatched the receiver from him with a glare. "Yes?" Even before the harsh words were grating in her ear, she knew something was terribly wrong. She listened, the annoyed expression on her face slowly replaced with dawning horror. Her lips moved silently.

"What is it?" Vern asked sharply.

"All right," Keely said, suddenly breathless. "Yes. Bellevue. I know where it is. All right . . ." Her voice broke. Her eyes were tearless but glistening. "I know. I'm sorry. I'll be there."

She hung up the phone, put the heels of her hands to her eyes and pressed.

Vern leaned forward, took one of her hands away and held it urgently. "Helen?"

She nodded. "Another stroke."

Vern was white around the lips, but there was a wild light in his eyes. "How bad?"

"I don't know. I've got to go. The puppy . . ."

"To hell with the puppy. I'll get a cab."

FOURTEEN

On the morning of the funeral, Helen lay in her Empire bed in Westerby draped in ice-blue silk, her apricot-colored hair carefully arranged in the bouffant style she had made her own. The mortician had puffed a tiny bit of rouge on her cheeks so that she looked blooming and only sleeping against the lace-embroidered pillow.

Keely was too stunned to cry. Even though she had known this day would come too soon, the dreadful finality of entrusting Helen's fragile, carefully nurtured body to the cold earth seemed more than she could bear.

As friends and business associates filed in and out all morning to pay their last respects, Keely lay on her own bed down the hall wondering if the bereaved "son" would return for his three o'clock performance at the funeral service. Added to her grief for Helen was remorse and guilt that she had been with Vern when it happened instead of at the Dakota apartment, and that Bryan blamed her bitterly. Last night they had had a fearful screaming match of recriminations, and he had slammed out of the house and not returned.

Bryan came at last, his manner and dress very correct, cold and formal. Sitting beside him at the service, Keely could detect a faint odor of liquor, and she wished she could find solace as easily. She declined his arm as they entered the limousine for the ride to the cemetery.

A fog-drenched day marked Helen Easton's burial. Prepared as usual for any contingency, Vern carried an umbrella, while Bryan stood to the side. Bareheaded and somber, he had turned up the collar of the trenchcoat Keely had bought him for his birthday, more to shield his ravaged face from view than to protect it from the elements. Keely's own face was hidden behind a black veil, and her posture revealed only stoic acceptance; her calmness acknowledged the uselessness of tears. When the service ended, Keely accepted Vern's proffered arm and the crowd parted before them, respectful of the uncontrived dignity of Helen's daughter-in-law.

Later, Vern Preston lingered at the mansion in Westerby, willing Keely to turn to him for comfort. But she did not. She remained calm, her grief passing into that deep well of resignation. Finally, she told him she wanted to be alone, and he reluctantly went home.

The night of the burial became a bizarre vigil. Periodically Mrs. Maguire came up the stairs with a fresh pot of tea, tending to each of the equally but separately bereaved Eastons behind closed doors, clucking and scolding in sympathy that a husband and wife should be together in time of mourning. But Helen had been the catalyst that had bound them together; without her they were lost to each other. If one had given a sign or indication to the other, they might have bridged the widening chasm; but neither did, and as the awful hours wore on, mutual exclusion and the weight of darkness drove the final wedge between them.

FIFTEEN

"I think we may begin if everyone is here."

Arthur Preston's words were spoken into the dead quiet of the room where twenty persons sat. There was no obvious anxiety on any of the faces, Keely thought, except possibly her own. In the week since Helen's death, they all had disciplined themselves with the knowledge that she was never coming back.

"I think the will is quite clear—but I'll answer whatever questions you may have when I finish reading."

No one spoke. They sensed the drama in the moment, with the two principal players sitting on opposite sides of the room. There had been much door slamming and acrimony between them; now came the moment of truth.

There was a stiff crackle of paper as the elder Preston unfolded the document. Keely let her gaze move upward to the carved stone mantel, the paneling, the sculptured ceiling, willing herself not to care about Helen's last testament. The bay window jutted out over the terraced summer garden where Helen once tended flowers for daily use in the house. She wished she was out there among the roses and sundials and Helen's memory, rather than here waiting for the axe to fall.

As the attorney began to read, Keely slid a look at the man who had duped everyone—everyone but Vern and her. He sat stonily correct, his irregular masculine features carefully composed to conceal the victory he must have known lay close at hand. How she hated him. He met her icy stare, but she knew he was not even seeing her.

She pulled her thoughts back to the will and gave her attention again to Preston's words: "To Lida Maguire and Robert Sikes, if they are still in my employ at the time of my death, each fifty thousand dollars outright and a pension as herein outlined, for life."

Sikes remained impassive, but Mrs. Maguire began weeping silently into her handkerchief, her husband patting her shoulder awkwardly. Smaller bequests were given to other members of the household staff.

Now Preston was saying: "To Keely Neal Easton, my beloved daughter-in-law, the island vacation home at Cape Cod, known as Turtle Cay, together with the ten acres and cottages that stand on the property, and the property on 61st Street in New York City. Also, the income for life on ten-thousand shares of stock in the Easton Publishing Company. The voting rights, however, are to remain with my son, Bryan Trevelyan Easton, subject to the conditions below."

Preston's eyes now flickered over his half-spectacles, moving over the group, as if waiting for a protest. The discipline held; no one spoke or moved. Preston went on.

"It is my wish that Keely Neal Easton shall continue to discharge the function of chief executive officer of Easton Publishing as long as it pleases her to do so. Her successor will be chosen by my son as Chairman of the Board."

Then followed the clause that everyone was waiting to hear: "The remainder of my estate, all real and personal holdings, stocks and investments, the property known as Easton Manor in Westerby, New York, the Dakota apartments and my interests in the Easton Publishing Company, I give, devise, and bequeath to my son, Bryan Trevelyan Easton. The condition of this inheritance shall be that he shall reside at Easton Manor at his convenience and shall assume an active interest in the publishing company. A further condition of this inheritance shall be that in the event of default by my son, and after the several bequests have been fulfilled, the remainder of my estate, all real and personal property, shall revert to Keely Neal Easton, with all the foregoing conditions to apply.''

Arthur V. Preston removed his spectacles. "Any questions?''

A dark chill settled over Easton Manor in the aftermath of Helen's death. Keely and Bryan refused to be in the same room with each other, and a brooding anger hung between them like a dark cloud until even the servants began to tiptoe uneasily.

At night Keely could hear his restless pacing through adjoining doors, or she could look down in the garden and catch a glimpse of his shadow. She knew his virulent headaches had intensified when his neurologist was summoned to relieve his excruciating pain, and she also knew he had been drinking too much.

The night Helen died was the night he had moved out of her room, but it didn't matter because Easton Manor was his house now. The will stripped Keely of all autonomy and irrevocably bound her to the man more tightly than a marriage contract. The final explosion was brewing, and Keely welcomed it. She wished with all her heart that she could believe his claim to be Bryan; then she could dump everything in his lap and escape through divorce.

But he wasn't Bryan, and he had stolen an empire. Could she let him get away with that? Helen had gone to her grave without learning that fundamental truth. Would it have changed anything to have told her, or would it have only hastened her death?

Movement across the table focused her attention on Bryan. He had tossed the morning paper aside and was just draining the last of his coffee.

"Will you have dinner here tonight or do you plan to stay in the city?" Keely asked, and was rewarded with a frown.

"Since when do you consult me about your dinner plans?" He rose abruptly and went to the door, where he paused to glance back at her, his face hard and expressionless. "For information about my scheduled activities, I suggest you ask your boyfriend or your spies."

She felt her color deepen, wondering how much he really knew about their spies. "We can't go on like this, tearing at each other. Whether you like it or not, I'm part of the package, and we still have business to discuss," she reminded him quietly. "If that's what's bothering you, maybe we'd better get it out into the open."

"There's quite enough out in the open." Those storm-blue eyes with their brooding, almost angry, light caught hers. "Particularly the fact that with my mother out of the way, my wife and her lover now have one less obstacle to contend with."

With difficulty, she suppressed a gasp of anger at his cruelty. The barrier he had erected between them since Helen's death was getting taller and wider, more unbreachable by the day. Before she could utter a word, he had stalked from the room and was gone.

Her hands began shaking so hard that her cup slipped and shattered on the tile floor. From the moment of Helen's death, almost before her very eyes, he had changed from a man of good humor and patience into a snarling stranger—detached, aloof, seemingly indifferent and uncaring to all but his own grief. Only Ace basked in the approval of his master, often going for long walks with him in the evening. It baffled and infuriated her now that he had her where he wanted her, he no longer seemed to want her. Instead, he pounced on every opportunity to degrade and humiliate her. He was—yes, he was like the Bryan of old, and that fact became more apparent every day.

Almost, almost, she could believe . . . but could she have been so mistaken? Could a stranger have suffered so terribly from Helen's death? Could it be just an act, an act

so convincing that he had even Keely in awe of his bereavement? It was becoming more and more difficult to
reconcile what she wanted to believe with what she knew
about the man.

She brought herself up short. No. She could not afford
to think along those lines. How dare he not "forgive" her
for being in Vern's apartment the day Helen died, present-
ing himself as the wronged, cuckolded husband! As if that
had been the precipitating factor in her fatal stroke! How
dare he work that one-and-only visit into some sort of
sordid, full-blown affair? His accusation that they were
plotting behind his back stung all the more, because that,
at least, was true.

And then this morning! How much more of this was she
going to be able to endure? She had never dreamed it
would be so soul-destroying to live in isolation from the
man she loved.

Love. Love?

Thunderstruck, she rose to her feet, her heart suddenly
pounding. With a cry she ran into the study, slamming the
door behind her. She leaned weakly against the desk until
the dizziness left her and she was more in control of
herself. She caught her reflection in the oak-framed mirror
over the mantel and quickly looked away from the naked
truth in her eyes.

So that was it. She understood it all with gut-wrenching
clarity that threatened to tear her apart. She had fallen in
love, not with Bryan or Bryan's reincarnation, but with a
man she believed was guilty of outrageous duplicity. How
could she love him with such a monumental deception
between them? How could she, dear God, how? And yet
she did.

"Keely."

She jumped and looked up with tearstained face to meet
Bryan's eyes in the oaken mirror. He stood in the doorway
of the study, his countenance pale and desperately tired in
contrast to his impeccable attire. His briefcase was still

clutched in one hand. Keely bit her lip, trying not to think about what a fool she was. Instinctively she braced herself, preparing for another emotional onslaught.

Their eyes were fixed on each other in the reflection of the mirror as he set the case on the chair and slowly moved to stand behind her. She could not tear her eyes away from his, the new knowledge of her love for this man a raw wound in her breast. His hands came down on her shoulders in a convulsive, almost painful grip that she welcomed, turning her to face him. And then she was in his arms, her head buried against his chest, breathing in his unique fragrance of cologne and fresh linen. His hands moved in soothing little circles on her back, and his lips found her temple, his warm breath ruffling her hair.

"I'm sorry," he said softly, almost too low for her to hear. "When I stop hurting a little, maybe then I can stop hurting you."

She raised her face blindly to his and he kissed her. When she would have clung, he averted his head to hide his emotion, put her arms away from his neck and was gone.

Before she could ponder the meaning of it all, she heard the front door chimes. Who could it be this hour of the morning and in this weather?

Vern stood on the porch closing his dripping umbrella before handing it to Mrs. Maguire. Wet snow melted on his Harris tweeds, and Keely had to fend off an unspeakable weariness at the sight of him. However tepid their relationship seemed in retrospect, Vern hung on with the tenacity of a bulldog, refusing to let their tattered relationship end with dignity. Her rash promise to marry him had unleashed a Pandora's box of troubles. Though she hadn't seen him but twice since the funeral, he had written, sent flowers, and telephoned almost daily. He was determined Helen's death would not be in vain, and that after the trauma of her loss had faded, Keely would come to her senses and back to him. He intended to be there waiting.

"It's important or I wouldn't have disturbed you so early, Keely. Actually, I'm here as your attorney with some legal matters." He allowed the housekeeper to take his coat. "I waited outside until he left to catch you before your first appointment of the day."

That was how they both had always referred to him—"he," "him," never "Bryan," but oddly enough, from Vern it now irritated her. Reluctantly, she led him into the library. "Mrs. Maguire, we'll have coffee in the study."

The housekeeper, grimly silent, carried in the coffee service and poured two cups from the silver carafe before taking her leave. No doubt there would be a detailed report to Bryan tonight from his own spy in residence, a report that could only add fuel to the fire.

For the first time Keely noticed Vern's agitation, poorly concealed. "Keely, I know what I'm about to say is in incredibly poor taste with Helen so recently gone . . ." A nerve twitched at the outer corner of his left eye, and he swallowed. "But she is gone, and we must strike now to rid ourselves of this leech before he becomes permanently entrenched. I . . . assume that we still share that objective?"

"And what do you suggest?"

"With Helen gone, you don't have to handle him with kid gloves any longer. You must contest the will."

She felt uneasiness and dread at the thought of that devastating undertaking. She knew it was her only remaining recourse to expose him, but strangely her heart was no longer in the battle.

Seeing her vacillation, he set the cup down on the table so hard that the coffee inside sloshed out onto the polished surface where it was immediately blotted up by the antique doily. "Kelly, what's got into you? Don't you care any more that he's a liar and a thief?" he demanded. He got up and paced the floor, gesticulating wildly while Keely sat in numb surprise at his emotional display. "Can't you understand the rage I feel, the powerlessness, watching him take you over the way he did Helen, to see him controlling you through her? And yet it never really was him who came between us, it was Helen. Helen called all the shots, right down to who would win access to your bed, blackmailing you with her frailty to keep you in line—''

"Vern, stop it! I won't listen to this from you!" Keely was repelled and frightened by the fevered hatred in his eyes.

"For God's sake, wake up before it's too late, Keely. Helen's gone. Gone! You don't have to consider her health or her wishes any more—you're free to fight him openly for the empire that's rightfully yours!''

Keely paled. "Vern . . . did you say something to Helen?''

"Yes, by God. I did what had to be done, and I'm not ashamed to admit it!'' He drew up short, his righteous rampage halted momentarily. "You wouldn't! You wouldn't even try to tell her this man was making a fool of her, so I did. I told her how you really felt about him, about our secret investigation, that you were only humoring her. And, yes, I told her that you had promised to marry me. Don't look so shocked. It's the truth, isn't it? I won't apologize for telling her. It was kinder, more honest than what you were doing, stringing her along with lies.''

Keely's voice was deceptively soft, unnaturally calm. "And when did you have this . . . discussion with Helen, Vern?''

There was a pathetic arrogance in the set of Vern's shoulders now. She had never noticed before how sloped and thin they were.

"When?'' Keely demanded, her voice rising.

Vern's pointed face hardened in defiance. "All right, I admit it was earlier in the same afternoon she had the stroke. But it was a coincidence, it had nothing to do with our discussion. It was a civilized conversation. She wasn't exactly . . . thrilled, but she was calm when I left her. She even thanked me for telling her. I called you to come over that evening to discuss our plans, to tell you I'd taken care of Helen's objections in a dignified manner. The stroke was just bad timing—''

"Bad timing—!" Keely was already screaming, half in horror, half in fury to realize that he had killed Helen with his monstrous, egotistical need to prevail over his enemy. And oh God, Helen had died thinking Keely had betrayed her! Suddenly, nothing would do—she had to feel his flesh beneath her nails, feel his blood spurting for what he had done to them all in the name of ''love.''

With a cry she fell on him, scarcely aware of what she was doing until the strong hands of the chauffeur pulled her away from behind. Vern lost no time; he bolted as soon as he could, and it was Sikes who half-carried her to the sofa. By the time Dr. Houten arrived, Keely had calmed down enough to refuse the tranquilizer shot.

When Bryan entered the study for the second time that morning, he was struck by her pathetically brave stance in front of the mullioned windows. She was calm, but her studied avoidance of his eyes told him she was still in shock. He had some idea of what happened from Sikes, and along with his own urge to tear Preston limb from limb was a stab of contempt for himself. Hadn't he hurt people too in the name of love?

He walked over to stand behind her. Something in the set of her shoulders touched him; he wanted to hold her, protect her, love her. The aster-pink dress she wore suited her vivid coloring, but he was conscious only that she was beautiful in so many other ways. A touch of her shoulder turned her slowly to face him. They stared silently at each other, adversaries who wanted to be lovers and couldn't.

He eased down to half sit on the edge of the desk and drew her against him so that she could feel the full comfort of his body. With the heat and muscular hardness of his thighs enclosing her own, his hands were free to slide down her back pressing her ever closer to that hungry part of him which instinctively sought her yearning softness. For several minutes they stood wrapped together in mutual commiseration, not really knowing who was comforter or who the comforted, not really caring. There was a terrible joy in knowing that in this embrace the last barrier between them might crumble at last.

Was he Bryan? . . . she didn't know, but with a singing consciousness that had only now awakened, she knew she didn't care anymore. If he was, he was a different Bryan, so changed in spirit that she hadn't even recognized him . . . a Bryan she could love again.

I love this man, whoever he is, she thought in wonder. When did it happen? When did she stop hating him? Frightened at such sudden total knowledge, she tried to draw back, but he leaned forward and captured her half-open mouth with his. Maybe he'd meant his kiss to be comforting, but it was anything but. It produced a raw jangling in her, an instinctive desire to move against him, a frightening longing to surrender body and soul to him completely.

It was time for reparations, for conditional surrender and tentative demand, and they could scarcely believe the message of their mouths. For long moments they kissed, broke, kissed again, dipping and tasting, nipping and savoring, starved for sensation and touch and closeness.

Reluctantly, he broke the kiss. "Keely. We have to talk." His voice was rough with restraint.

She felt driven by a fierce desire to cry: "I don't want to talk! I love you, I believe you, I trust you," but some warning voice inside her head stopped her from it. She moved away to hide a sudden shimmer of tears and began arranging things back on the coffee tray.

"What happened between you and Vern?" he asked darkly, coming to stand behind her and grip her shoulders.

She turned her head to drop a kiss on his hand. "It's tempting to let Vern take all the blame, but if there's fault to be found in the way Helen died, then it's mine."

"You were honest," he said with force.

"Was I?" Her voice was toneless as she stepped away

from him to rinse out the cups at the bar and replacé the creamer lid. "Maybe what you said about me was true about losing the money and the power and the prestige—"

"I may have said those things to hurt you, but I never really believed them," he interrupted. "You were honor-bound to protect Mother's interests, and you did it with love."

"And look what that love did! She's gone, and it's too late to make things right." She turned to the window, hugging herself, struggling to blink back hot tears. "I guess good intentions aren't enough."

The silence was so protracted it approached pain. When she finally glanced back at him, what she saw frightened her. More than just his composure had been disturbed by her words; he looked thunderstruck.

"What is it?" she whispered.

Something was mattering to him very much, but his words jolted her from introspection. "Good intentions aren't enough," he repeated. He sat a moment more, as if listening to some hidden chord that had been struck in him. "We've all been guilty of good intentions. Vern, telling Helen 'for her own good.' You, fighting me tooth and nail to protect Helen. Mother, playing hardball to patch our marriage together. And then there's me, Mr. Fix-it Man, just chock-full of good intentions. My God, oh my God."

"I don't understand—"

Then shaking himself as if from a dream, he straightened with abruptness from his half-sitting position against the desk, brushed past her, and took the stairs two at a time.

Moments later, she surprised him in his bedroom. He had pulled down a soft leather weekend bag from the closet, and was stuffing socks and shirts and underwear into it. She stood in the doorway, the light behind her outlining the curves of her body, but there was no ac-knowledgement of her presence as he strode past her into the bathroom for his toothbrush and razor.

Keely watched in mounting alarm. "What are you doing? Where are you going?" Her heart contracted and a thousand incoherent thoughts shot through her mind, and she could not capture a single one. All she could do was watch with an incredulous sense of impending loss as he moved like chained lightning from closet to armoire to bed. When he straightened up from his packing, his eyes glistened oddly.

"Thomas Wolfe still says it best—you can't go home again. I was a fool to try." He quickly strapped the case and buckled it closed.

She moved to the bed and blocked him with her body, and then she was saying things, things that made no sense, disjointed thoughts and words tumbling from her lips in a torrent, falling on unhearing stone. "Don't do this. I know I've put you through hell with my doubts all these months. Won't you let me make it up to you now? We could be happy if you'll only forgive me . . . oh, darling, I—"

"Don't," he interrupted sharply. "Don't say any more."

Once he would have rejoiced at her capitulation. How could he pretend he didn't want her, when just a moment ago he was kissing her like a starving man! If he wanted to hear her beg for making him suffer, he was entitled to his pound of flesh.

She drew a quick breath at the hot, swift current running through her now. "I've fallen in love with you! Doesn't that mean anything? Isn't it what you told me you came back for? I'm yours if you want me, just don't leave me now—"

"Keely, Christ," he groaned. "Not now, don't say these things to me now—I can't bear it . . ."

She was perilously close to a wild outburst of tears. "Why? But why? Talk to me, please—" She was thinking frantically: I was only half alive until he came here, and now I'm losing him. And if I lose him, nothing else matters! Not the money or the publishing empire or a career. Nothing. How can I survive Helen's loss without him? Something was wrong, badly wrong, something far beyond his grief at Helen's death, more than Keely's antagonistic hostility.

She lifted her chin and her voice trembled. "You've humbled my pride by making me beg, but I won't risk your contempt by groveling."

He stopped packing and his cerulean eyes were grudging in their respect, which turned her even colder with dread. But whatever it was that was making him leave, she was determined to know the reason, and she bored in with her advantage. "I can see your mind is made up, but at least have the guts to tell me why. I think you owe me that much."

He drew a short despairing breath, turned around, clenched his fists first in his pockets and then stretched one arm up the wall where he rested his head against it. He turned his face away, but not before Keely saw along with the anguish another expression that baffled her—self-hatred.

"Keely, what I owe you could never be paid," he said at last. "And you do deserve an explanation, although nothing could excuse what I've done to you." He ran a hand over his hair and rubbed the back of his neck. He sat down on the edge of the bed, then got up and went to the window. He returned to the bureau and picked up a framed miniature portrait of Helen and studied it, his eyes brilliant with unshed tears while Keely waited in bewilderment. "There's just no easy way to say it." Finally he turned the picture face down on the dresser and when he spoke at last, it was as if the words were torn from him. "Keely—I'm not Bryan Easton."

SIXTEEN

Her first reaction was numbed suspension of belief. Then devastating disappointment. Then incredulous anger at a criminal duplicity that had finally pulled it off. And now, when she had just made the cataclysmic turnabout in her own mind—this! But hadn't she always known the truth? Had she really thought her love for him would miraculously change the fact that he had been lying, lying, lying?

"Keely?" His voice was husky with concern as he waited for her anger to subside.

She jerked away. "Damn you! Why did you have to tell me this now?"

He arched his head back and pressed his temples to ease their throbbing. "Please listen to me, Keely," he said wearily. "Even if good intentions aren't a legitimate defense, there is an explanation." He leaned forward and rested his elbows on his knees, fingers laced, so deep in thought that for a moment she wondered if he had heard her at all.

Finally she broke the silence. "I'm waiting."

When he spoke, he threw his head back to implore of the ceiling, "God, why is this so difficult to explain?" Sighing impatiently, he plunged in. "Have you ever heard the old catch-22 theory that no sound exists in the forest without a human ear to hear it? Well, when I was a child in the center of my universe, I secretly believed nothing had reality, importance, or meaning unless I experienced it. Other people were only props on my stage and existed only for my own consciousness. I guess I never outgrew that juvenile fantasy.''

"Is that your explanation for all this—?" Keely began, her eyes stormy and uncompromising.

"Let me have my catharsis, Keely," he interrupted. "I need to work it through. If nothing else, this fiasco has taught me what an egocentric bastard I am." His deprecating laugh was at once rueful and self-mocking. "In that prison camp, isolated from reality for so long, I called on all those old childish coping mechanisms to keep my sanity."

The dark-gold flash of Keely's eyes was the only hint of conflicting emotions roiling beneath the surface. "I grant that you suffered," she countered. "But right now I need to know who you are."

His eyes flicked over her without expression. "Keely, if I gave you a name you still wouldn't know who I am. For now it's enough to know that I'm a rootless misfit."

"But you could be an ax-murderer running from the law, a drug dealer from Colombia, an alimony dodger. Who have I been living with these past months?"

He laughed, the sound more bitter than amused. "None of the above. I never claimed to be a choirboy—or a Rambo, either. Before my luck ran out in Central America, I was training chopper pilots, running ordnance into Nicaragua, evacuating villagers." His voice became as staccato as the machine-gun fire that had brought the helicopter to a crash landing in the trees. "I remember the ground fire and the chopper tilting forward before it plunged into the trees. I don't remember being rescued from the wreckage. I woke up a prisoner."

Keely was suddenly very still as his ordeal came to life in frightening clarity. A dark fire glimmered in his eyes as he saw her forcing herself to stare blankly in front of her, trying not to shiver. "Are you very, very sure you want to hear this story, Keely? It isn't very pretty."

Nervously, she licked her lips. "I can handle it."

There was an odd ripple in his voice as he continued the story dispassionately. "When they were through 'interrogating' me, I was thrown into an abandoned latrine pit camouflaged with heavy boards. Whenever they remembered me, food was thrown down like garbage on my head. Other than that I was left alone—days, maybe weeks. Down there in semidarkness, without any contact with the outside world, I was literally in danger of losing my mind. I was scared and suicidal, or in a tearing rage against fate that bordered on madness. But when one day my captors came back, I almost welcomed them, hoping they'd finish me off. Instead, they threw another prisoner down into the hole."

"Bryan." Her breath sucked in, and her gaze fell to his hands, dark and veined, rubbing the tips together, the tips that had been burned until the prints had melted away. Until now she had scarcely allowed herself to think about the inhuman pain and deprivation that this man—and her husband—had endured together.

The words were now painted in swift, angry brush strokes. "He was more dead than alive, but his greater need gave me something to take my mind off my own plight. I set his broken leg with a root and tied it with strips torn from his shirt. It was in one of his pockets that I found the photograph that had somehow escaped our captors."

"The wedding picture," Keely breathed, caught up in the story now.

He rose suddenly and going to the window, he drew the curtains and looked out intently as if he were seeing another world beyond the darkened glass. "Most of the time he raved with fever, and during his worst times, I kept the photo safe. The bride was a little darkhaired thing clinging to his arm and looking up at him adoringly. For some reason, the intimacy of it, her whole shining attitude just—tore me up. She was such a victim too, yet untouched by this dirty war. I could almost taste what it would be like to have a woman like that waiting for me, how she would welcome me to her arms, how she would love me on clean sheets perfumed by the fresh air of freedom. But this time my fantasy was another man's reality.''

At last he turned to her and Keely was stunned with the force of his emotion. ''He was wracked with malaria. In delirium, he'd thrash around and scream until I was frantic they'd kill us to shut him up. Every time they'd come with food I'd beg for quinine until they threw an assortment of stale drugs into the pit. He began to come around. They were feeding us better, too, probably to get us in shape for trading. As the weeks dragged by, we became friends of sorts with nothing to do but talk to each other.'' He glanced up swiftly. ''Escape was out of the question— even if we'd had the stamina we were too well guarded. So we talked. Sports, music, books. Then politics, religion, and all the places we'd been. Our families, friends, favorite dogs. Finally, all that was left were our most intimate experiences.''

''So, that's how you were able to impersonate Bryan enough to fool even his own mother—you literally picked his brains,'' Keely accused. ''I just can't understand how Bryan could discuss our most intimate moments with a stranger—''

He glanced up swiftly, the blue-black depths of his eyes an enigma. ''Then don't judge what you can't understand,'' he warned in a rough, unequivocal tone. ''It may seem an incredible invasion of privacy to you, the secrets we told each other in the dark of that pit, and yes, we discussed things a man could never tell even his wife or closest friend, but at the time we were dead men.''

''All the same, you had a good time drooling over the lurid details,'' she said bitterly, remembering his intimate knowledge of her body.

"It wasn't like that, Keely," he interrupted wearily. "You were more than just a flesh-and-blood woman—you were a symbol. Can't you—won't you—understand? You were my hope for the future and Bryan's regret for the past."

"Yes, I can see that the Eastons were indeed your hope for the future," she said caustically. "But I'll never believe that Bryan regretted the past."

"That's a hell of a presumption on your part," he responded angrily. "I dare you to look me in the eye and accuse me of conspiring to have my face beaten in so I could impersonate Bryan Easton."

Keely tried to look at him, but her eyes betrayed her. "That was a cheap shot, and I'm sorry. It's just that—this whole thing is so very difficult—"

"I know." His look was quick, somber, almost tender. "And you're wrong about Bryan—you were the cipher in his life, his torment. He was conscience stricken about the past and vowed that if he had another chance he would come back and make things right again."

"So when he couldn't, you did."

"With all good intentions. It was never a conscious plan. But you should know that whether it was love or hate, he was so obsessed with you and eaten up with guilt that I couldn't have stopped him from telling me everything, even if I'd wanted to."

Her fingers moved convulsively, but she could not bring herself to look at him. "What did he say about me?"

"Wonderful things. How a beautiful sky or a field of wildflowers or a violin concerto could move you to tears. Your passion for chocolate, how you loved the smell of fresh-cut grass, leaves burning, the sea. The name of your favorite perfume, the schools you went to, and the color of your eyes when he made love to you . . ."

Involuntarily her eyes flew up to his, then dropped in confusion somewhere in the vicinity of the deep cleft in his chin. In the periphery of her vision, she saw his mouth curve in a tight, compressed smile. "God help me—a doomed man wildly in love with another man's wife—a real Oscar Wilde farce. Where was the harm? It was a love that demanded nothing of anyone, least of all expression. In the privacy of my own mind, I was free to touch you, love you. My love was as pure as the sun caressing your skin as you lay on the beach at Cape Cod, or the waves licking the salt from your breasts, or the wind ruffling the fragrance of your hair. I was in hell, but in heaven, too.''

From beneath her lashes she risked a glance up at him, afraid to let him see how his admission had affected her. "But—what about your own past?" she asked. "There must have been someone."

He shook his head as if reluctant to relinquish the memory even now. "My own life was empty, peopled with images too vague to care about any more. I shed it eagerly like a skin for Bryan's life, Bryan's wife. The only way I could experience you totally was through his memories, and I pumped him shamelessly about every intimate detail until I felt I knew you better than he ever could.''

Keely felt the color flooding up from her throat in a hot tide. She felt stripped naked to the eyes of a voyeur. "Can't you see that's sick?" she finally managed in a strangled voice.

"I was sick, I admit it," For all the self-contempt in his voice, Keely sensed the underlying need, and it intrigued her. "I was obsessed with pain and longing, and like an addict, soon a cerebral love affair was not enough. I craved the reality of the body to make it complete."

Keely's gaze iced over. "So much for pure motives."

"Maybe I deserve that from you, but I loved Helen like a son. I wanted to make her last years happy."

Her taunt had cut him, but she refused to apologize. "Tell me the rest," she prompted.

When he recovered himself, his voice was devoid of all emotion. "One afternoon there was an air raid from the border. Our captors were in such a tearing hurry to get out they couldn't take us with them. The last thing I remember was the muzzle of a gun, the spurt of blue fire. Thank God

I was unconscious when they beat my face beyond recognition." He rose quickly and began to pace, a wounded male animal whose restless vitality quickened her blood even in its extremity.

He went on with quiet intensity. "When I woke in the hospital with my face swathed in bandages, tubes and monitors were sticking out all over me, I felt disembodied. There was an absence inside me, a bottomlessness, a feeling of something unfinished. For a while I wondered if I had been crazy and was now sane, or had been sane and was now crazy. I couldn't remember anything until they showed me the picture and then it all came flooding back— all the familiar memories, and I latched onto them like a drowning man. After tests, the neurologists ruled out brain damage, and the amnesia was considered transitory because I was able to recognize the picture and had perfect recall. Only it wasn't my life I remembered—it was Bryan's."

Keely drew a deep, shuddering breath as if she knew what was coming next. "Are you saying that your existence got traumatically deleted from your brain and you were miraculously absorbed into Bryan's?"

His voice was curiously taut, as if he'd opened himself to ridicule. "Have I finally stretched your patience too far, Keely?"

Tears sprang to her eyes. "No," she whispered. "And that's what frightens me."

"I can understand that total amnesia can happen as a form of self-preservation, a kind of protective brainwashing. I also know enough about psychology to recognize both denial and the loss of control over one's own destiny. But a total switch in personality—" He shook his head dazedly. "It's too unreal."

"Maybe not. The concussion you suffered during that last savage beating could have split your own personality away and crystallized it into an illusion—delusion—that Bryan and you were one and the same person."

His somber gaze went past her and his moody eyes

stirred her so much that she believed his sincerity implicitly. "It's hard to accept that my mind could slip to that degree, but I have to admit it would explain how I lost track of where one of us stopped and the other began."

Keely took a deep breath to steady her voice, and when she spoke again her voice was low and surprisingly soft. "What happened to Bryan?"

His eyelids went down, leaving his face a dark blank. "Dead, I assume. I never saw him again."

Keely looked away, less disturbed at her lack of grief for her departed husband than her inability to pretend something she didn't feel. "Now that we know who you aren't—" she turned to face him, her expression perplexed. "Who are you? I have to know."

He arched his head back and a gust of humorless laughter escaped him. "You want to know what's truly funny, Keely? I still don't remember."

She drew in her breath. "Then how—?"

"How do I know I'm not Bryan?" He shrugged and spread his hands. "I don't, not really. I still haven't any recall of my own—I'm still thinking from Bryan's perspective, using Bryan's store of memories. But you, Keely— you knew from the beginning, even if I didn't, and isn't that the bottom line?"

"But I knew it on an intuitive level," she argued. "Are you telling me this entire story is just speculation and you don't know yourself if it's true?"

"You wanted an explanation and I gave you one."

"But we're right back where we started unless you remember Bryan and yourself as separate persons."

"Of course, he was a separate person—how else would I know what I know?" he countered. "Maybe going back to Honduras will jog my memory."

A shock coursed through Keely. "No! You don't have to go back. You can see a doctor here—a psychiatrist, hypnotist, private detective, anybody who can help you recover your past . . ."

"Keely, even if we knew, what then? How can I stay

after everything I've told you, after all I've done to you and Helen?'' His breath came out in a hiss of self-loathing. ''How could it never cross my mind that the stress of my return—Bryan's return—might kill her, or that it would screw up your inheritance? Maybe I got hit on the head harder than I thought!''

Beneath the self-contempt in his words she could feel the violence against himself that made her more afraid than if it were directed at her. In railing at his perceived dishonesty in posing as Bryan, she had been confused by the contradiction of his innate morality, the tenderness and humanity in him that had been at odds with what she knew of Bryan. Those very qualities that made her doubt his identity were the very ones that made her fall in love with him. He had brought new happiness to Helen, mended unhappy relationships, and turned Keely from an inevitable fate as a man-hater.

''So what now, my love?'' he said bitterly. ''Helen is gone, and I can never bring her back. As you put it, good intentions aren't enough. All I can do is restore her estate to you by defaulting on the terms of her will. And I can get the hell out before I cause any more damage to the people I . . . care about.'' He had to force himself to avoid the word love.

Panic caught in her throat. ''There must be another way!''

''Then let's discuss the alternatives rationally. Public confession? While it might salve my conscience and give Preston great satisfaction to prosecute me, the publicity would damage everyone. Besides, I've had a bellyful of prison and I utterly reject any risk of it.''

''But you're a victim, too, and under the circumstances no doctor or jury would believe that what you did was with criminal intent!''

''Thank you for that. Divorce? Unfortunately, divorce is a legal acknowledgement that I am Bryan Easton.'' He paused while searching her face earnestly. ''Keely, let's face it. The only way out is for me to take a repeat walk into the twilight zone."

"And leave me in legal limbo another seven years?" she demanded, fierce and quick.

A wintry smile touched his lips. "Not this time." He pulled out a beautifully tooled, monogrammed kangaroo-leather wallet. "Short of producing my body, which I am not yet ready to relinquish, my wallet found in a combat zone on the Nicaraguan border will be convincing evidence that I died. I'll leave the announcement details to you."

"Wait! There's another alternative."

He raised a sardonic eyebrow.

"You can stay here."

"As what?"

"I don't care—husband, lover, friend . . ."

He shook his head. "Without an identity? We can't live like that."

"But how can I explain a second disappearance? People will think I'm a dreadful woman—"

He laughed gently at her feminine vanity. "There's just no 'honorable' explanation, Keely. Tell them the truth—I'm an impostor, and you knew it all along." He paused, his brow furrowed and a puzzled smile on his lips. "Why? When everything I said was letter perfect, when my total immersion in Bryan's persona fooled everybody else . . . how did you know?"

Now it was her turn for confession. But could she tell him the secret that had lain hidden in her heart like a festering wound for the past seven years? Keely withdrew from him to sit in the bay window overlooking the garden, knees drawn up under her chin and encircled with her arms. Her gaze was fixed on the opaque glass, but she was seeing something beyond the cold rain drizzling against the panes.

"Tell me."

"It really doesn't matter any more." She kept her gaze

averted from that penetrating gaze that made her feel curiously naked and vulnerable.

"You're lying," he accused quietly, waiting. "It still matters very, very much."

Keely ran nervous fingers over her temples. "He's gone. Can't we leave it at that?"

His voice cut into her like a cold, steel blade, his persistence stronger than her silence. "I opened myself to you, Keely, and for my own peace of mind, I need the last piece of the puzzle. It isn't just because he deserted you. There's something else."

"Bryan didn't tell you everything." She glanced away to hide the sudden shimmer of tears, determined to remain as dispassionate in the telling as he had been. "In pouring his heart out to you, he must have left out the fact that he—forced me the first time we were together. I wanted to believe that terrible first time had been an impetuous mistake, and I was determined to put it behind us. But after we were married, I was never able to respond . . . sexually to him." She swallowed and plunged on, aware of his sudden tensing, finding it incredibly difficult to verbalize the shame and pain she had never overcome after all those years. "Frustration eventually turned him into a brutal, selfish lover. He hated 'perfunctory sex,' but he hated it even more when I tried to pretend feelings I didn't have. It somehow struck at his very perception of himself as a man, and every encounter between us turned into—rape, for lack of a better word. The more he tried to force a response from me, the more I withdrew emotionally, until I became almost pathologically afraid of any intimacy." She was crying softly now. "Our troubles were probably all tangled up with his anger with his father and his personal insecurity, but I was too young and naive to help him deal with it. Because I hurt and humiliated him, he hurt and humiliated me."

Unwanted, unbidden, the memories came flooding back— Bryan's hostility, Bryan's crudity in the bedroom. When

Keely submitted to him that last night, unable to even feign passion, he had flown into a fury and called her frigid and a prude.

"If I am, it's what you've made me," Keely had trembled. "All I get from you is three minutes of pain when you're in the mood. You don't care about my feelings."

"And you obviously don't give a damn about mine. But after tonight you'll never treat me with indifference again," he had raged. She had thought he was going to hit her, but instead he had pushed her down on the bed and there followed the worst nightmare of humiliation she had thus far endured. Afterward he was contrite, but she would not be appeased. Finally, apologies rejected, he got up and slammed out of the apartment.

"He never came back," Keely whispered. "I cried all night from fear he would come back, and after the news came of his death, I cried from relief. Neither of us had known I was pregnant at the time, and when I miscarried a few days later, I knew that Bryan's last attack had killed our baby. I'll never, never forgive him for that."

Stunned, his breath escaped him in a soft hiss of comprehension. "Keely. Oh, my love—"

"You asked me once if I wanted that baby," she cried brokenly. "I never had a chance to find out. Bryan snatched it away from me before I even knew it existed. It was as if he had reached out to torment me even from the grave."

"My God," he whispered, his face drained of all color.

"When you kissed me in Mexico City I was fairly certain you weren't Bryan. And when you finally made love to me, so sensual, yet tender and caring, so different in every way—" Tears scalded the back of her throat. "I knew beyond all doubt when I responded with the first real emotion I've experienced with any man."

"So that's what you meant when you kept saying I was nothing like him." He sounded almost aggrieved. "No wonder I couldn't get past all the barriers you'd thrown up between us. Keely, I've been such a damned fool."

"Stay with me," she begged.

He wouldn't look at her as he shook his head firmly. "How very tempting you are, Keely. But no."

"If we were married . . ."

He had to quell the temptation to give in and let her take care of the fallout. "Keely, we've been over this already." He was maddeningly reasonable. "It's one thing to truly believe I was Bryan, but it's quite another to pretend to be. There's no way out of this dilemma but for me to walk away."

"But where will you go? What will you do?"

"I told you—back to Honduras."

She wrung her hands in frustration. "I can't—I won't let you go! Not yet—not now, until I get this all sorted out in my mind. You could stay if you really wanted to! There's nothing keeping you from it except—except—"

"Honor?" he asked quietly. "Keely, don't ask me to continue the lie—I'd never have your respect, let alone my own. And how could we even be happy together knowing that if I hadn't played God, Helen might still be alive?"

Powerlessness, pride, and anger warred within her. "You're still playing God! How can you enter my life at will, turn it upside down, then bail out when the going gets tough? Maybe you're not so different from Bryan after all!"

He blanched, and she knew she had hurt him. "Don't make this any harder than it already is, Keely. I'm going because that's how it has to be." He turned his back on her, signaling an end to the conversation.

Keely held her peace, returning to her old room to regroup. She knew that the true battle would have to take place in an entirely different arena. She dressed for bed, too mentally distraught to even cry. Since her early marriage to Bryan had failed, Keely had learned to live her own life rather than living vicariously through a man, and until now her existence had been far from arid—for the most part it had been satisfying enough. Now to find her thoughts and feelings so possessed by another person, defined by his mere presence in the room, frightened her. Then why couldn't she let him walk away?

Without putting on a robe or finding her slippers, Keely rose with a new sense of purpose. She stood in the darkness of the corridor separating their rooms, gathering the courage to turn the knob of his door. It opened, almost of its own volition.

He was writing something, a letter, a large book propped on his knees, a bath towel thrown carelessly across the lower half of his body. She knew he was still nude from the shower. A faint tingle of fear, intermixed with expectation, touched her as Keely stepped from the shadows into the deep glow of his lamplit room. She stood for a moment without speaking until he glanced up at her, not at all surprised, almost resigned, as if he had been expecting her. Then he slowly folded the letter and placed it on the low table. She didn't try to hide her trembling from him, but crossed slowly into the pool of light and stood beside the bed.

She wanted to call him by name, but he had no name, and "Bryan" had always stuck in her throat. He must know that by whatever name he chose to be called, she wanted him to stay, to be her husband, her lover, her man.

Compulsively she reached out and lightly touched his flat, hard stomach. His muscles recoiled beneath her hand, and jackknifing from the bed in one movement, he walked away from her to the window. As he raked his hands through his hair, the interplay of muscles on the perfect symmetry of his bare back reminded her of the supple, silky flanks of a quarter horse.

Oh, God, I want this man, she cried out inside. *Give me this man.* "I came to say goodbye," she said in a soft rush.

"Goodbye, then."

"Make love to me before you go."

"I can't."

Her pride already in tatters, she moved behind him to

lay her smooth cheek against his back, her hands sliding around his torso to hold him, and his skin quivered. He took her hands away and bruised the fingers in his grip. "Don't do this, Keely. Let's say goodbye to each other with dignity."

Her heart leaped in sudden hope. Why, he was afraid of her! Afraid that if he gave into this last intimacy he would be unable to leave her! A new strength and purpose rose in her. He had given her sexual power in that tacit admission, and like Delilah, she would use it against him.

She hesitated only an instant, then threw caution to the winds. In one swift, graceful movement, she opened her negligee and dropped it to the floor in purposeful abandon, her golden eyes holding his, wide and luminous as the moon.

He would have been all right if in that one split second he hadn't looked. Quickly he averted his eyes, but it was too late. The glance was fatal, and they both knew it as desire battled with reason, as need warred with caution. He had seen her body, all amber and coral and wild honey, warm, exciting, alive. He could not hide his catch of breath when she lifted his hand and placed it on her breast, and when he felt the wild thudding of her heart under that perfect pink-tipped mound, all was lost.

Somehow he was on the bed, pulling her down on top of him, kissing her throat and breasts and lips with all the pent-up fury of a man provoked beyond human endurance, a man on the verge of losing everything of value in his life. There were no preliminaries. His hands slid down her naked back with provocative strength to pull her hips astride his, where his powerful thighs chafed maddeningly between hers and the tumescent surge of his vital force took swift possession, driving the breath from her. Closer, cradling, cup and pull, rocking and twisting, pausing in sweet fusion on the brink of thrilling fire, with murmured love words and gasping cries, they stroked and pleased each other, hands rhythmic, breaths mingling, mouths tasting their very essences, until the woodsy fragrance of his male-muscled body sent the voluptuous flame rippling like quickfire through every nerve to the core of her being. The center disintegrated within her, all consuming, searing her with almost unbearable pleasure. The rich, deepening beat of her blood rose in tempo to the surging crescendo of his rhythmic counterpoint. She cried out as the slow, delicious friction of heated hips carried them to an erotic explosion so intense that her body twisted and together they flew to the edge of the universe.

"Stay with me," she choked the command.

"Keely, oh Keely," he groaned. "What have you done to me!"

Locked together in wave after wave of residual clasp-ings, their passion faded gracefully into a drift of elusive sadness.

How can he leave me now? she thought triumphantly, nestling in sated contentment against his chest, her lips against his moist throat. He had become hers, truly bound by sexual and emotional ties too strong to break. She knew it with a cat-and-cream confidence; and as she sank into sleep, the knowledge gave her peace.

A sensation of chill awakened Keely the next morning. She turned to nestle against a warmth that wasn't there. She bolted upright, sudden panic taking hold of her where inner radiance had glowed all night. He was gone.

Her gown, so hastily discarded in last night's hectic passion, was neatly draped across the foot of the bed. She threw off the satin coverlet and donned it hastily.

The dressing room and adjoining bath were neat, empty. The bureau top was cleared; his cufflinks and diamond jewelry lay in the rosewood box. All his clothes still hung in the closet, his shoes neatly paired in a row. The Burberry trench coat hung there in silent reproach.

The only thing missing was his leather duffel bag which he had packed earlier. He intended to leave this house the same way he had come, with only the clothes on his back.

Now she saw propped against the pillow a plain white envelope with her name scrawled on it. Inside was the letter he must have been writing last night.

Frantic now, she ripped it open. His neat handwriting, so similar to Bryan's it had divided the experts, now set the stage for his second disappearance.

"Darling: (she read) Please pick up my gray suit from the tailor's Wednesday. I should be able to wind up my business in Honduras soon—two weeks, a month—at most. I'll phone every chance I get. Take care of Ace for me and remember that you're ever in my dreams. Bryan."

In that prosaic note, he had given her a month's grace before the baying of the press was loosed on a juicy second disappearance, an event that would dwarf even the first those seven years ago. In a sudden excess of grief, with the door locked and the world shut out, Keely flung herself on the bed in helpless abandonment to tears.

After what seemed like hours, she lay back exhausted, eyes dully fixed on the ceiling. All feeling was suspended. She was battered, numb. But soon numbness gave way to pain. She got up and went into the bathroom. She ran a sink of cold water and laved it over her face, dried on a hand towel. In the mirror, she inspected her eyes. They're not even red, she thought. Just dead.

The bedroom phone rang. Hope surged and she snatched it up. It was Frank Cabell. She listened with total lack of comprehension, then during a pause she told him to make the decision himself, she wouldn't be in today and, without waiting for a reply, she hung up.

Under the telephone she noticed the corner of a white business card. She fished it out and looked at it. It said, "Ricardo Castillo. London. Mexico City. New York."

In a sudden fever she picked up the telephone again and dialed.

SEVENTEEN

The flamingos rose in an aerial ballet from the marshy swale where the sea had been trapped in a shallow inland lagoon on the sweltering, shark and mosquito infested coast of Honduras. Abandoning the brackish water to the braver ducks, the neon-pink cloud of birds exited by the hundreds, shattering the mirror-like surface in a colorful burst of spray.

The pilot anchored the little pontoon-footed plane near the shoreline where it could disgorge its supplies and passengers to a rubber raft. In addition to Keely and Castillo, among the plane's occupants were two Pipil *indio* guides and three Miskito porters.

The day was drawing to a close, and with great difficulty Ric persuaded Keely to make camp there by the lagoon and wait until tomorrow before attempting to reach the mission enclave where U.S. troops were on maneuvers.

After a canned dinner, Keely withdrew from the mosquito fire. At twenty-nine, she was an extraordinarily beautiful woman, with all the lovely audacity of youth, yet a serenity and aloofness that intrigued his warmer Latin temperament. He had mixed feelings about the way she had taken charge of this expedition—admiration for her decisive, indomitable spirit, irritation at the way she had brought him to heel with fear for her safety in this foolhardy adventure. He had briefly entertained the thought of taking her hostage in Jucuapa and physically preventing her from embarking, but it would have been a Pyrrhic victory and he knew it. You didn't handle a headstrong, independent woman like Keely the way you would a girl brought up to be submissive to a man's wishes.

He watched her now, the fire flickering on her skin, casting tawny shadows on her creamy, November complexion. She reminded him of an American girl he had loved many years ago—not so much in looks, but in manner. It was inborn in American women, he supposed—that freedom of spirit which challenged the dominance of more traditional males. He had never been attracted to passive women.

Keely seemed unaware of her unique beauty, and even unembellished it was an adornment here in these primitive surroundings. Without makeup, her face had an almost exotic quality, a deceptive fragility. Thinking what it must be like to be loved by such a woman sent an unexpected and unwanted rush of blood to his groin. He rose swiftly to break it. It wasn't him she wanted.

Keely left the camp reluctantly to retire to her tent. Ever since they had arrived, she had felt a growing sense of Bryan's presence within her, growing even stronger as the night progressed. She halfway expected him and his commandos to stride into the circle of tents, but of course he would not. She could hardly wait until morning when she and Ric and the *indios* would backpack to the spot where they had sighted the mission from the air.

Outside the circle of tents, the forest was alive with night sounds. A cat screamed in the distance as Keely removed her blouse to allow what little air there was to circulate around her body.

Lost in thought as she applied insect repellent to her skin, she at first didn't hear Ric silently lift the mosquito flap, or see the disturbed intensity of his expression as he watched her smooth the liquid over her shoulders, her head thrown back to anoint her throat, feathering the emollient over her breasts. Finally, she sensed his presence and looked around, startled to see him there but with enough poise to calmly reach for her shirt.

"Is everything all right?" She buttoned only the middle button as he entered like a shadow. She saw that he was bare chested, too, under a loose white cotton shirt, and the gleam of perspiration in the hot humid night gave his smooth skin an oiled appearance; he was very brown. A gold crucifix adorned his neck and a large pistol was strapped at his waist.

Her firelit gaze swept over him, and her voice was cool. "What is it?"

He spoke. "Did you hear the puma?"

"Yes."

"I came because I thought you might be afraid." He smiled. "Another woman, perhaps. Not you."

"I've never been afraid of four-legged creatures."

His eyes glinted. "Just two-legged ones?"

"Maybe once, but no more." Her words implied far more than they actually said. "You were right to leave me that night in Mexico City, Ric. You said I'd be grateful for it, and I am."

A slow flush crept up past the rigid plane of his jaw as he realized that she knew what he had come in here hoping for, like a moth to her flame. Before he could utter a face-saving word, an explosion sounded in the distance.

Ric pushed past her so abruptly she almost fell backward as a pepper of gunfire and fullbodied explosions ripped open the night. She followed his rush out of the tent where he began kicking and shoveling dirt on the dying embers of the fire. The frightened *indios* were rushing about babbling and pointing.

Keely looked inland against the black monolith of the cordilleras. Far up the mountainside orange fire and white smoke boiled up against the inky western sky. The whine and drone of the planes emerged from the sporadic explosions and the ak-ak of antiaircraft ground fire carried on the warm night air.

"Run, Keely!" Ric shouted. "They're going to strafe us!"

She ran.

The planes were overhead and the chatter of automatic guns spat bullets in straight lines of fire through the camp, ripping through the tents. In the dark, she stumbled and tripped over insidious vines, trying to dodge the peculiar dull whuff of bullets as they missed her by inches in the marshy undergrowth. There was no thought of snakes or alligators in her wild flight to safety.

She huddled, trembling from head to toe, waist deep in water and sucking mud. The planes made two strafing runs, then disappeared to hammer the mountainside outpost again. All she could think of with sickening clarity was that Bryan was up there on the escarpment and might truly not survive this surprise raid.

When Ric found her and led her back to the bullet-ridden tent, she was a miserable sight. She had stepped into a hidden ravine and tumbled down several feet before catching on a tree root. Her lip was bleeding, beginning to swell, her hair and body were caked with mud. Ric was very gentle with her and she allowed him to carry her to the lagoon, entering it with her clothes and all. He bathed her and cleaned her scratches with antiseptic soap, talking to her in a soothing voice about inconsequential things to calm her. She was shivering, but it was not from cold. He washed her mud-filled hair and dried her with his shirt and helped her put on some clean, dry clothes.

All was quiet now and the great marsh slowly resumed its nighttime chirr and rattle, and the bass roar of the alligators could be heard in protest. On the mountain, orange fires and pale smoke raged. Keely began to weep, deep sobbing cries for Bryan that alarmed Ric. Unafraid of the jungle and its animals, she was only afraid for the man she loved. Ric pulled her close and held her, comforting her. He stroked her hair until she had no tears left and fell asleep in his arms. He leaned his head against a tree but his mind could not let go. She slept fitfully. More than once he woke her from a nightmare and cradled her head on his shoulder. He slept little, troubled. Bryan's chances looked very grim, but he didn't need to tell her that.

In the morning, he was relieved that she seemed more herself . . . pale, but composed and full of purpose. Their situation was not good. During the night the terrified indios had deserted them. They were stranded on the beach miles from Jucuapa with a ruined two-way radio, no guides or porters and, after last night's raid, no point of destination.

They pored over the map together. "We'll go on to the mission," Keely decided.

He straightened up, annoyed at her imperious assumption after last night's lapse into feminine passivity. "We'll walk up the beach to the nearest village," he contradicted. "We can get word to Lozano to send the seaplane for us."

The implacable gold of Keely's eyes flashed a warning. "Bryan may be up there on that mountain, and that's where I'm going." There was a silken whip in her voice.

"Keely, if they evacuated, the place could be crawling with enemy soldiers. Bryan could have been killed in the attack or gone with the survivors. My concern now is your safety. I can make inquiries—the commandos will regroup nearby, and if he's dead or alive we'll find him."

"But he may still be at the mission," she said firmly.

His voice was infinitely patient. "Without guides, it will take two days to reach that mission. It may look like it's just over the rise and up the hill, but that's rugged, jungle terrain up there with deep valleys and rivers in between and impenetrable undergrowth. We could be captured. Then what good could we do Bryan?"

There was a dogged, single-minded determination in her that alarmed him. "This is the Honduran side of the border. Honduran and American troops will return," she said stubbornly. "There will be transportation, radios. If we take the beach route our supplies will run out too soon, we have no boat, and we'll be fighting mosquitoes, alligators, and sharks.''

There was a curious bleakness in her gaze that he'd never seen before. "If he's dead, I have to see the body, Ric. Otherwise I'll never know if he's truly dead or merely used the mission attack to drop out of sight.''

For another hour as they packed their gear, the argument raged back and forth, ending in Ric's angry ultimatum and Keely's grim announcement that with or without him, she was going.

In the end, Ric was once again forced to give in to her implacable will. They decided to cut around to the Patuca River and follow it northwest in the general direction of the mission. Following the river gorge would add but two miles to their journey, but it would be easier than trying to cut straight up the face of the mountains through rugged terrain. Keely gazed in awe at the purple shadowed pyramids rising before them, choked in rampant greenery and infested with strange bugs, animals, and birds.

It took them all day to reach the Patuca where it made its descent into the coastal lagoons. They were overloaded with as much food as they could cram into their backpacks, along with ammunition, axes, and machetes. The first night out they were able to string their hammocks.

Keely lay awake for a long while, looking up into the night sky and watching the stars prick the vibrant tropical blackness. Bats swirled out of hiding, swooping erratically for the airborne feast of mosquitoes. The swampy lowlands breathed about her, and she could almost hear the night creeping out from its dark recesses to spread across the river. Tonight everything seemed out of reach; the birds, the animals, the stars: Bryan. She abruptly turned her head to stop the thought.

Before closing her eyes she looked over at Ric in his nearby hammock. He was lying on his back, his arms cradling his head. She knew he was awake and counting the stars, too. In the exhaustion over the day, they had withdrawn into themselves, scarcely speaking, until Keely felt an almost schizophrenic isolation in the midst of the teeming wilderness. She adjusted the waterproof sheet at the foot of the hammock where she could pull it over her head if rain came, lowered the mosquito netting over her upper torso and closed her eyes.

An apologetic sun put on a spectacular sunrise the next morning. After they rose stiffly and improvised a cold breakfast, in Ric's disapproving silence they once more shouldered their backpacks. Being practical, Keely accepted the lightest one without protest. Ric swung the rifle strap over his shoulder and they sat out toward the mountains now shrouded in early mist.

By steaming mid-morning, they had left the marshy coastal plain and begun their ascent into the foothills. At times the growth was so thick they had to hack a path with their machetes, protecting their right hands with the only pair of gloves shared between them. Even minor blisters were dangerous in the bacteria-infested tropics.

At four o'clock, after having climbed some three hundred feet in elevation, they camped on a narrow, rocky ledge perched above the now swiftly moving river.

Keely took a towel and some antiseptic soap and went upstream some distance from Ric to bathe. She found a spot where the river was not too swift or deep and sat on a rock in the water, letting the current soothe her tired muscles. Then she washed her hair and her clothes. She was amazed that in this heat the water could be so cool; delighted that the small luxury of cleanliness could make her feel so refreshed. She reluctantly drew on her hot boots and made her way back to camp, feeling better than she had in the past two days of sweat and strain. When she arrived, Ric had already shaved and bathed and was repacking the gear.

He greeted her with a look that was unmistakable. She knew what he was thinking. She met his gaze levelly, her golden eyes clear and steady, until he swallowed hard and averted his gaze. He was angry with her, she knew, yet her independence somehow heightened her appeal as a woman.

She moved away and sat on a rock to sun dry her hair. They were alone in a world that was light years removed from New York City, election campaigns, gentle living. She cursed herself for not having anticipated that thrown together without the buffer of indios, with danger all around them, the possibility of Bryan's death, the unforgotten episode in Mexico City when she had thrown herself at him, that Ric's arms' length affection for her should develop into a healthy desire to make love to her. She had never really told him she was in love with Bryan; only that they had unfinished business. Ric was an attractive man; she might even have enjoyed a relationship with him . . . before. But now she couldn't bear the thought of being touched by another man—even if Bryan were dead.

She knew the chances that he had survived the guerrilla attack in the mountains were very slim. The thought sent a stab of pain through her so deeply that she almost cried out. No, it was better to keep a blank mind on the subject of Bryan. Time enough to deal with his loss after they arrived at the mission outpost.

The next day they trekked less than a mile, five hundred feet of it straight up. As they laboriously made their way through the narrow gorge, they caught glimpses of waterfalls thundering down three-hundred-foot spills into a rainbow of mist below. They watched flights of toucans and thousands of green parrots. They were followed and scolded by tiny monkeys. All the land animals were frightened away as the little party noisily hacked their way through the undergrowth. The vegetation seemed to grow taller and lusher with the altitude, and the jungle intruded everywhere, even springing out of rocks where there appeared to be no soil at all. Although remote from her, Ric always seemed to be there with an outstretched hand whenever

Keely found the path too steep. Each time she found herself looking directly into those disturbing black eyes she quickly released her grip on him as soon as she could.

Twenty feet above the boiling river, they were inching their way single file across a ledge when the earth trembled under their feet. Keely knew earthquakes were an almost daily occurence in this volcanic zone, and most were harmless, including this one. The ground shook only long enough to dislodge fragmented rocks above them, sending them bouncing and leaping in a lethal shower around them. Quickly they slipped off their backpacks to lessen their profiles, and Ric swiftly pulled her under an overhang to shield her body with his.

It was a a gallant but foolhardy thing to do, Keely thought wryly, more for effect. Both would have presented less of a target surface if pressed singly against the cliff wall. But she said nothing. Latin men didn't appreciate females who usurped their protector roles, and Ric had already suffered far too many defeats at her hands. He seemed now on a subtle campaign to bend her to his will through sexual mastery.

The river churned and twisted below; the small but deadly rock shower peppered around them as they waited tensely to see if the quake would intensify and shear the whole face of the cliff into the gorge below with them as passengers.

Residual bouncing stones kept them trapped under the ledge for nearly ten minutes in intimate contact. She started to pull away from him, but his arms tightened around her. ''Not yet,'' he said.

Perspiration had collected in the hollow of his throat and soaked through his shirt, and she knew her own back was wet under his hands. She acquiesced, resting her forehead against his chest, but resisting the smell and feel of his body pressing against hers.

Almost without realizing what he was doing, she felt his lips on her damp temple, then he continued on down to press his mouth to her neck. Suddenly stunned by what was happening, Keely knew then his trembling was not from fear or exertion. She averted her head and said in a low tone, "Ric . . . please . . ."

He stiffened and stopped immediately. Without a word, he levered her away from him and swung his backpack over his shoulders. Then he turned and, expressionless, helped her into her harness, not once looking her in the eye. His pride had been stung, she knew, but she also suspected his anger was with himself rather than with her. She left him alone, and he left her alone.

It was almost dark when they made camp for the night. Ric expected to reach the mission by midmorning the next day, and he wanted to approach it cautiously until they discovered who occupied it. But they were saved the trouble.

On the trail the next morning they literally ran into a group of Honduran scouts. With apprehension, Keely watched the tense young faces of the soldiers while Ric identified themselves in rapid Spanish to the young officer in charge. Then they were escorted at gunpoint into the U.S. military encampment set up outside the bombed-out mission.

Footsore and weary, they were marched past the still-smoking ruins of the buildings to the tent of the American military adviser. Two camouflaged helicopters crouched like ugly insects in the crater-pocked courtyard. Honduran and American soldiers mingled with pickaxes and shovels, clearing the rubble to look for bodies. Several bodies lay stretched out under tarpaulins. The stench was unbelievable. Keely almost gagged, but she could not keep her eyes off them while she and Ric were escorted into the tent.

In his large Operations Headquarters tent, Lieutenant Keith Putnam sat studying and making notations on a report of the attack on the mission outpost across the border from

Pegualpe. A young Honduran aide was marking a map with a small red cross and circle.

The officer rose and came around his desk with hand outstretched to Ric, but his lively brown eyes lingered curiously on Keely. "So. You're Richard Castillo—I've read several of your Amnesty reports at Headquarters. What are you doing in the middle of all this?"

"Rather bad timing on our part," Ric agreed equably. "We're looking for this lady's husband. Lieutenant Putnam, this is Mrs. Bryan Easton of Easton Publishing in New York."

Keely put out her hand. "I hope you can help us, Lieutenant. My husband was supposed to be with Tiburon or Suarez in this camp. I'm worried he might have been killed in this attack."

"Unfortunately, that's entirely possible. Any Americans at this post with Suarez weren't official U.S. issue, and we don't keep files on guerrilla personnel. We haven't been able to identify all the casualties."

Keely lifted her chin bravely. "I saw the—casualties outside. May I take a look?"

Ric pulled out a photograph of Bryan as he appeared now, but Putnam gave it only a cursory examination. "We're mop-up," he said carefully, admiring her guts, knowing she wanted it straight, no frills. "Those bodies out there were found today, ma'am, three days old. They aren't very pretty and they smell worse. There are more under the rubble, and tomorrow they'll be four days old. Are you sure?"

"I'm sure."

The officer was impressed and intrigued. Not many wives came looking for their men, much less to view a bunch of corpses. She must be one helluva a woman. "All survivors were evacuated after the raid, Mrs. Easton. As for the men still buried, you'll have to wait to check them at the hospital and morgue in Tegucigalpa. Mr. Castillo could arrange that for you."

Seeing Keely's white face, Ric intervened quickly. "Perhaps we could look over the personal effects left behind—clothing, passports, photos—things that would have been emptied out of pockets at night when the attack took place."

The lieutenant signaled to the aide. A large box was removed from a locked cabinet to the side. Not a word was spoken as Keely moved alone to the table. With her heart in her throat, she began to examine the contents. She wanted to retch at the pitiful remains of once living men—medallions, letters, address books, a small volume of poetry.

Toward the bottom she found the wallet.

EIGHTEEN

She knew it was his with a sinking in the pit of her stomach. She opened it, knowing already that it bore his embossed initials, BTE, in the soft, now discolored leather. Inside were *lempira* notes, a spare key to the Jaguar Helen had given him for his birthday, and a small photograph of Helen with a wisp of her apricot hair taped to the back, snipped just before she was buried. The last item was the last will and testament of Bryan Trevelyan Easton, type-written and notarized by his attorney in New York. Keely folded it back up without reading it, unable to swallow the terror in her throat. He had left nothing to chance; everything was arranged to prove that Bryan Easton had died here.

But now it was no longer a controlled illusion—the possibility was very real. If his body wasn't outside under a tarpaulin, and he wasn't found at the hospital or morgue in Tegucigalpa, how could she be sure whether he was really alive or not?

Keely felt as though she were going mad, trapped in some sort of Dantesque nightmare from which there was no waking. They moved outside, and one by one the body bags were opened enough to view the faces of young men who had died so senselessly in the violent raid. Keely kept her composure through it all with relief that each soldier viewed was not the man she loved. When it was over,

Ric took the wallet from her unresisting fingers and looked deeply into her eyes. He saw anguish there, but hope as well.

"I'm very sorry, Mrs. Easton," said the lieutenant. "It's a damnable, dirty war."

"May I have the wallet?" Keely interrupted, no longer sure she could remain calm once she had submitted to his sympathy.

"Of course. It's been catalogued."

"Thank you. Lieutenant, until we actually find his body, I hope we can delay any premature speculation or publicity about this . . ."

"I understand. We'll do everything we can to spare you."

"You're very kind."

"But you must leave the area at once," he pressed on with the urgency of a man with much to do and not enough time to do it. "There will be further strikes along the border and I don't want civilians mucking up the works— beg pardon, ma'am. You'll have to wait for the rest of the casualties to be shipped to Tegucigalpa."

He shook hands with Ric and turned again to Keely. "You're welcome to my tent to clean up and rest until we evacuate you this evening." He hesitated, then plunged. "I want you to know we enjoy *EastonWest* magazine all the way down here, Mrs. Easton. You're quite a lady."

She blinked back tears at his kindness and held out her hand to him. "Thank you very much."

Putnam signaled the young aide, and Ric stepped forward to accompany her to the lieutenant's tent. She stopped him with her hand on his arm.

"Don't come, Ric. I think I'd like to be . . . alone for awhile."

He nodded in understanding, and Keely followed the young man with her shoulders held as if there had been a gunstock up her back.

Keely flew home to New York alone, exhausted and

unutterably sad. The only comfort she could derive was the hope that Bryan was still alive after the air raid that had swallowed him without a trace. She had done everything humanly possible to convince him to stay, and failing that, everything to find him. What was left but—acceptance? Such a bitter pill! Even knowing he had sacrificed himself on the altar of love and honor did not ease the pain in her heart or the ache in her loins as night after night she lay alone in the bed where he had made love to her. Acceptance? She only accepted that she loved him without reservation, that she would love him forever.

She knew that only professionalism and a sense of duty could keep her from falling apart. Dreams of him by day and nightmares by night crowded everything else out of her mind. While intellectually she understood his reasons for leaving, emotionally she couldn't accept such gadfly intangibles as honor, sacrifice, and self-respect. It was a puzzle without a solution: I love him, he loves me; why aren't we together?

Her grief went through stages—denial, anger, then the unkindest cut of all—acceptance. Her psychological impasse was manifest as a tropical flu, and Keely took to her bed with a kind of torpored ennui disguised in depression, crying jags, and vomiting. Time spun out into an eternity of fevers and fears, tangled in fantasy and reality.

Keely could not remember how long she had been ill, but when she opened her eyes, everything was still there, familiar and somehow reassuring; the multi-paned window, the shadow of the barren tulip tree, and the spire of the Methodist church beyond it. Faint but clear she heard the chatter of birds. This moment as she lay, now cool and dry, she felt the world at last solidify around her. Slowly she remembered she was alive, in her own bed, in her own house, in Westerby, New York.

Alone. Without Helen. Without Bryan. Without love.

Feeling weaker than she had expected, Keely pushed back the coverlet and stood up. She felt her way unsteadily to the alcove and looked out at the winter world just a few weeks from Christmas. The trees in the garden reached skeletal fingers toward the gray flannel sky, and she thought of the steaming jungles of Honduras. Here the barrenness of the trees seemed a parallel to her own life, an appalling sterility that made the verdure of South America seem an impossible dream.

She turned uninterested eyes as Mrs. Maguire ushered Dr. Houten into the room. The doctor, a dapper man with mustache and toupee, stood surveying her until the door closed behind the housekeeper.

"So. We've decided to rejoin the human race?"

Keely attempted a smile and gave up. "I'm alive. Is that a good sign?"

Dr. Houten moved to the alcove and took her wrist. "Hmm. Pulse fast but good. Eat lightly, my dear, drink lots of fluid. In two days you'll be a new woman."

"Was it malaria, Garry? I took my pills every day."

He shook his head, flicking the fingers of one exquisitely manicured hand in dismissal. "Not malaria. Not even a tropical fever. I'd say it was stress and overwork complicated by pregnancy."

Keely's head whipped around. "What?"

"I said," he repeated tersely, "that an expectant mother cannot traipse about the jungle, eating and drinking God knows what and come out of it unscathed. You were lucky—you could have lost the child."

"But when—how—?"

He chuckled. "I think you can answer that better than I can. I had the positive test results right after your routine physical two weeks ago, but you rushed off on that trip before I could tell you." He said much more, but Keely heard none of it. All that registered was that she was carrying the child of the man she loved. Her mind flashed back to his reaction when he learned about her miscarriage so long ago. His grief had been real, whether he had believed himself to be Bryan or not. And now his own child would grow up fatherless. It seemed almost more than she could bear.

Then a sudden thought struck her. "This illness. Could it have hurt the baby—? All the drugs—?" Alarmed, her hands went to her stomach.

"Everything's fine," he soothed. "You do your job and let me do mine. Right now, yours is to get enough rest and good nutrition, and mine is to deliver a healthy baby."

She sank back in relief. The rest of the doctor's visit passed in a haze of mixed happiness and despair. When he had gone, she stood by the window, pressing both hands on her stomach. His child! Suddenly she could see a small replica with curly chestnut hair and serious blue eyes, and the enormity of her joy overwhelmed her.

Mrs. Maguire, fussing and clucking about people who tried to get out of a sickbed and carry on as usual, wheeled the breakfast cart into the room. But Keely felt too breathlessly disturbed by the news to eat. Finally, she felt as if she would pop with the news.

"Mrs. Maguire, I'm pregnant!" she blurted. Then unable to maintain her poise, she burst into tears.

Mrs. Maguire was flustered to see her mistress so undone, never having seen Keely any way but in complete control. Knowing the marriage between her beloved Bryan and his wife had been less than ideal, she was unsure how to react. "My, what a surprise, ma'am," she managed cautiously.

Keely wiped her eyes on the napkin, remembering that the housekeeper did not know of Bryan's second defection to Central America. Keely had carefully maintained the pretense to everyone that he was merely away on business. "I'm so very, very happy . . ."

Mrs. Maguire's eyes lit up in relief. "Does Mr. Bryan know?"

"Not yet, I just found out myself." She broke out into fresh paroxysms, her tears mingled with laughter.

"It's happy I am for you, ma'am. It'll be nice having a

little one running about the place." She plumped up the pillows. "And if I know Mr. Bryan, he'll be so thrilled he'll take out an ad in all the papers to let the whole world know!"

Keely blinked, and her head swiveled around. "Say that again, Mrs. Maguire!" she commanded.

"I said, your breakfast is probably stone cold by now . . ."

"No, no! About taking an ad in the newspapers. What a wonderful idea!" Keely was gripped with sudden excitement, and she hugged the bewildered housekeeper and whirled away to the window to gaze with dazzled eyes over the garden below.

The world had never looked so beautiful. The sky was clear and brilliant blue, fresh washed by the cold front out of the north which had caused the temperature to plunge into the teens. Even the branches of the trees, the shrubs that lined the path, the blades of grass in the lawn, were transformed into objects of beauty, encrusted as they were with a thin layer of ice that sparkled like diamonds in the sunlight.

With shaking fingers, Keely dialed the office, whipping out disjointed instructions to the bemused Mrs. Maguire as she did so. "Will you be a dear and get my long dressing gown? And take this egg away. All right, I'll eat the toast, but that's all."

Mrs. Maguire kept sneaking glances at her transformed mistress, clearing the tray away without argument. She lost no time closing the door quietly behind her.

Keely tapped her fingers impatiently on the desktop while waiting for the call to go through. "Frank? Keely."

The editor's voice instantly warmed. "Boss lady! Feeling better? Not still contagious, I hope."

"Not my particular malady," she responded dryly. "I'm still a little weak, but the nausea is better. Dr. Houten says I'm confined to the house for a couple more days. Look, Frank, I need to discuss a few things for the magazine."

"Sure. Shoot."

"No. I mean in person. Are you free sometime this morning?"

"If I leave now, I can be there in a couple of hours."

"Fine. And Frank, bring the paste-up for the Christmas issue of *EastonWest*."

"Will do."

She hung up, and waltzed through the room with her arms around herself, feeling strangely elated. She took a shower, blow dried her hair, applied makeup. Strange! She thought she'd been ill! Now she felt imbued with new vigor and life. Life! She laughed out loud at her pale but newly vibrant image in the mirror. She was full of life— Bryan's life and hers, all centered in that little bit of protoplasm growing in its protective cocoon. This child was going to have its father, she vowed silently.

Mrs. Maguire knocked and stuck her head in the door. "Mr. Preston is downstairs for the fiftieth time with more flowers. We're beginning to look like a funeral parlor."

"Send him up."

Vern tapped presently and entered with his arms laden with red anthuriums and white poinsettias, looking anxious and subdued. He set the flowers down and approached the bed where Keely now sat propped against lace-trimmed pillows in her pretty dressing gown, looking pale but radiant. She smiled, held out her hands and raised her cheek to be kissed. Surprised at the unexpectedly warm reception, Vern accepted the offer in gratitude and sat on the edge of the bed.

"Keely," he said deeply. "Thank God you're all right. I've been frantic . . ."

"I'm fine, Vern," she responded lightly. "I thought you'd be in Washington rounding up your new staff."

He brushed his impending move aside. "I couldn't leave without seeing you first."

She reached over and took his hand. "Vern, I'm sorry for the way we parted. I was upset, and—"

"No, no, it was entirely my fault. I just couldn't bear the thought of your thinking I had hurt Helen purposely . . ."

She realized with amazement that all of them, even Vern, had been guilty of good intentions. "Oh, Vern—"

His head bent forward and he drew both her hands to his lips. "I'm not here to plead my cause. I'll always love my Galatea, but I realize now I'm not strong enough for a woman like you."

Keely suddenly realized that she had bullied all the men in her life—Vern, then Ric, and she was going to bully Frank today. There was only one man she had never been able to dominate.

"I'm reconciled to losing you, Keely." He searched her expression. "I just want to understand what went wrong . . ."

Her luminescent eyes played over his face with regret for his pain, and she realized just how mismatched they had been. "I'm in love with him, Vern."

"Well, I suppose my ego's a bit dented to see him succeed with you where I failed," he admitted with an anguished smile. "Keely, if it was passion you wanted, I'm not altogether a cold man. Our relationship was cerebral because you wanted it that way."

A warm flush suffused her throat. "It's—more than that, Vern. I'm pregnant with his child."

He blanched visibly. When he could speak, he got up from the bedside and went to the window. "Then he gave you the only thing I couldn't—a child. You led me to believe it didn't matter. That hurts, Keely."

"None of this was planned, Vern. It just—happened."

"Then you accept his claim to be Bryan Easton?"

"I've accepted the man."

For long moments they looked at each other, each avoiding truths that must remain unsaid. Finally he spoke. "I see. Well, I guess I'll have to be satisfied with that."

"I hope you'll give us your good will, Vern."

He shrugged. "You'll always have that, Keely, whatever happens. I won't stand in your way."

"Thank you." She was saved from further recriminations by a tap on the door. Frank Cabell stuck his head in, followed by his arm, sleeve pushed up to expose his watch. "Ninety minutes on the nose. Ready or not, here I come." He opened the door and strolled in, saluting with two fingers to Vern. "How are you, Senator?"

"Fine, thanks," Vern replied, rising reluctantly. "I was just leaving." He kept Keely's fingers for a moment longer. "May I call you before I leave for Washington?"

She met his look, trying not to be caught by the unspoken pleading there. "Of course."

Still he lingered. "Well, I'll be off," he said finally. "Don't work her too hard, Cabell."

"Don't worry, sir, everything's under control," Frank returned good-naturedly.

The moment Vern closed the door behind him, Frank lost no time unpacking the crudely blocked-out magazine and spreading it over the bed. Preliminary pleasantries about the office and weather helped Keely put Vern out of her mind and get down to business.

Borrowing his blue pencil, she blocked out her idea on the photostated copy of the mock-up Christmas issue of *EastonWest*. She worked quickly, then passed it over. "This goes in before you go to press," she said briskly. "Include it as a sidebar and eliminate one of the photos on that story about the Sandinistas. I want it edged in mistletoe and holly."

Aghast, Frank snatched the article copy from her hand to read it more carefully. Then he swore softly under his breath. "What the—? You're going to use *EastonWest* magazine to tell the entire world you're going to have a baby?" he croaked. He flung himself out of the chair and paced across the room waving his arms. "A goddamn giant birth announcement? Boss lady, gimme a break. I'll have to move heaven and earth, it'll cost a fortune—"

As if he had not spoken, she went on calmly, "And I want this photograph right on top." She handed him one of Bryan and herself taken after Vern's election, with the candidate carefully cropped out.

He stared at her. "Keely, you've finally flipped. You're nuts. You're—"

"—the boss," she finished sweetly.

A full minute passed before his shoulders went down in a great exhalation, and he slumped in disgust. "Okay. I can see you're not going to tell me the reason for all this, so I won't ask. But wouldn't it be cheaper just to rent a billboard or a skywriter or run it across the marquee in Times Square?"

At Keely's delighted laugh, he grinned, lifted by her buoyant mood. "Not bad, Cabell, but Bryan's not in New York. I want him to see it in Central America."

"You mean he doesn't know yet?"

"I didn't know myself until this morning."

"Well, I'll be damned. You Eastons really know how to put on a show. When the kid's born I guess you'll order a special-issue, full-color layout and run its picture on the cover."

"Don't tempt me, Cabell," Keely laughed, realizing the impossible task she had just laid on him, and grateful for his professionalism. She could always depend on him to get the job done. "Thanks, Frank."

He grinned and flipped his coat over one shoulder, heading for the door. "Welcome back, Boss. We miss your bulldozing style down at the office."

She made a face and blew him a kiss.

Owen Neal came down for Thanksgiving and they went out to dinner, ostensibly to give the servants the holiday off, but really because Keely's heart wasn't in a holiday celebration. Her father was overjoyed about the baby, surprised that Keely was, too, and concerned about his son-in-law's absence. He asked some very penetrating questions which Keely preferred not to answer. She was determined to stick to the fabrication that Bryan was on extended assignment in Central America, and she saw to it that articles continued to appear in *EastonWest* under his byline to keep gossip and speculation down. Wherever he was, she was gambling everything in the hope that the news of the baby would bring him home!

When the Christmas issue of *EastonWest* came off the presses, even before it hit the stands, Keely sent large shipments of the magazine to Ricardo Castillo, all Central American Amnesty offices, Senor Lozano in Jucuapa, U.S. Army and Marine training centers in Honduras, El Salvador, Guatemala, and the American Embassy in Tegucigalpa. Another shipment went directly to Lieutenant Keith Putnam, along with a case of Scotch and a note thanking him for his help and hospitality, asking him to distribute the magazine among his men as a season's greeting from her. She desperately hoped that someone might recognize Bryan and show him the issue, or perhaps that he would run across a copy himself. She knew he was alive; surely his baby would bring him home!

And then finally, all there was left to do was wait.

As the days marched on toward Christmas, her self-imposed deadline before publicly giving up hope and admitting to the world she had been deserted or widowed once again, she was seized with a morbid dread of the uproar and publicity that would attend this second disappearance, this time with the added fillip of a posthumous child! She had no intentions of exposing him as a fraud. Better to leave an escape hatch to come back as Bryan Easton for the child's sake. She would deal with his other identity if and when the time came.

Ric phoned to report the safe arrival of the magazines. "Is it true?" he asked without preamble, and they both knew he was referring to her pregnancy. "Not just a ploy?"

"Certainly it's true," Keely replied quickly. "But it's also a ploy."

"Rather inconvenient timing, is it not? With Bryan gone

and you not sure if he's alive or dead.'' His tone was distinctly unhappy.

"He's alive," she flung back. "If he weren't, we'd have found his body in Tegucigalpa. And even if he never comes back, at least I'll have his child.''

"I want you to know, Keely," he said softly into the receiver, "that if Bryan is alive in Central America, I'll find him.'' He paused. "And if he's dead, then I'm volunteering as godfather to your little one.''

Tears misted her eyes and the lump in her throat made it difficult to talk. "Thank you, Ric.''

"I miss you,'' he said roughly. "Much more than is proper to miss another man's wife.''

He didn't have to elaborate; his feelings for her were very clear. It seemed an irony that now, more than at any other time in her life when she needed the support of people who loved her, she had to let both Ric and Vern go. She had never felt so alone.

Her voice caught on a sob. "Feliz Navidad, Ric.''

"May Saint Nicholas be good to you, Keely. I will call you if I hear anything.''

Long before Macy's Thanksgiving Day Parade, New York had been geared for the garish Christmas whirl. Keely gift shopped for the house and office staff and a few personal friends, but without Helen her heart was empty of holiday cheer. She went to work each morning, going through the motions, professionalism alone carrying her through. The child in her womb and its father in her heart occupied most of her thoughts.

"I know the holidays won't seem the same this year without Miss Helen," ventured Mrs. Maguire. "But don't you think we should get a tree before Mr. Bryan comes home for Christmas?''

"Not yet,'' Keely replied.

Mrs. Maguire tightened her lips disapprovingly, but she said no more. Boxes of decorations came down from the attic and soon boughs of evergreen and holly decorated the mantel. Fairy lights twinkled in reproach from the window of the carriage house from a small tree positioned there. The nativity scene appeared on the foyer table, apple logs burned fragrantly in the grate every night, and the good smells of holiday baking filled the house in Mrs. Maguire's determined campaign to keep up appearances and bring a smile to Keely's white face.

Nature cooperated the weekend before Christmas with a fresh blanket of snow and the skies were crisp and blue beyond twinkling rooftops. But holiday spirit was sadly lacking in the big house. Owen Neal was spending the holiday with his brother's family in Vermont. Keely was invited but she begged off, citing Bryan's imminent return and work commitments.

On Christmas Eve Keely dined alone, but she was scarcely able to taste the food. Even with Christmas carols drifting in the background, the big house echoed with loneliness. Thoughts of Helen on past Christmases contributed to her morbid mood. To the staff, Keely kept up the pretense of waiting for Bryan. She donned a new, daring black strapless jumpsuit with a black and silver sequinned top. She had spent a fortune on her hair and makeup and perfume for the "homecoming" in the hope that positive thinking would prevail.

She sat curled up in the big chair in the study sipping Kir, listening to Boston Pops Christmas carols. When the strains of "Blue Christmas" came on, the sharp breath Keely took went no farther than the lump in her throat. He wasn't coming, now or ever, she knew that now. He must be dead.

She set the wineglass down, unable to bear being in this house one minute longer. There was no reason to hang around and ruin Mrs. Maguire's evening, too. At least she had a husband to go home to.

"I have some work to finish up at the office," she told the silently pitying Mrs. Maguire. She slipped into her coat and fled before the tears began.

Toward midnight, as Christmas Eve turned into Christmas Day, Keely wandered through the big, dimly lit offices at Easton Publishing. The litter of the sixth floor office party was heaped into the trash baskets—torn Christmas wrap, paper plates stuck with fruitcake, broken Styrofoam cups, empty champagne bottles. The decorations were still up—plastic holly garlanded over the cubicles, sprigs of mistletoe over strategic doorways. Idly, Keely plugged in the lights of one of the funny, little Christmas trees decorated with leftover satin balls and silver tinsel, garish when contrasted with the perfect two-story designer-decorated tree in the massive marble lobby. But the sight and symbolism caused her heart to feel as if it were splintering into a million pieces. Restively, she pulled the plug, plunging the room again into gloom.

It seemed impossible to escape Christmas, but Keely tried. She passed the empty personnel department on her way to her office. The publisher's suite included offices for three secretaries and a larger one for the associate publisher which Bryan had occupied so briefly. The foyer served as a trophy room, and awards presented to the magazine over the years, along with photos of Alfred, Helen, and Keely Easton in the company of notables, from U.S. presidents to labor negotiators to various domestic and foreign government leaders, crowded the walls.

Her office looked out over the East River and the Brooklyn shore, but she was uninterested in either the spectacular view or the exquisite Renoir on the opposite wall. Instead, she cleaned out her files and dictated a few letters for one of her secretaries to type Tuesday, then left the office to roam restlessly down the corridor toward the conference room, her high-heeled shoes clicking hollowly between Oriental runner rugs on the polished parquet floors.

The conference table and plush upholstered chairs that by day looked so rich and tasteful now loomed like hulking shadows. How many battles had she fought across that table, over issues that at the time seemed important? Now it all seemed so trivial. Looking up at the oil portraits of Alfred and Helen Easton, she realized with a pang that she didn't even have a likeness of the man she loved.

Behind her there was a muffled bang. Someone had left the elevator and was walking rapidly toward the conference room. She turned with just a faint frisson of alarm. A security guard? Even the janitors had Christmas Eve off. And no one knew she was here except Mrs. Maguire.

"Who's there?" she called sharply.

The hoary chill of winter seemed to sweep around the shadows in the doorway, then the light flooded on.

"Ho, ho, ho," said Bryan.

NINETEEN

Keely's heart somersaulted into her throat. Rooted to the spot, her coat slipped from her bare shoulders to the floor. In a state of suspended animation, she saw the epaulets of snow frosting the shoulders of his topcoat, the clear eyes hooded and watchful. Looking up into his rugged face as in a dream, she scarcely dared to breathe. Her entire life lapsed into slow motion; and she knew she was alive because she could feel, could hear, her heart pounding crazily.

And then he opened his arms. With a cry she collapsed against him, and his open coat enfolded her like the wings of a seraphim. Round and round they revolved in a wordless, timeless waltz, pressed tightly together, luxuriating in the exchange of smells and textures of cold, crisp snow, clean juniper, the satin warmth of woman skin and perfume.

Her face was buried in him, overcome with the joy and wonder of this moment after weeks of despair. "Oh Bryan, I'd almost given up . . ." Kisses peppered his neck, his chin, his jaw, and her humbled voice vibrated with emotion.

"No more 'hey you'?" He drew back, his aconite blue eyes searching her face. The leaping light she had expected was not there, and something in his tone stopped her dead. It was then she realized he had not held her a moment ago so much as she had held him, and suddenly she was very, very frightened.

His voice was heavy with fatigue. "I can't stay long, Keely. I've already booked a return flight."

She had expected him to say almost anything but this. Stunned, she stared at the tense expression on his face until she finally found her voice, trying to lighten the mood with a little laugh. "What? After I turned Honduras upside down looking for you, spent a fortune on bribes, littered all of Central America with the message to come home—you're leaving?"

"Damn it, Keely, this isn't a social call. Castillo said you needed to see me, so here I am." He turned away from her, raking his hands through his hair. "You found my wallet in Honduras weeks ago, and I've been scouring the papers for news of my disappearance ever since. What the hell is holding up an announcement?"

Keely stood motionless, transfixed, literally shaking inside. "Then—you didn't see the Christmas issue of *EastonWest*—you don't know—?"

"Know what? I've been in seclusion in Panama since the border raid. I called Castillo Tuesday, but all he would tell me is that there's been a snag and it was urgent that I speak to you personally."

She laughed on a sob. "A snag. Yes. You might call it a snag."

She touched his arm, then bit her lip when he took her fingers away. "Nothing's changed, Keely," he warned.

"Nothing—! Oh, my God, Bryan, everything's changed! I'm pregnant."

His breath stopped, and a sudden tiny flame in his eyes was quickly extinguished. He turned away so she could not see his face as he spoke, slowly shucking his gloves from his fingers. "I see. Preston didn't lost any time staking his claim."

The back of her throat was dry and burning, and the tightness in her chest intensified. "It isn't Vern's."

He exhaled slowly before turning around to face her. "Then I won't insult you by denying it's mine."

"Thank you."

His eyes were flat. "Of course, he'll insist you correct our little . . . indiscretion."

She felt as if he had slapped her after all. "Vern and I were finished long before you left. And I plan to have this 'indiscretion.' "

"You'd pass the child off as a blooded Easton?"

Keely flushed. "My legal name is Easton and so his will be, until you remember yours."

They measured each other for a moment without speaking, and she struggled to control her trembling. This wasn't going at all as she had planned. After a moment he reached out to adjust the lopsided star on the tip of the Christmas tree. His voice was guarded, almost bitter. "What is it you want with me, Keely, aside from telling me that I've now added insult to injury? I have no legal claim to your child."

"My child? Bryan, he's your flesh and blood, too," she choked.

His expression was hard. "Don't call me Bryan. I'm a stranger with no name."

"I don't care who you are. Come home to me. Our baby needs its father."

"How can I? To assure the child's heritage, we'd have to present me to the world as the late Bryan Easton."

"Stop it!" She leaned forward, tears of frustration in her eyes. "You've made your point, Bryan, but to leave me now cancels out all honor and makes it cruel and unusual punishment. I'm sick of hearing why we can't be together. With Helen gone, there's only you and me and our baby to consider."

Watching his reaction to her strong words, Keely saw temptation conflicting with reason, and she knew he was wrestling with his inner demons. "You make it sound so simple, so sensible, Keely. But once it's done we can't walk away from the lie."

"Our love isn't a lie." If Keely had learned nothing else over the past year, it was that she could not bulldoze this man in a head-on confrontation, so she abruptly changed tack. "Oh, darling, I understand and respect your honorable intentions, misguided as they are." She smiled through a sparkle of tears, desperate for a temporary truce to gain time. "All I'm asking for now is that we forget about our problems and enjoy Christmas together."

She didn't wait for an invitation, but moved into his arms and pulled his head down to still any objections with her lips. He resisted only a moment before melting into a kiss full of unrequited longing and sweetness, and she knew that the homecoming she had waited for so long was at hand. His mouth drifted across her face, his tongue tasting her warm scented skin and he stroked her body in the slinky jumpsuit until the heat of their bodies became explosive. After long moments, he dragged his mouth away from hers, and his whisper thundered in her ear. "You little witch. You're not playing fair—"

"Who said life was fair? All I know is that it's Christmas, and you're the only present I want tonight."

Wild, sweet hunger caused them to move together again and their mouths clung in a fevered kiss. It was a while before either of them was calm enough to speak again.

He drew back his head to smile his surrender into her eyes. "This is one Christmas present I'd rather open at home—in our own bed." Then, "Have you bought a tree yet?"

"No. I was waiting—hoping you'd come."

"It's after midnight. Think we can get one at half price? All I have are pesos in my pocket." His voice was a rough gasp against her mouth, and she laughed. It was so wonderful to laugh again.

They found a lot that was open all night, but the trees were nearly gone and the selection was poor. They settled for a scrawny pine, flat on one side, and waited laughing, their breaths puffing white in the crisp cold air, her hands stuffed in his coat pockets, while the lot man flocked it to fluff it out and tied it to the top of the car.

"You've already been home," she accused, noticing the Jaguar for the first time.

"You're just jealous that Lida saw me first," he teased, and she knew it was true.

The snow began to swirl around them, transforming the garish Christmas lights of Fifth Avenue into a fairyland. The long drive from the city to Westerby flew by. They both talked at once, kissing and fondling at signals like a couple of high-school kids.

At home the discreet but absent hand of Mrs. Maguire was evident. All the boxed tree decorations were stacked and ready to use. A fire crackled merrily in the grate. A crystal bowl of cranberry punch, wickedly spiked with champagne and cloves, beckoned from the sideboard along with plates of decorated hazelnut cookies and wedges of rum-soaked fruitcake.

They fed each other tidbits amid much soft laughter, kissing, and all the little nothings that pass between lovers, and Keely was hardly aware of anything but the terrifying pleasure of being with him and the promise in his smoky blue eyes as they scorched over her.

An hour later, the spindly pine had been transformed into a glittering miracle and stood proudly in the mullioned bay windows facing the deserted street. The tree lights were all strung and Bryan tested them to make sure they all worked.

"Blink or twinkle?" he asked, continuing the double entendre repartee that had kept them on the edge of sexual tension all evening.

"Both."

"Didn't anybody ever tell you you can't have it both ways?"

"Says who? I intend to have it in every way possible." Her eyes glowed with promise.

His laugh was almost a groan. "I can hardly wait."

Soon little fairy lights flickered like fireflies in rainbow colors. The garland spiraled around the branches like silver fire and the della Robbia ornaments glowed like rich wine. All that remained to be placed was the antique snow-haired angel on the top of the tree. Even on the three-step ladder Keely had to stand on tiptoe to reach the top.

"Steady there." As she wobbled, his own response was lightning quick. One hand shot out to grip her thigh while the other reached up to steady her waist, so that suddenly Keely found herself almost lifted, her hips and legs crushed against his torso.

"I'll fall on you, Bry!"

He grinned at the implied threat. "Promise?"

He lifted her clear of the ladder and kicked it aside. Now there was nothing under her feet but air. Then she was poised precariously above him, looking down from her height and gripping his flexed and muscular shoulders. Their laughing eyes were like stars as his lips found the soft valley between her breasts. He relaxed his grip and inch by inch her body slid past his hungry lips and body in sensuous apposition: breasts, slender shoulders, silken throat, all tantalized and inflamed by brushstroke kisses.

At last the floor rose to meet her stockinged feet, but even that contact with reality could not stem the exquisitely slow enravishment of her senses. Keely closed her eyes and let her head fall back, savoring the rasp of his jaw and nip of his teeth as he caressed her hot, bare skin.

By that time she could hardly bear standing next to him. He kissed her closed eyelids, the fevered warmth of her cheeks, hovering above the moist beckoning embrasure of her mouth. Keely felt shock waves on her scalp, in her breasts, in her groin. She couldn't breathe, panting as if at a high altitude. "Aren't we finished yet?"

"Nope. We forgot to hang the mistletoe," he teased against her lips.

"Damn the mistletoe!"

"Tch, tch, such language, and on a holy day."

"In another minute I'm going to make love to you under the Christmas tree."

"I'm sure that's sacrilege."

"Take me upstairs," Keely begged, lifting her arms to encircle his neck and draw him closer. She felt his laughter against her mouth, felt herself being lifted into his arms and carried toward the stairs, whirled upward into the welcoming darkness. There was no sensation of deja fait in the reenactment of another night when she had been carried up these very stairs. They had been another man, another woman in another time. She was conscious only of the tense, expectant, determined passion that connected them with an electric current that would soon fuse them together forever.

Once inside the bedroom door, Bryan set her down and pulled her to him and kissed her hard on the mouth. Crushed against him with mounting excitement, Keely wanted him as she had never wanted anything before. Her knees trembled when she felt him hard against her stomach. One hand held her quivering flesh firmly against him while the other unzipped her black sequinned jumpsuit, tracing the outline of her spine down to its base with a wicked thumb that produced a shudder of need through her.

With an effort he pulled himself away long enough to push her gently down on the bed, where she lay back on her elbows, her head thrown back in wanton ecstasy. He bent to lick the pulsing curve of her throat and taste each nipple before peeling off her stockings and bikini panties from long silken legs, his fingers detouring and delaying deliciously along the way.

When she was naked, she lay back against the pillows to watch through lash-shuttered eyes as he stood beside the bed to undress himself. He even knew how to take his own clothes off erotically—looking steadily at her body with sultry hooded eyes and a sensual bottom lip, loosening his tie with two fingers, slowly unbuttoning first his cuffs, then his shirt, dropping each article carelessly on the carpet. He was inviting her, inciting her, playing the delaying game that was just as pleasurable and arousing for her as it was for him. And when he was naked at last, he bent slowly and pressed his mouth to hers in a long hot kiss before coming down to her in the bed.

Shivering in anticipated pleasure, she yielded wholly to his touch, his fingers, his mouth. She savored the smell and feel of him, his warm breath on her cheek, his hands lacing through her hair.

Unlike her, he was in no hurry. He leaned on his elbow and explored her in the glow from the firelight, one finger lazily tracing a firm, pink nipple, until her whole being leaped toward him in response. How gently he kissed her and stroked her satin shoulders! How sensitive the fingers that slid into her, one, then two, dipping and sliding with a soft, steady rhythm, drawing forth the essence of her until she relaxed and was conscious only of the voluptuous sensations flooding her body. There was not another man in the world like him—certainly not Bryan!

A great, shuddering sigh came from him. "Is this real, Keely, or am I back in the jungle dreaming of you again?" With an arm across her shoulders, he rolled over onto his back and pulled her on top of him until they were face to face.

Searching his eyes in the fireglow, she whispered, "I don't know and I don't care. Just don't make me wait any longer . . ."

His laugh was a husky growl in his throat as he turned again and bore her down into the pillows, his mouth warm and fierce on hers. She felt the strength of rough muscular thighs against soft ones, broad, gentle hands cradling first her buttocks, then her tingling breasts. He cupped, caressed, stroked, then pressed her nipples to his own bare chest in sensual abandon, and she could feel his heart in wild tattoo against her own.

She swooned into semi-awareness, feeling as if the bed was swirling up toward the ceiling, about to fly through the window on a tornado of sensation, over the rainbow, into the sky. She felt hot, excited, yet strangely peaceful, swirling into a mounting vortex until all thought was blown from her mind and her senses alone commanded her body as he drew her into the violent erotic eye of the storm.

With every roughly tender touch, she exulted that he was not Bryan after all, but her own true love.

Then the lull in the storm enveloped them both and she received him as softly as a sea anemone, curling, cupping, stroking in dream-like beauty until she could feel him high against the core of her, his energy pulsating inside her. She wanted this! She wanted to couple with this wild, hard-muscled man forever. He was her love.

Slowly, strongly, driven by his hard insistent rhythm, she felt the pull from the other side of the storm, a mounting, quickening pressure that sucked at her relentlessly, and suddenly through the mist she knew it was going to happen. And when it did, the sweet drowning of fulfillment poured over them both in soft, intense, golden waves, arching her toward him in ecstasy until all too soon he fell back with a low cry that echoed its way to heaven.

Afterward they lay connected, neither wanting to leave the other's body. Still and silent, they gloried in their completion, warm together in the big bed tucked beneath the satin coverlet as the snow outside the window floated as gently earthward as they had done.

But reality was inexorable. Though she lay next to his heart, Keely began to sense his troubled preoccupation. She moved her head around, relieved to see that his expression was tender. When he spoke, his voice was curiously rough, yet gentle. "I wish it could always be like this—no questions, no doubts between us."

Keely's lips curved into a contented smile. "I hadn't noticed anything at all between us."

But he refused to be diverted from his sudden melancholy mood. "I want to believe this is enough, that love is enough. But is it? The past would always be there to haunt us. You'd always secretly wonder who I really am, and I'd always feel I was with you under false pretenses."

"False pretenses?" She twisted her neck around to look up at him, acutely aware that he wanted to stay and was asking her to convince him. "How can it be false when we both know the truth? It isn't Bryan I want, it's you."

"I want—need—to believe that so badly." His hand came up to caress the contour of her face. "While I thought it was Bryan you loved, I wanted to be Bryan with all my heart. Now, knowing that you hated him, I want to be anyone but him."

She lifted her head to brush her lips against his throat. "Darling, it doesn't matter any more. The name 'Bryan' is just a word. I'm not in love with a name, I'm in love with a flesh-and-blood man. And that man is you."

"But what if I should remember some day, and I turned out to be Bryan after all?" he agonized. "Would you love me then?"

She put a finger over his lips. "But you're not, now are you? And when you make love to me the way you do, I'm never more certain of anything in my life. Nothing could change the way I feel about you."

"God help me, I want your love so much that I can't think rationally." He buried his face in her breasts and she knew that if she handled him carefully she could win him back.

"Darling," she whispered, turning to him. "You can't go on tearing yourself apart like this. Let's not live even one more day regretting the past and fearing the future. All that matters is the moment."

They held each other for a long time before he spoke again. "It was eerie watching the papers for news of my 'death.' I was in limbo, waiting, wondering, dreading the finality of it . . . and when the announcement never came, I almost felt—reprieved."

Her fingertips scratched a lazy trail over his shoulders. "Did you know that Ric and I were camped on the beach the night of the attack in Honduras?"

His half-closed eyes shot open to regard her in disbelief. "You went to the mission? And pregnant! You little fool, you might have been killed!"

"I just couldn't let you walk out of my life," she confessed. "I had your wallet removed from the effects of the dead men so your name wouldn't show up on the official casualty list. I knew as long as I withheld it you were still technically 'alive' and you could openly come back.'' Tears shimmered in her eyes at the memory. ''Oh darling, you put me through hell!''

He pulled her close to stifle the memory. ''I know, and I'm so sorry, my heart,'' he said fiercely against her hair. ''Oh God, if only I could be sure . . .''

Her answering laughter was husky with emotion. ''Of what? Of me? My love?''

His voice was serious as he caught her fingertips to his lips and kissed off the reasons one by one. ''Me. Who I am. How I'll fit into your life. Most of all, who you really want me to be.''

It bothered her that he remained insecure even after her assurances. ''I want you to be my life's partner, my other half. I want us to be together in all we do.''

''Not the publishing company, Keely. I'd have to be involved in some other line of business.''

Keely was disappointed, as he had proved himself to be a valuable, talented, intuitive addition to Easton Publishing. ''I can understand your feelings. I guess I didn't make you feel very welcome.''

''It's not that. Your blood, sweat, and tears are there, not mine. I'd still be the carpetbagger.''

''What will you do?''

''With my background, I think the government might be interested in my services as a consultant on aviation and materiel in Central America.'' Instantly alarmed, she sat up to protest, but he pulled her down again and tucked her head under his chin. ''Take it easy. I said consultant, not pilot, and I could do it from the Pentagon. I've had enough jungle to last me a lifetime, and I found out very quickly over the last month that my priorities—not to mention my reflexes—aren't what they used to be.''

She snuggled into him. ''I can't help it. I suppose I'll worry every time you leave home. I—we—need you so.''

''Home,'' he said dreamily. ''It will be heaven to live

with you and our children in this wonderful old house surrounded again by all the old Easton family traditions. I just wish my parents were here to share our happiness . . ." His voice throbbed with emotion as his hand caressed her still-flat stomach, cherishing the child they had made together.

Keely's eyes opened wide as a thousand needles prickled down her spine. Did he realize the enormity of what he had just let slip?

For a fearful moment, the terrible accusation trembled on her lips: You got your your memory back when you went to Honduras. Didn't you? Didn't you!

One word, one misstep . . . and their tenuous reunion could be destroyed forever. She had promised him there would be no more questions, no more doubts or reservations, that his name and past were of no consequence, that she loved him until it didn't matter where her flesh and blood left off and his began. She realized then how deeply she had counted on his being some other person than Bryan Easton and how that conviction had freed her to fall in love with him. Could she live the rest of their lives together suspecting, even knowing, that he was the man she had hated and feared all these years? Perhaps. But could she ever forgive him for the death of that other unborn child?

She waited, troubled at the dilemma and struggling to sort out her mind before she committed herself to the unknown. Was he hiding the truth from her because it might cost him her love?

He turned restlessly toward her, bending his head to brush his lips against her forehead, and a surge of intense feeling swept over her in a familiar tide. She twined her arms around his neck. There were no decisions to make.

They had all been made long ago.

SHARE THE FUN . . .
SHARE YOUR NEW-FOUND TREASURE!!

You don't want to let your new book out of your sight? That's okay. Your friends can get their own. Order below.

No. 5 A LITTLE INCONVENIENCE by Judy Christenberry
Never one to give up easily, Liz overcomes every obstacle Jason throws in her path and loses her heart in the process.

No. 6 CHANGE OF PACE by Sharon Brondos
Police Chief Sam Cassidy was everyone's protector but could he protect himself from the green-eyed temptress?

No. 7 SILENT ENCHANTMENT by Lacey Dancer
She was elusive and she was beautiful. Was she real? She was Alex's true-to-life fairy-tale princess.

No. 8 STORM WARNING by Kathryn Brocato
The tempest on the outside was mild compared to the raging passion of Valerie and Devon—and there was no warning!

No. 9 PRODIGAL LOVER by Margo Gregg
Bryan is a mystery. Could he be Keely's presumed dead husband?

No. 10 FULL STEAM by Cassie Miles
Jonathan's a dreamer—Darcy is practical. An unlikely combo!

No. 11 BY THE BOOK by Christine Dorsey
Charlotte and Mac give parent-teacher conference a new meaning.

No. 12 BORN TO BE WILD by Kris Cassidy
Jenny shouldn't get close to Garrett. He'll leave too, won't he?
